# BAD PRESS!

Know All You Present, That on the Second Day of August, in the Year of Our Lord 1232, the Notorious Brigand, Sir Conrad Stargard, Did Feloniously and with Malice Aforethought Attack a Caravan of Goods, the Property of the Teutonic Knights of Saint Mary's Hospital at Jerusalem.

In this Evil Attack, He Murdered Five of the Members of Our Holy Order, and Maimed a Sixth Member for Life, while these Honorable Men were Peacefully Attending to the Business of Our Order.

We pray to God that He may Strengthen Our Champion's Arm, That he might Smite the Brigand Sir Conrad, and Recover for Our Order All Our Property, Including the Heathen Slaves.

May God Uphold the Right.

By Leo Frankowski
*Published by Ballantine Books:*

**THE ADVENTURES OF CONRAD STARGARD**

**COPERNICK'S REBELLION**

# THE
# HIGH-TECH
# KNIGHT

**Book Two in the Adventures of
Conrad Stargard**

## Leo Frankowski

A Del Rey Book

BALLANTINE BOOKS • NEW YORK

## DEDICATION

This series is dedicated to Clovis, King of the Franks, (A.D. 466-511), the first man in recorded history to want a time machine.

On hearing an impassioned telling of the crucifixion of Christ, he said, "Oh! If only I could have been there at the head of my gallant Franks!"

I'd like to thank Phillip C. Jennings for his kind help in proofreading this series, and for his many valuable suggestions that have improved this work.

A Del Rey Book
Published by Ballantine Books

Copyright © 1989 by Leo A. Frankowski

All rights reserved under International and Pan-American Copyright Conventions. Published in the United States of America by Ballantine Books, a division of Random House, Inc., New York, and simultaneously in Canada by Random House of Canada Limited, Toronto.

Library of Congress Catalog Card Number: 88-92183

ISBN 0-345-32763-2

Printed in Canada

First Edition: March 1989
Sixth Printing: December 1993

Cover Art by Barclay Shaw

# Author's Note
# Medieval Time

Monks got together eight times a day at approximately even intervals for prayer. Since they rang the bells at these times, everybody else got into the habit of using the same designations, even when there wasn't a monastery around.

*Prime*. The first hour. Daybreak.

*Tierce*. The third hour. Halfway between dawn and noon. About nine A.M.

*Sext*. The sixth hour. Noon.

*None*. The ninth hour. Halfway between noon and sunset. About three P.M. Actually, this is where the term noon came from, as a joke. There was once this monastery, the inmates of which, as a mark of their austerity, swore that they would not eat each day until the none bell struck. Well, since they were the ones who were in charge of ringing the bells, and since a guy gets awfully hungry sitting around and praying, the none bell sort of got to be rung a little earlier each day. The townspeople, noticing this, got to calling mid-day "none," to ridicule the monks, and the name stuck, eventually turning into "noon."

*Vespers*. Sunset.

*Compline*. Halfway between sunset and midnight. Around nine P.M.

*Matins*. Midnight. Actually, matins means "morning." A matinee was the morning show back in the days when theatrical performances were normally given in the afternoon. With the advent of artificial lighting, the main shows were moved to the evenings and the matinee was moved to the afternoon. Then recently, I was invited to an "evening matinee," and then somehow the performance got delayed until midnight. In the course of things, we have wandered entirely around the clock.

*Lauds*. Halfways between midnight and dawn. About three A.M.

Please note that the hours are not the same size, but change with the season. In a high latitude area like Poland, this meant that some hours could be three times longer than others.

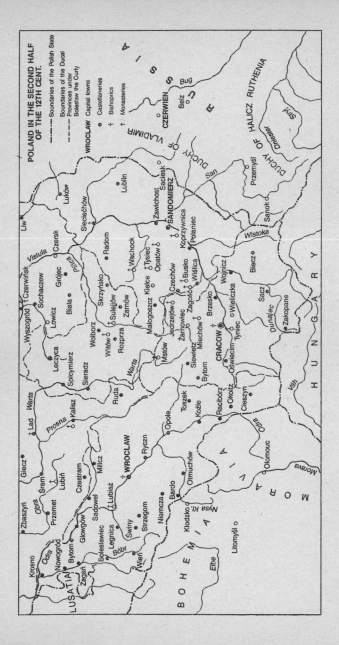

POLAND IN THE SECOND HALF
OF THE 12TH CENT.

---·---·--- Boundaries of the Polish State
---------- Boundaries of the Ducal
           Provinces under
           Bolesław the Curly

WROCLAW  Capital towns
      ○   Castellaneries
      †   Bishoprics
      †   Monasteries

# Prologue

He unloaded the temporal canister, glanced quickly at his new subordinate, reloaded it with his previous superior, and hit the retrieve button. That had to be done quickly. Holding the canister in 2,548,950 B.C. was *expensive*.

He examined her frozen, nude body. It was just over four feet tall and skinny. The skin was dark brown, the hair black and tightly curled, the breasts small yet pendulous. An excellent imitation of a type twenty-seven protohuman. The biosculptors had done a good job.

He switched off her stasis field.

Her eyes opened, she stared shocked at the stalactites on the ceiling of the cave. She noticed the naked brown man bending over her, noticed her own nakedness and yelped, covering her breasts and groin.

"Yeah, the uniform here is a bit skimpy." He chuckled. "The protos haven't invented clothes yet, so what can we do? Hey. Don't look so shocked. I'm not going to rape you. You're not *my* adolescent fantasy any more than I'm yours."

"Damn it! I have five doctorates!"

"I'm sure your mother is very proud of you. Are any of them in finding carrion or grubbing for grubs? Anything else isn't very useful around here."

She glanced furtively at the cave's rock walls, at the torch that was its sole illumination.

."What is this place? When is it? And who are you?" She was still clutching her groin.

"You weren't briefed? This is anthropological research station fifty-seven. The time is half past two million B.C., and I am your charming host, Robert McDougall. I'd tip my hat, but you see the problem. The tribe here calls me 'Gack,' so you might as well, too. No point in being formal when you're naked. I'll be your boss for the next fifty years."

"Fifty years . . ."

"Right. Then I go home, a new chum arrives, and *you* get to be boss for fifty more."

The cave was cold and wet. She shivered. "This is all some horrible mistake!"

"How can there be a mistake? You replaced the asshole I used to work for. Not that I really had anything personal against her, but you'll understand that after fifty years with only one person to talk to, you just naturally start to hate each other's guts.

"Anyway, the computers don't make mistakes, so you're supposed to be here because you've arrived at the proper time and in a body properly tailored for our research."

"This body!" She bawled, "I used to be *beautiful*!"

"All part of the high price of science," he said. But she had pulled herself into a fetal position and was sobbing louder. "Hey, you're serious, aren't you? You actually didn't volunteer for this post?"

"No! I mean, *yes* I didn't volunteer. I was in twentieth-century Poland. I spent *one day* on my new assignment and the monitors came and I woke up here! I'm in the *Historical Corps*. I don't know anything about anthropology!"

"Why, those filthy bastards . . ."

"Yeah," she said, grateful for any sympathy.

". . . sending me a totally untrained recruit! My God! That means . . ." He stooped down and found a sliver of bone on the cave floor. He grabbed her right hand.

"This doesn't hurt. You won't feel it at all." He slipped the bone under her index fingernail and moved it sideways. She stared openmouthed as he repeated the operation on her left hand.

"What..."

"They were both turned off, thank God. Look. You have some fairly powerful equipment built into that little body. Your right index finger contains a temporal sword. With it, you can cut a tree in half at six paces. Your left contains a fire-starter. They can save your life, but if you don't know how to use them, they can kill you. Or me!"

"There's more?"

"Some recorders, communicators, beacons, and so on. But that can wait. I want to find out what you're doing here." He squatted in front of a large flat rock by the cave wall. He pressed four nondescript spots on the rock. Glowing white letters appeared in the air before him.

READY

He started tapping the blank rock as though it was a typewriter keyboard.

INFO REQUEST PERSONNEL RECORD. HISTORICAL CORPS WORKER NO....

"Hey. What's your number?" She told him, he loaded it and started reading. "Hmmm...born in North America, 62,218 B.C....approved for child rearing; eleven children...at forty-five, attended Museum University 62,219 B.C. to 62,192 B.C....doctorates in medicine, Slavic languages, psychology, and Greek literature... accepted into the Historical Corps...assigned to Periclean Athens, forty-one-year tour of duty. Performance unsatisfactory..."

"That wasn't fair!" she said.

"Fair? What's fair? If you want to talk about 'fair,' go talk to one of our protos after her kid's been eaten by a leopard!" he snapped. "...Returned to university and obtained a doctorate in ancient Egyptian languages... turned down on four assignment requests, ninth through thirteenth dynasties...assigned twentieth-century Poland...caused a situation which resulted in unauthorized transport of local citizen to the thirteenth century. Involuntarily assigned to anthropological section as disciplinary action..."

"The bastards! Turning *my* station into a penal colony!"

"But all I did was leave a door open!"

"We'll *see* what you did." He backspaced a few lines and requested an information expansion. "Good Lord! You're *her*! They used to tell stories about you in school. You're the worst screw-up in our history! *You're* the one who sent the owner's own cousin back to the Polish Middle Ages, ten years before the Mongol invasions, when the guy didn't even know that time travel existed. They couldn't bring him back because he wasn't discovered there until the invasion was actually on. The owner himself found his own cousin on the battle lines, so they had to leave the guy there for the ten years or violate causality. When you make a mess, lady, you don't kid around!"

"But all I did was to forget to close a door!"

"You screw up here and I'll feed you to the leopards." He pulled up four more files and scanned them. "Well, if it's any consolation, your last boss was punished for failing to brief you properly. He'll be here in fifty years as my replacement and *you* get to break *him* in."

"I think I'll just quit and go back to North America."

"Fine. You'll get your chance to do that in a hundred years, subjective."

"But—"

"Lady, this far back we get one canister every fifty years. The last one just left and the next one is taking *me* out of this flea-bitten pest hole.

"So cheer up, kid, and make the best of it. Hungry? Come on, I'll show you where there's a good rotten log. Lots of grubs."

# Chapter One

MY NAME is Sir Vladimir Charnetski. I am a good Polish knight and a true son of the Holy Catholic Church. I was born in 1212, the third son of Baron Jan of Charnet.

I write because my instructress felt that I could improve my literacy by recording the events of my life, but on reflection I find that there is very little to say. I had an ordinary upbringing. At sports I was better than most, but not the best. I am good at arms, but there are some who can knock me out of the saddle. My chess is solid but uninspired.

Who would want to read the tale of so ordinary a knight? None but my mother and she already knows it.

But in my twentieth year, I met a most extraordinary nobleman and I think it fitting to write about *him*.

His name is Sir Conrad Stargard and I met him in the following manner. In the fall of 1231, word came from my father's liege lord, Count Lambert, that we should send a knight to Lambert's castle town to attend there on Easter and for the three months thereafter.

This was a duty that I eagerly sought for myself, for rumor had it that Okoitz was an excellent place for many reasons. Lambert's table was reputed to be one of the best in Silesia and his wine cellar the best stocked in Poland. Also, Lambert took his *droit du seigneur* in a most unusual and, it seemed to me, a most delightful way.

The lord of a manor naturally has the right to enjoy his peasant girls on the night before their wedding. My father is a vigorous man in most respects; but encouraged by my mother, he had long since declared himself too old for this duty and delegated the task to his sons.

My brothers and I diced for the responsibility and occasionally I won. Now, while the worst of copulations can fairly be described as excellent, these bouts were often less excellent than they could have been. While unmarried girls were presumed to be virgin, in fact they rarely were and a considerable number of them were obviously pregnant.

Then, too, they were often frightened and sometimes actually in love with their future husbands; circumstances which degraded their enthusiasm.

Oh, one could always encourage a wench to meet one in a secluded wood, but this entailed a certain amount of sneaking around, a thing I am loath to do.

My Lord Lambert's solution to the problem is as straightforward as he is. He picks the best-looking of his girls just as they are blossoming and persuades them to move into his castle as "ladies-in-waiting." The advantages he offers are such that scant persuasion is needed; indeed little more than a permission to come. He turns the management of his household over to the "ladies," and enjoys them at his leisure until such time as they are with child; he then procures for each an acceptable husband, provides a suitable dowry, and pays the wedding expenses.

Most importantly, Lambert, with his usual largesse, permits his attending knights full use of this harem, which often numbers a half dozen.

Lambert's custom is the envy of all the noblemen around and he gets away with it because his wife stays on her family's estates in Hungary. Or perhaps she stays there because of his custom. For my purposes it was inconsequential. I wanted to go.

As this pleasant obligation must, of necessity, fall to one of us three brothers, they suggested that we dice for it. I refused, saying that three months was a long time and that the matter ought to be discussed carefully over several days. My real reason was that, while I was a bach-

elor, my brothers were both married. I was sure that once
their wives heard about the matter (and I saw to it), I would
be given the task without the risk of the throw.

And so it was that my father informed me that I would
go to Okoitz. My mother was in tears as I left, acting as
if I were going off to war, or some less honorable way of
finding death. My father and brothers were cordial and
polite with the vague certainty that somehow I had
cheated them.

It was an easy day's ride to Okoitz and, since the
highwayman, Sir Rheinburg, had been killed, a safe one.
It was Holy Saturday and the Truce of God was in effect,
yet prudence and courtesy required that I be fully armed,
covered head to toe with chain mail and astride my war-
horse, Witchfire.

But there was no need to be grim, so I took the precaution of carrying a three-gallon sack of wine over my
saddlebow, and had a plentiful supply of bread and
cheese in my bags, this being the last day of Lent.

It was a pleasant spring morning and I found myself
singing old songs. I aided Witchfire by lessening the
weight of the burdensome wine sack and came to some
assistance with regards to the saddlebags, as well.

Horses like you to sing to them and soon Witchfire
was galloping for the sheer joy of a clear springtime
morning. But while crossing a small wooden bridge he
threw the shoe from his right rear hoof.

This was serious, both because of the high cost of
steel and because a charger cannot possibly be ridden
unshod without injury. I could not walk to Okoitz and get
there by the morrow, and to not get there would stain my
father's name.

I searched the bridge, the stream and its banks for
hours without finding the lost shoe. At last I went down
the road, walking in full armor and leading my horse,
searching for a blacksmith.

I found a small side trail and followed it to a peasant's
hut. The peasant's wife assured me that there was a village with a blacksmith two miles up the side trail.

In full armor, I trudged fully four miles to this village,
only to find that the blacksmith was away, visiting his
mother for Easter. But the filthy churls informed me that

but three miles further on the trail there was another village and here the smith was sure to be home, as he was the brother of the local smith and it was their custom to alternate, year by year, visiting their mother on Easter and Christmas.

I walked more than eight miles without finding the next village. Witchfire was limping badly, the wine skin was nearly exhausted and night closed in on us. There was nothing for it but, like a hero in a fireside tale, to stretch out under a tree and sleep in armor.

I unsaddled Witchfire, rubbed him down as best I could with some weeds and hobbled him for the night.

I had my flint and steel with me, and by dint of a half an hour's puffing and cursing, I managed to get a decent fire going. I gathered a supply of wood, doffed my helmet and unlaced the coif at my throat. I took another pull of wine and dozed off.

At perhaps midnight, I woke to the sound of a wolf howling. It was shortly answered by another and yet another, *and they were close*!

The fire was down to a few dying coals and Witchfire was whinnying nervously. I went to him and tripped in the dark, which spooked him worse. I had to speak to him a bit before he'd let me come close enough to take the hobble off. A damned nuisance when time was precious, but no beast of mine will ever be taken without a chance to defend himself! I could hear the wolves, snuffling, gathering both their courage and their numbers.

I went back to the coals of the fire and found my helmet and sword. Then I threw what kindling and wood I had left onto the coals and said a silent prayer in thanks to Saint Christopher for the blessing of enough time to get ready.

The fire blazed up as I belatedly laced shut the chainmail coif at my throat and donned my helmet. I slipped on my shield and drew my sword, for this was not the place for the lance, though I love that weapon above all others. The wolves grew louder, and I could tell that they didn't like the fire. I could imagine some impudent young wolf complaining, "Sooner! We should have hit them sooner!" It's sure that I heard one of the animals yelp as though bitten!

Witchfire, trusty friend that he is, came into the circle of firelight to join me. He knew that this must needs be a fight afoot, but he none the less meant to get his share of it. I grinned at him and they rushed us.

A huge gray wolf burst out of the darkness and at my throat. It was skinny, gaunt and hungry, yet it was fully my own size and weight none the less. These murderous beasts must have traveled far for the pains of winter to still be on them!

My sword caught the huge gray brute fair on the side of the skull and I heard the bone crack. His body rammed me square on the shield with such force that I was nearly knocked over, and indeed would have been had not a second wolf hit me but a moment later in the back. A foul blow, that, but one I was glad of, for once down, it was not likely that I could defend myself with any alacrity!

The wolf at my back was trying to bite into my neck, but the armor my father bought at great price was proof against it. I swung my sword back hard as though preparing for a forward blow. It caught the beast on the back. Again, I heard bones crack and it was at my feet whining and snapping.

I had no time to give it mercy, for my war-horse was sore pressed. Three gray forms were snapping around him and he had a fourth in his teeth, shaking it as a small dog will shake a rat. He threw it high into the air. It came down on the fire, screamed, and lost all of its fighting spirit. It ran away, yelping, its coat burning merrily.

I waded into the beasts that were harassing my mount and broke two gray necks with as many blows. The third turned to charge me, but Witchfire dropped both front hooves on its back and it moved no more.

Suddenly, all was quiet. We'd killed five of the foul creatures, and the one who got away would think long before it again approached a human fire!

Witchfire seemed unhurt and I was unwounded. I gave each of the dead animals another blow to see to it that they stayed that way, then laid myself back down to sleep. I didn't bother hobbling my mount. He wouldn't be wandering far from the fire again this night!

Yes, I was unharmed, but only because I was armed

and armored and with a trusty war-horse. One can well see why the peasants lock their doors at sunset and dare not leave until dawn. Even in daylight, many are killed when caught alone in the wilds. But what can be done about it?

I left the carcasses to rot on the ground. Wolf skins are worthless—even a peasant can afford better. And maybe the other wolves would get a meal off of their brothers instead of killing some hapless commoner.

The next morning I gave the *coup de grace* to the last of my wine, cheese, and bread and found the village not a quarter mile down the trail. I caught the smith and his family on their way to church.

"But, my dear sir knight! This is Easter morning, the holiest day of the year! Surely you can't expect me to work on this greatest of feast days!"

"Surely I can! Know that I am sworn to attend our liege lord, *Count Lambert himself*, on this very day at Okoitz. I cannot get there without my horse and my horse cannot travel without a shoe. You are the only blacksmith available and therefore you will do the job. Bid your family to church without you, and come with me."

"But to miss mass on Easter would be a great sin!"

I loosened my sword. "Not nearly so great a sin as committing suicide, which is your alternative."

His wife kissed him worriedly and hustled their children before her toward the church. Thus she made the decision for him, though I intended the man no harm. He started to call to her, but I took him by the upper arm and moved him to his shop.

"But I am in my best clothes! I must change."

"Very well. Do it quickly." He went into his house and I followed. It was well built, as peasant huts go, with a brick fireplace and a real wooden floor. He stopped and looked at me hesitantly, so I drew my sword and placed it before me, point down with my palms on the pommel. He changed clothes rapidly.

"But, sir knight . . ."

I ground the point of my sword into the floor, twisting it. He darted out to his shop. I followed.

Once he had a fire going in his forge, he said, "But I

have forgotten! I have no more iron! I used the last of it Thursday and no more will come until tomorrow."

"No iron? Then we must find you some. Hmmm... the hinges on this door are iron. It's a start." I ripped the door from the frame and threw it at him. It's a pity to have to use such techniques on such a sniveling wretch, but he had exhausted my patience.

"But that's not nearly enough and hinges are so hard to make!"

There were plenty of iron tools about, but I hate to deprive a man of his livelihood. I stalked back to his house. "That crucifix is iron."

"But that was blessed by the priest! We can't..."

"No, I guess we can't. Those candlesticks... the two of them will make a shoe and nails and we can spare your hinges."

"But I made those for my wife!"

"If your wife demands gimcracks while you lack the wherewithal of your trade, she deserves a good beating! Take them!"

It was eight hours of welding and forging, filing and fitting before my horse was shod. While I waited, his wife returned. I sent her out for wine and meat. Lent was over and I had a craving for a thick slab of roast pork.

What I got was small beer and chicken, the best—she claimed—to be had in that festering dump.

Finally, it was past none when I saddled Witchfire.

The blacksmith ran up. "But sir knight, you owe me for the shoeing!"

"The last time I had a shoe put on, it cost me eight silver pennies, so that's what I'll pay. And here's another penny for the meal, though it wasn't worth it." I rose to the saddle.

"But the candlesticks alone were worth twice this!"

"Then next time be better prepared." I rode out of town. Actually, I'd paid him half the money I had. My father was not a wealthy man.

We were an hour getting back to the main trail and though we pushed on as fast as I dared, darkness overtook us many miles from our destination. I had failed.

There was no moon and perforce my charger and I spent yet another night under a tree.

The tierce bell was ringing as we rode into Okoitz. An old friend was at the gate; we embraced and exchanged the kiss of friendship.

"Sir Vladimir! You arrive late!"

"Aye, Sir Lestko. Witchfire threw a shoe and finding a smith on Easter...But I must apologize to Count Lambert. Where is he?

"Your apology will be delayed as well; Lambert left at gray dawn to make his spring rounds. He may not return for months."

"Damn! Damn and thrice damn!"

"Fear not at all. Lambert said that if you arrived today, all would be well; but if not, we should search for you on the morrow. He knows no son of your father would fail him."

"Sir Lestko, we serve the finest lord in Christendom."

"Agreed. But come. You have just time to wash off the road dust before dinner."

We entered the bailey where a vast tower was under construction. "What on Earth is that thing?"

"A device of Sir Conrad's planning. They say it will suck power from the winds and force it to do man's bidding."

"That smacks of witchcraft."

"Sir Conrad claims not, though by all accounts, he's as much warlock as warrior and a giant besides."

"Sir Conrad? Is he the man that killed the brigand, Sir Rheinburg?"

"Rheinburg and his entire band and each killed with a single blow of the sword!"

"Unbelievable!" I said.

"But true. That German bastard's arms are in the storeroom here without a mark on them. Sir Conrad caught him straight through the eyeslit and cut his skull in half without harming the helmet."

"Some might call that luck."

"Not when he killed all the others besides. I tell you he brought in four suits of armor and all of them intact save for bloodstains."

"What manner of man is he?"

"I haven't met him yet myself, having arrived only a day before you. They say he's in Cieszyn and will return in a week or two. I must watch the gate until sext, but you go up to the castle; the ladies will see to your comfort."

"Indeed!" I asked, "Is Lambert's board and bed all they say it is?"

"Better. He has eight of them now and there are only five of us knights to keep them pleasured."

"The poor things." I grinned. "Well, we can only do our best."

No one met me at the castle door, but a remarkable noise was coming from within. It sounded like a dozen mad drummers going at once, or like carpenters trying to be musicians. I followed the sound to the great hall and found there an incomprehensible flurry of activity.

There was a great table around which sat a half dozen pretty wenches. Each had a cartwheel in front of her that seemed to spin of its own accord. There were big balls of wool and complicated arrangements of thread and spools spinning with astounding speed.

Unconsciously, I made the sign of the cross.

Against one wall, two more ladies worked a great wooden machine of incredible complexity, with thousands of strings and levers and moving parts.

Against the wall opposite stood three huge bolts of cloth.

One of the girls at the spinning wheels noticed my entrance, stopped her work and greeted me.

"What . . . what is all this?" I asked.

"Lambert's loom and spinning wheels, of course. Our lord would have us make our own cloth and stop paying our silver to those awful Waloons. You must be Sir Vladimir. Let me show you to your room."

As she led me down a hallway I said, "These wheels and such. They are something this Sir Conrad has built?"

"Who else?"

"You know him then?"

"I don't exactly *know* him." She rolled her eyes and grinned. "I mean I was still only a peasant girl when he left, but I hear he's just marvelous!"

"But you've seen him?"

"Oh, yes. He's enormously tall and absolutely beautiful!"

"I fail to see how a man can be beautiful."

"Then you haven't seen Sir Conrad. This will be your room." She scurried about, seeing that the water pitcher was filled and the chamber pot was empty. The place was remarkably clean, with a huge bed, a stool, and a wash stand.

"This will do nicely. Uh, would you help me get out of this armor? This is my first chance to remove it in three days. Two nights sleeping in chain mail is entirely too much."

"Of course, Sir Vladimir...Oh. You need a good scrubbing, besides."

"That is a glorious thought." I sat on the stool and she gave me a thorough sponge bath. Very thorough.

Once dry, I sat on the bed and said, "I'll rest a bit. Take off your dress and join me."

"I thought you'd never ask."

Much later I said, "That was good, wench. Very good."

"Thank you, my lord. Ah. There's the dinner bell. We must dress."

"Right." I got into my tunic and hose. "Uh, what is your name?"

"Annastashia."

At dinner I met Sir Bodan, a friend of my father, and he introduced me to Sir Frederick and Sir Stefan. They each sat down with a woman by their sides, so I bid Annastashia join me.

"I believe I'm still senior here and so am in command," Sir Bodan said. "Sir Vladimir, I observe that you have arrived late. In punishment for this, you shall take the graveyard shift and watch the gate from matins to prime."

"This seems just, my lord." I downed a bowl of beer and motioned for it to be refilled.

"Well, somebody has to do it."

"I make no complaint. But tell me more of this Sir Conrad."

"He does seem to be the main subject of conversation hereabouts," Bodan said. "First off, he rides a mare."

I stifled a giggle. "A mare?"

"A mare. Furthermore, they tell as many stories about the horse as they do of the rider. She refuses to be shod and goes without horseshoes, yet she gallops over rocks without splaying her hoofs. She doesn't soil her stall, but removes the bar and goes out in the bailey like a house-broken dog. Then she returns to her stall and replaces the bar!"

"Incredible!"

"She is fully war-trained and Conrad claims that two of his kills were made by her alone. Yet she has no objection to wearing a horse collar and working with the peasants. And under her influence, Count Lambert's best stallion hauled logs last winter, two war-horses guided by a single little peasant girl. The commoners here claim the mare is so intelligent that she can talk!"

"What?"

"Oh, it's just a matter of shaking and nodding her head. Yet she does it in response to questions; myself, I think it just a carnival trick."

"But what of the man himself? Who are his people?"

"That's another mystery. It seems that some priest laid a geise on him, that he may not tell of his origins. Some say that he is a socialist, though it is not clear just what that means. It might refer to his country, his military order, or his religious sect. Myself, I think it must be a religious sect, for he is uncommonly gentle with children, peasants, and other animals.

"All we really know is that he came out of the east in the company of a merchant, Boris Novacek."

"Ah. I know the man."

"Then you know that Boris is no fool and that he wouldn't lie unless there was a profit in it."

"True."

"Well, Boris claims he took this true belted knight out of a monastery in Cracow, where he was engaged in writing books."

"A knight who can read and write? That's unmanly!"

"There's nothing unmanly about him, though he claims to have spent seventeen years as a student in schools."

"Indeed. How old is this Conrad?" The beef stew was excellent.

"He claims to be thirty, but he looks no older than you and there's not a scar on his body. Then there is his equipage. They say he has a pavilion light enough to hold in the palm of your hand; it's said to have the property of keeping out noxious insects. He has silver pots and plates, lighter than a cobweb. He has a knife with a dozen blades that fold to a size smaller than your finger. He has another instrument of the same size that produces fire at the touch of a lever and a sleeping cloak that grows shut to keep the cold out. He gave Sir Miesko a device with a needle that always points north, to guide him in the dark. That needle burns with a green fire but never is it consumed."

"I could have used that last night," I said. The beer was truly fine.

Sir Bodan ignored me. "He gave Lambert an object that makes far things look close. Some of the girls here can show you incredibly tiny needles they had of him. And the peasants! He gave hundreds of parchment packages of seeds to the peasants, each package with writing and a beautiful painting on it. Most of the seeds are sprouting and there are some damn strange shoots coming up in Okoitz!"

"He must be a man of great wealth."

"Fabulous wealth. He arrived here with a chest of gold and silver worth *120,000 silver pence!*"

"Then . . . then why does he stay in a back woods place like Silesia?" I asked around the bread in my mouth.

"Who knows why a wizard does what he does?"

"Ah, yes. I saw his wheels and loom. He's a mighty wizard."

"Yet there's no magic in those machines in the great hall. I've been over every inch of them and there's nought there but boards and thread. They're clever, mind you. Damned clever. But they're still just things of wool and wood."

"Indeed?" A wench refilled my bowl.

"Then there's Conrad's sword. It's a skinny thing with but a single edge, yet with it Count Lambert—in front of a hundred witnesses—took the head off a fully grown pig with a single blow; and when Conrad became angered with a blacksmith, he chopped the anvil in half."

"Well, *I* can sympathize with that," I said. "But you haven't told me much about the man himself."

"I was coming to that." Bodan took another pull of beer. "He is huge and must duck his head to walk through that doorway. His hair is a dark blond and he wears it very short, inches above his shoulders. He has a proper moustache, but he shaves the rest of his face every day with a strange knife that never goes dull. Mostly, he wears ordinary clothes, but sometimes he dons garments of a thin, eldritch cut, with hundreds of buttons, clasps, and closures. There's something odd about his boots, though I haven't heard a good description of them."

"You mean you haven't seen him yourself?"

"What? No. None of us have, except for Sir Stefan and the wenches. Looking forward to it, but all I've told you is hearsay. Oh, yes. Besides all else, Conrad's a surgeon, a mathematician, and a great chess player. He beat Count Lambert for the first two dozen games they played and no one but he has beaten Lambert since. Ah. I've talked until my food got cold. You, girl! Throw this back into the pot and bring me more that's goodly hot."

"Well, I know that foul warlock right well," Sir Stefan said. "Too well! I've served here since Christmas, almost every night from dusk to dawn without relief and I know the bastard for what he is."

"Dusk to dawn?" I said. "Long hours! Weren't you to serve with Sir Miesko?"

"Sir Miesko took Conrad's place in the service of a merchant, to do an errand for Count Lambert. Then Conrad bewitched Lambert with dreams of wealth and fame and spent his days building the warlock's gear that you see in the hall and bailey. I was forced to stand guard seven nights a week and they were long cold nights!"

Sir Bodan said, "I've already shown that there's no witchcraft in those looms."

"*No witchcraft?* Do you realize that Conrad used this very table we're now eating from and drenched it with human blood!"

"I was there," Annastashia said quietly. "One of the

men from the village was hurt while cutting down trees. His foot was all smashed. Sir Conrad had to cut it off and sew him up to save him."

"And that peasant was dead within a month! The witch's rite didn't help much!" Stefan shouted.

"But, Sir Conrad was trying . . ."

"Shut up, wench!"

We were quiet for a bit, then Annastashia said softly, "I remember Sir Conrad at the funeral of a peasant child. He cried."

# Chapter Two

Two WEEKS slid pleasantly by. The weather was lovely; supplies of food and drink seemed inexhaustible; my fellow knights were excellent comrades; and the ladies, ah the ladies. I'd sampled them all by that point, but in the end I found that the best was at the beginning. I spent most of my nights with Annastashia. Well, my evenings at least, the graveyard shift being what it was.

Often Annastashia would come to me when I was on duty; sometimes we would talk and sometimes we simply held hands and watched the stars wheel by. I was quite taken by her, although of course nothing could come of it. For all her absurd status as a "lady-in-waiting," she was a peasant and I was a knight and my parents were very . . . traditional in their outlook. Yet . . . yet I tried not to think about my departure from Okoitz.

I looked forward to meeting Sir Conrad with a mixture of joy at the arrival of a hero and of fear at the coming of a warlock; yet when I finally met him and got used to his astounding size, I found him to be the most courteous and pleasant knight that could possibly be.

He had a fine voice and he knew thousands of songs; except on request, I don't think that he ever repeated himself. He could dance and recite poetry for hours. The ladies insisted that we learn his polka and mazurka and waltz. Sometimes Conrad would hire a few peasant musicians and we danced and laughed into the night.

The warlocks of legend are all taciturn and secretive. Sir Conrad was eager to teach his skills to all comers, peasant and noble alike; I found his mechanic arts to be fascinating and in time I came to appreciate his reasons in the machines he planned, and even hoped that one day I would be able to imitate them.

Yet in some ways he was decidedly odd. The peasants had stopped cock-fighting because "Conrad doesn't like it." The winter before, when Sir Stefan had brought in a bear for baiting—that is, to be tied to a stake and be ripped apart by the castle dogs for sport—Conrad attempted to purchase the bear, slew it with a single stroke of his remarkable sword and ordered the hide to be tanned and the meat served for supper. He did not do this in sport. As he killed, they say, there was a look of great sadness on that noble face.

Then there was his attitude toward children. Now, a normal man leaves children to the women until they are old enough to be human, but Conrad took great pleasure in their company, sometimes preferring it to that of his fellow knights. He always took time to explain what he was doing and never lost his temper with them as he often did with adults. He paid the priest to teach them their letters and taught mathematics himself. Moreover, he made them toys and taught them new games and sports.

Conrad was an absolute master of the sword and soon he was teaching us regularly every afternoon. He disdained to use a shield, trusting only to his blade for blocking. Indeed, he had a low regard for the usefulness of armor! Yet he was absolutely ignorant of the use of the lance and was remarkably clumsy with one on horseback. Nor was he good with a bow, yet somehow these things only increased our affection for him; it was a joy to find that I was better than him at *something*!

Lastly, there was Krystyana. She was a wench from Okoitz who had traveled to Cieszyn with Conrad. It was obvious that she was hopelessly in love with him; and somehow, much of his charm and courtesy had rubbed off on her, but in a most feminine way. She had the bearing and grace of a fine noblewoman to such an extent that none of the knights could treat her as a peasant girl, but accorded her the courtesies due to one of high rank.

Soon, some of the other "ladies-in-waiting" began to imitate her, my Annastashia among them. I found this charming—indeed, I found everything that Annastashia did to be charming!—but the other knights often reacted oddly. To tumble a village wench was one thing. To have intercourse with a noblewoman was something else!

Eventually Count Lambert returned, and with almost royal company, for with him rode his liege lord, Duke Henryk the Bearded, and that lord's son, young Prince Henryk, called the Pious. I was not privy to their conversations, but they stayed closeted with Sir Conrad for much of the afternoon.

The day after, there was to be a hunt and Count Lambert invited me to go. I am famed for my ability as a huntsman and perhaps Lambert had heard of this. Perhaps also he did not know that I stood daily guard from matins to prime, but when your father's liege lord invites you to hunt with *his* liege lord, you go!

So after duty, I went hunting rather than to bed. It was a good hunt and as Fortuna would have it, Sir Conrad took first blood on a winset. Being inept with the lance, he botched the job, only wounding the bison on the shoulder. Then he lost its trail entirely and even lost himself. In the end, I finished the animal and Count Lambert retrieved our crestfallen Sir Conrad.

I missed the feast that night, falling asleep in bed still in my armor, but I was up before matins and at my post at the proper time.

But within an hour, Sir Bodan relieved me and instructed me to attend Duke Henryk in his chamber.

I had never before had conversation with so high a personage and I was nervous as I knocked on his door.

"Come in, boy. Sit down and share a cup of wine with me." The duke was an ancient man, fully seventy years old. His face was lined and cracked and sunburned; his thick white hair brushed his wide shoulders and his huge white beard hung to below his finely tooled swordbelt. He was dressed all in purple velvet, heavily embroidered with fine gold wire.

Yet there was nothing foppish or feeble about him.

His bearing was robust, his arms still powerful and his eyes...*his eyes knew all things*.

"Thank you, your grace." I made a full Slavic bow to him, on my knees with my forehead to the floor.

"Up! Up child! No need for that nonsense when we're alone. I told you to sit."

I sat and he filled a huge golden wine cup from a silver pitcher. He drank deeply and handed the cup to me. I took a pull as great as his and set the cup down empty.

"Good! You drink as well as your father. If you're half the man he is, I'll expect great things from you." He refilled the cup.

"I try, your grace."

"You try right well. I know it's a hard thing to live up to, being the son of a great father. I remember him at the Battle of Fulnek. The Moravians had us outnumbered two to one, but Sir Jan led a charge that broke their line in half. It seems like yesterday...He took their first knight with his lance, splitting shield, armor, and breast bone. He rode on with the Moravian's shield still threaded on his lance and broke that lance on a second knight moments later, bashing him from the saddle to be trampled beneath our Polish chargers. Then he drew sword and cleared a swath through them as wide as he could reach, and his men behind him widened it. He broke their impetus and gave the rest of us time to regroup and charge the breach he'd made. We caught them on the flank, rolled them up like an old map, and the day was ours!"

"I heard he was sore wounded in that fight."

"Yes. It was before you were born, wasn't it? I saw a filthy peasant put a spear under his byrnie and into his gut. For a long time I feared for Sir Jan's life, but stamina and your mother's nursing carried him through. You know, I marked that peasant and when he turned up among the prisoners, I let all the others go, but him I hung for his impudence!

"Ah, you look so much like your father that you could almost pass for his twin, barring age. You have much of his skill—I missed your kill today but I saw the carcass. A single thrust, straight to the heart, on an animal maddened by Sir Conrad's clumsy blow."

"Your grace, I heard that Sir Conrad had never before been on a hunt."

"As did I—and that's odd, isn't it? A knight who could slay that almost invincible brigand, Sir Rheinburg, and singlehandedly wipe out his entire band; yet who never hunted an animal! Tell me, what do you think of him?"

"That's hard to say, your grace. He's such a mixture of things. Half hero and half child; half craftsman and half poet; half warlock and half saint! All I can say is that I like the man and that I trust him."

"Tell me, would you stay with him if you could?"

"Well . . . yes, your grace, were it consistent with my duty and honor."

"So. You missed tonight's feast . . ." I started to explain but he held up his hands. "I know you did right. It was your duty to be alert and on guard tonight; missing the festivities was the honorable thing to do. But know that during them, Count Lambert settled lands upon Sir Conrad. He leaves for them at dawn and I want you to go with him."

"But, your grace . . . My duty here . . ." Dammit, I couldn't tell him about Annastashia!

"Do not concern yourself. I will square matters with Lambert and your father."

"But what is it that you would have me do?"

"In truth, boy, I don't know. I, too, am uncertain about Sir Conrad. He could be the greatest good that has ever happened to Poland, or he could be the greatest evil. I only know that I would feel better if he had a trustworthy knight beside him, to protect him from harm and . . . and to let me know anything that you think I *should* know."

"Then your desire is my command, your grace. I shall do my duty unto the death, if need be."

"I know you will, my son. The blood of your father runs strong in you. Mind you, this is a privy conversation. Not one word of it to anyone save your father. Now to sleep with you. There's a long ride waiting at dawn."

So my stay at Okoitz was to be cut short and when next I saw Annastashia, she'd likely be a peasant's wife with dirty children crawling around a smoky fire.

I did not go straight to my room, but stopped in the great hall. The remains of the feast had not yet been cleaned up. I found a nearly full pitcher of wine, a cup, and a joint of cold meat. It suited my mood to eat and drink alone. Endings are such sad things.

The lauds bell struck as I stumbled into my room and dumped my armor on the floor. I got into bed and found Annastashia already there. In an instant we were crying in each other's arms.

"Sir Vladimir," she bawled, "I don't want to leave you."

So much for Duke Henryk's secrecy, I thought. The girls always knew everything that was happening.

"And I don't want to leave you, my love."

"Your love? You never called me your love."

"Perhaps because until this hour, I never realized how much I truly do love you."

"Oooowww! Don't you see that that only makes it worse! I mean, why do we have to do what everybody else says? It isn't fair! Why do I have to leave because Lambert says so? I don't want to go anyplace else!"

"Wait a moment, love. It is I who must leave and you who must stay."

"But no! Lambert says that I must go with Sir Conrad."

I am sure that my laugh woke half the castle.

"And I shall accompany him as well!"

Our joy was such that we got no sleep that night. At dawn we were packed and ready in the bailey before Sir Conrad got there. When he arrived, he was in the company of Krystyana and three other ladies besides. Indeed, it seemed that he had picked those who were most gracious of manner.

"Well, Sir Conrad. It seems that our lord sends you out well provisioned."

"Indeed. He is most generous. But why are you saddled up?"

"I hoped to accompany you and help you guard these treasures."

"More treasures than you know, Sir Vladimir." Conrad slung a pair of small, heavy saddlebags over his horse and lashed them stoutly to the cantle. "Your presence is needed, and I hope you'll come as my guest. It looks like I'm not the only one who needs you." He winked at Annastashia, for of course he knew of our relationship.

The girls felt obligated to cry at leaving their families and homes, and Annastashia joined them in this even though her parents had been dead for a year. But in an hour their tears were dry and the joy of adventure was on them.

Our company made a rich appearance on that clear morning. Conrad and I were in full armor on our chargers, our ladies well dressed on fine palfreys and we had three good mules loaded with provisions and clothing. Conrad took the lead with Krystyana at his side, so perforce Annastashia and I rode rear guard with the others between.

After a few hours, I said, "Annastashia, do you know where we are going?"

"Why, to Sir Conrad's lands."

"But where are those?"

"Well, I suppose in *that* direction." She pointed forward.

I found this location to be inadequate, and questioned my love more closely. I was amazed to learn that not only had she not the slightest concept of geography, but that this was the first time since early childhood that she had been out of sight of Okoitz. Her blind faith in me and Sir Conrad was touching, but I feel best when I know what I'm about.

Our trail had been winding through a dense forest and the dangers of being taken unawares was such that I dared not leave my rear-guard post. But when we found ourselves among plowed fields, I spurred Witchfire to the head of the column.

"Sir Conrad, I would speak with you."

"You've picked a fine day for it. How can I help you?"

"You know that I missed the feast and did not hear Lambert's settlement on you. Where are we going?"

"That's a very good question. When we started, I didn't know myself. I've been worrying about it all morning. You see, I've been given a huge tract in the mountains south of here. There's an old coal mine on it that I hope to reopen. But there's not a building there, not so much as a shed, and we can hardly dump these girls in the middle of a forest."

"Lambert gave you lands but no people? How odd. Perhaps my father could supply a few dozen peasants."

"Well, thank you, but I'd hate to impose on a man I've never met. Anyway, there are plenty of people out of work in Cieszyn. I think our best bet would be to go there and put together a construction crew before going to Three Walls."

"Three Walls?"

"I've decided on the name because the valley we'll build in is boxed on three sides by high mountains. God has built three of our walls. We need only build the fourth."

"A nice thought. Hmm...at this speed we'll not make Cieszyn by nightfall."

"Right. The girls couldn't stay in the saddle that long anyway. I think we'll call on Sir Miesko and Lady Richeza for the night. There's a stream and a meadow an hour ahead. We'll break there for dinner."

Sir Conrad's language was always colorful. At the meadow, we helped the ladies off their palfreys, unsaddled the mounts, unloaded the mules and hobbled all the animals save Conrad's Anna, who refused it. Conrad treated Anna as an indulgent father treats a favorite daughter, permitting her to race about the woods around the meadow. Only after she had completely circled the meadow twice, once near and once far, did she come in to drink and crop grass. It was just exuberance on her part, I know, but I had the uncanny feeling that she was searching for possible ambushers.

I turned from these musings expecting to find the ladies preparing dinner, but the fact was that they could barely walk. Conrad himself was busily chopping wood and in a remarkably short time he had a merry fire going. He seemed to be enjoying himself, proud of his woodcraft, and made no suggestion that any should aid him.

Yet seeing him indulge in this woman's work embarrassed the girls such that they limped up and took over the preparation of food from him, which left him free to join me lying on the grass.

He was silent for a while, so I said, "Share your thoughts, my friend."

"Well, I'm thinking about that coal mine. It's filled with water and we'll need some sort of pump to empty it."

"Another of your windmills?"

"I don't think so. The valley is surrounded by fairly tall mountains with only a small entrance between the two cliffs. There won't be much wind there."

"It sounds easily defended."

"There is that advantage. But pumping that mine is going to be a problem. Wind power is out. There is no stream, so water power is impossible. Animal power? The area is heavily forested and it will be years before we're self-sufficient in food. Importing animal feed would be expensive. But, if we have coal, I wonder if we couldn't come up with a crude steam engine. Pistons, cylinders, and high-pressure boilers are well beyond us, but perhaps a condensing steam engine..."

"Sir Conrad, you have lost me again. Please explain how it were possible to raise water with vapors."

"Let's see... I've explained that matter exists in three phases—solid, liquid, and gas. If you heat a solid enough, it melts. If you heat a liquid enough, it boils."

"That much is obvious."

"Okay. Now ordinarily the gas phase is much larger than the liquid phase. A given amount of material takes up much more room."

"I'll take that on faith."

"You don't have to take it on faith. You have observed it! You've watched a pot boiling. Look there, where the girls are cooking. Steam is going out of the pot, overflowing it. Further, that steam was once water, as is proved by the way the water level in the pot gets lower as more steam goes out."

"I *said* I believe you!" I sat bolt upright.

"You said you had faith! What I tell you about science should *never* be taken on faith! Each and every step should be proved by direct observation. I am trying to teach you how to understand and manipulate the physical universe. I am *not* trying to teach you a religion! That's not my job!"

"I'm sorry, Sir Conrad. Please continue." He has such a temper! I think he doesn't drink enough wine.

"No, I owe the apology, Sir Vladimir, and in fact there is a certain religious aspect to science. You see, God made all beings, all things, the whole of existence. He is the Grand Planner, the Master Designer, the Chief Engineer. When we study the world around us, we are studying His works, His thoughts. It's almost blasphemy to ignore that and have faith in the words of a mere man."

I lay back down. "Now, *that* is a *remarkable* thought! That it were possible to study the mind of God by observing His works—in the same manner that I have studied your mind by observing your mills and looms. Incredible!... I think that it will take me a long time to absorb it."

We were silent for a while and then our ladies called us to dinner. They were still walking stiffly and were not at all cheerful.

"Why such downcast faces?" I asked.

"My love, it is not my *face* which is troubling me," Annastashia replied.

"Well, cheer up! We shall be at Sir Miesko's in four more hours."

*"Four more hours!"* came five simultaneous feminine cries.

"Well, I'm sorry," I said. "But there's nothing for it. The fault is all in those sidesaddles you persist in using. With the possible exception of teats on a stallion, they are the stupidest things imaginable. There is nothing to keep the rider in place but the horse's good intentions, an untrustworthy thing at best. Look at that rig! The rider must sling her right knee over a knob designed to numb her leg, put her left foot into an inadequate stirrup and then put her right toe under the back of her left knee to obliterate sensation in that member as well. Its sole purpose seems to be to permit a woman to ride while wearing a dress and destroying her body."

"Well... what are we supposed to do about it?"

"Don't ask me, my love. I am taxed to my abilities being a fighter and a lover. Sir Conrad is our master of technical devices."

Five pairs of eyes turned on Conrad.

"It's obvious. Put on pants and ride on a man's saddle."

"That's scandalous!" Krystyana said. "The very thought that a lady would be *seen* in a man's clothing..."

"Then there's the key word, pretty girl, 'seen.' Make an outfit that looks like a woman's dress but functions like a man's pants."

"Uh...I don't follow you."

"Take one of your dresses. Slit it hem to crotch in front and behind. Sew in a fold of cloth between them. If you're careful about it, you can make it look acceptable but still be able to fork a horse."

The girls looked at each other anxiously and then grew a communal grin.

Suddenly, Krystyana said, "But how would you get into it?"

"Well...you could make it in two pieces, top and bottom, blouse and skirt; or you could slit it down the front and button it up like one of my shirts."

The grins returned.

"But that's not going to get us to Sir Miesko's. You girls clean and pack the gear while we saddle the horses."

The sun was still high when we arrived. Sir Miesko was out inspecting his fences, but Lady Richeza greeted us well. She is easily the most courteous and gracious woman in Christendom. She was common-born, like my Annastashia, and seeing her well-run household gave me visions of my own domestic bliss. But Sir Miesko was base-born as well, and knighted on the battlefield for valor. He was not faced with a heroic father and twenty generations of nobility.

Sir Conrad was talking intently with Lady Richeza.

"Yes, Sir Conrad, Gretch arrived safely and the girl's a wonder! This new mathematics of yours is a fascinating thing. I have no doubt that we'll have a dozen good instructresses by Christmas."

"And how about the schools?"

"It goes well. Eight villages are fully committed, and

by winter I think that the problem will be the lack of educated teachers."

"A dozen the first year is better than we had hoped. Textbooks?"

"We've made a start, buying supplies out of Cieszyn. But at the rate it's going, we won't have four dozen sets in time."

"That's skinny. Haven't you heard from Father Ignacy?"

"Not yet. But there was a delay in finding a merchant going to Cracow."

"Well, if you don't hear from him in a few weeks, inquire about professional copyists in Cieszyn."

"But that's expensive, Sir Conrad, and we're already close to your budget."

"Well, going over budget is not as bad as blowing the whole project. We need the books."

"Excuse me, Sir Conrad," I interrupted. "What is all this about?"

"Lady Richeza and I are organizing a school system. We'll have a dozen schools going next winter, from Christmas to spring planting."

"Schools? To teach what? To whom? By whom?"

"Schools! Reading, writing, and arithmetic, for starters. For Lambert's people. By Lady Richeza's gallant ladies."

"For the *peasants*? With some *peasant* women teaching them?"

"Sir Vladimir. May I point out that you show all the signs of being in love with a lowly peasant? That you are under the roof of a man who was born among these unfortunate people? And, while I am at it, that in the long run, the truly important thing is that women bear children and raise them properly—which includes education—and that the best that we males can do is to support them in that function? Now start apologizing and start with Lady Richeza."

Damn! Damn and thrice damn! But I had sworn to protect the man. Fighting him was out of the question and there was nothing for it but to apologize.

I had only begun when Sir Miesko came in and Conrad called to him.

"Sir Miesko! Say hello to your new neighbor!"

"What? You, Sir Conrad? What is this?"

"Count Lambert has granted me lands adjoining yours."

"Congratulations! But . . . that can only be in the hill country. There's not much good farming land up that way."

"True. But I plan to make mortar from limestone and coal, do some lumbering, and perhaps raise some sheep."

"Well, it might work. But how are you going to feed your people?"

"Obviously, I'll have to buy food, which is one of the reasons I wanted to talk to you. I hope to be your best customer."

"Well, I'd rather sell to you than a Hungarian merchant, but this wants talking. I have a new vat of beer in need of breaching. Let us retire to my chamber."

Lady Richeza was in rapt conversation with Krystyana, with most of the others gathering around. Soon they moved off to the kitchen. I thought I was abandoned, but, no. I had my Annastashia.

# Chapter Three

▲▲▲▲▲▲▲▲▲▲▲▲▲▲▲▲▲▲▲▲

THE NEXT day, on the road to Cieszyn, I said, "Sir Conrad, you were speaking of a machine with vapors..."

"A condensing steam engine. Yes?"

"Tell me the way of it. This is something that you've seen before?"

"Well, I've seen a walking-beam engine in a museum, but what I've seen won't work in our situation. You see, there is an existing mine shaft that slopes down at about a forty-five degree angle." Observing my facial expression, he gesticulated, drawing the angle in the air so that I understood. "I don't know how far the shaft is straight, but I think that I have an even simpler mechanism that should work."

"Indeed. I have seen a walking-beam and to my eyes it was no simple thing."

"Have you! Where?"

"At the salt mines near Cracow."

"Sir Vladimir, we are going to have to visit that place. But back to my engine. Imagine a barrel with two holes in the bottom and one in the top. One of the bottom holes is fitted with a valve that will let water in but not out. It has a long pipe on it that leads down into the water. The other bottom hole has another long pipe on it—say about eight yards long—that leads up to another barrel with another valve on the bottom that lets water in but not out. These valves can be simple pieces of leather that loosely cover a hole."

"I can imagine that."

"Okay. Into the top of each barrel, we run a pipe from a boiler, a big kettle with a good lid. Between the kettle and each barrel we have a valve that is open and shut by hand. Still following me?"

"Yes."

"Right. Now we open the steam valve which fills the lower barrel with steam. Air in the barrel is forced out into the upper barrel."

"Uh . . . oh. You have a fire under the kettle."

"Of course. Now we close the steam valve. Steam in the lower barrel cools, condensing back to water which takes up much less space than the steam. The valve in the upper barrel will not let air back in so water is sucked up the pipe to fill the lower barrel."

"Uh . . ."

"Have you ever drunk through a straw?"

"A straw? No, but once when I was ill my mother had me drink hot beer through the shaft of a heron's feather."

"Same thing. As the lower barrel is filling, we purge the top barrel of air as we did the lower barrel. Once the lower barrel is full, we open the bottom steam valve again and close the top one. Thinking about it, these two steam valves could both be worked with the same handle. The water runs out the lower barrel and up to the top one, having been lifted sixteen yards. Closing the steam valve repeats the process.

"Now, I don't know how deep that mine is, but I'm sure it's more than sixteen yards. Still, I see no reason why we can't cascade any number of barrels, each feeding the one above it. We'd only need two steam lines, one for odd barrels and one for even."

"Why, that sounds wondrous, Sir Conrad." We rode a while in silence as I tried to digest it all. Then I said, "But why would you need many barrels? Why not just put a longer pipe on the first one?"

"Well, there's a limit on how hard you can suck. Actually, I've said 'suck' because it's easier to visualize. In truth, you can't pull on water. Fluids lack tensile strength. What we're really doing is lowering the pressure in the barrel and letting atmospheric pressure push the water up."

"Atmospheric pressure . . . ?"

"Yes. Consider that we live at the bottom of an ocean of air . . ."

"At the bottom of an ocean!" There are times when Conrad pushes too far!

"Of air. Come on now, Vladimir. Can you really doubt that you are surrounded by air? What do you think wind is, but the motion of air? What do you think you're breathing?"

"Well . . . yes. But I've never thought of it in those terms."

"Okay. Now air has weight and . . ."

"There! You are doing it again! If air has weight, why doesn't it fall down?"

"Huh?" Conrad said.

"It's up in the air, isn't it? . . . or maybe I can't say that, but it's up there, isn't it? If it weighs something it should fall down!"

"But . . . it *has* fallen down. It's on Earth, isn't it? It hasn't drifted off to the Moon, has it?"

"How the hell should I know?"

"Well, it hasn't. If you go to the Moon, you must take your air with you."

"If I go to the bloody damn Moon! Dammit, Sir Conrad, I am trying to engage in a simple, civil conversation. We are talking about accomplishing the mundane task of getting water out of a flooded mine. I may not have your education, but I am no idiot child to be fobbed off with tales of fairies and dragons and trips to the Moon!"

The girls had dropped back as our argument heated up. We rode in silence for a bit, letting our tempers cool down. Then Conrad said, "Okay. I'm sorry. I didn't intend to insult you. Now, we were discussing atmospheric pressure. Let's suppose that you were walking at the bottom of a lake— No! Let me take that back. Suppose that a turtle was walking on the bottom of a lake."

"Very well," I said.

"Now, the turtle can look up and see the water above him, right? But you know that water has weight, always flows downhill, and settles in the lowest spot possible. Right?"

"I see. So if I could stand like an angel above the world, I might see you riding at the bottom of an ocean of air."

"Well put, Sir Vladimir. Now, air weighs very little, but it is many miles deep. The weight of it over a single square yard is something like ten tons. Hey, don't fly off the handle again!"

I said with some resignation, "My back must be half of a square yard. Please explain how it is that I can carry five tons of air on it with ease, when one ton of stone would squash me flat?"

Sir Conrad rubbed his neck with his fingertips, grimaced at the dirt of them and muttered, "Two weeks without a bath," then said, "A fluid pushes equally in all directions. While it is pushing down on top of you, it is also pushing up from the bottom. Those two areas must be the same, so they cancel out. The push down equals the push up and you don't feel anything."

"I have tons pushing down and tons pushing up and doubtless tons pushing at all sides! Were that true, I would surely be squashed!"

"Without the air pressure on you, you would quickly die. You might say that you are already squashed, that you are used to being squashed."

"My mother would not be delighted to hear it."

And so it was that we talked out the morning.

Conversation with Conrad can numb the mind more than all the wine of Hungary! My one moment of glory was when Conrad thought that a "walking beam" was a log that somehow had a walking motion, whereas in truth a walking beam is a beam that a man walks on. A small victory, but something to hang the pride on.

The none bells were ringing as we entered the gates of Cieszyn. I started heading for the castle, as was my custom, but Conrad directed us to the Pink Dragon Inn.

"You and I would be welcome at the fort," he whispered. "The girls would not."

I saw the wisdom in this. I had heard that Conrad owned the Pink Dragon Inn, and I suppose that I expected it to be filled with more of his mechanical contrivances. What I found surprised me. The place had a large carved wooden sign, as brightly painted as a statue in church. It had a large and fat pink dragon, beer mug in hand, staring with great lechery at a small and remarkably feminine pink rabbit. This strangely proportioned rodent was grinning back at the dragon.

We were met at the door by Tadeusz, the innkeeper. He was a huge man, as round as a ball, with a full beard and a clean white apron, yet for all his size he moved with remarkable speed.

"Sir Conrad! Welcome, my lord! It is joyous to see you again!"

"Nice to see you, too, Tadeusz."

"This noble lord and these fine ladies, they are your guests, my lord?"

"Oh, yes. They lodge at the inn's expense."

I was relieved to hear this. You see, while my father is hardly a pauper, his expenses in recent years have been high. Not only had he provided three sons with horse, arms, and armor, but he had provided a total of seven large dowries in the course of getting my six sisters married. (It happened that one prospective brother-in-law had the affrontery to drop his dowry into the Odra River while on a ferryboat. To his credit, he did try to retrieve the sack, but was unfortunately wearing full armor at the time. Or perhaps fortunately, for had he not drowned, my father would surely have dealt the fellow a less honorable death. I suppose every family has a skeleton or two about.)

Be that as it may, my father does not see fit to provide lavishly for a son who has remained a bachelor. My services to Lambert had been in discharge of feudal duty, so of course I had not been paid. The duke had not mentioned money, so I could hardly broach so mundane a subject to so high a personage.

The result was that I had in my possession a total of nine pence, enough perhaps for a meal and lodging for a night. After that, well, I would always be welcome at Cieszyn Castle, Count Herman's wife being my mother's second cousin. Also, since my father is one of eleven living children and my mother one of seventeen, there was always a relative nearby who would be happy of company. In fact, I once computed that it would be possible to spend four and a half years visiting them all without spending a pence, without overstaying a welcome, and without imposing on the same relative twice. My family may not be wealthy, nor high in the nobility, but we are prolific.

The duke, however, had charged me to stay with Conrad and this would have proved difficult had not Conrad himself paid my way.

Conrad and I dismounted and helped the girls down. A half dozen stable boys scurried out and took away our horses.

"Curry them down and feed them of the best!" Tadeusz shouted. "The very best, mind you!"

Conrad stopped the boy who was leading off his horse, removed his small, heavy saddlebags and draped them over the innkeeper's shoulder, which visibly sagged under the weight.

"See that these are put in a safe place, Tadeusz, and have something sensible done with our baggage."

Conrad introduced his party, but the innkeeper became increasingly fretful.

"But you did not let me know that you were coming, my lord."

"Well, it's not like I could phone ahead."

The innkeeper paused to let that strange statement pass, being perhaps more used to Conrad than I was.

"Business has been extremely good, my lord. The inn is full."

"That's wonderful!"

"It is wonderful that I cannot provide my liege lord and each of his noble guests with rooms?"

"It's wonderful that our inn is doing well." At the time, I was shocked by Conrad's use of the royal plural, but on getting to know him better I found that he thought of the inn as belonging to both himself and the innkeeper. Conrad owned it legally and Tadeusz managed it, so it was "theirs." He actually thought that way.

"We don't all need separate rooms," Conrad said, rubbing at the dirt on his neck. "What about the room that you were supposed to keep reserved for me?"

"Why, your accountant, Piotr, uses that, my lord. I know! Those merchants from Prague! I shall evict them. I never liked Bohemians anyway!"

"Hey, none of that! If we've rented them rooms, the rooms are theirs. Look, for tonight, put Piotr up with the stable boys, find a second bed and put it up in the room for Sir Vladimir and Annastashia. Three of our ladies can sleep with the waitresses."

"Ah, my lord. Some of these maidens wish to be waitresses?"

"I'm afraid that they don't qualify. For now I want a tall beer and a warm bath before supper.'

I later found that to be a waitress at the Pink Dragon Inn, a maiden must needs be a true intact virgin; a thing my Annastashia had ceased at months ago.

Although the sun was still high, the common room of the inn was full of customers. At a whispered word from our host, a party of young men quickly smiled, bowed and vacated a table for us. It seems that they worked at the brass foundry, which Conrad also owned.

A pair of fast-moving waitresses quickly cleaned the table and brought us pitchers of cool beer from the cellars. They were maids of exceptional beauty and most immodestly clad.

To start from the bottom, they wore shoes with extremely high heels; two or three fingers high. They wore no dress, but a tight fitting cloth that barely covered their breasts and privy members. The back of this skimpy garment had an absurd puff of fur, like a rabbit's tail. Their legs were covered with tight hose of a material suitable for netting small fish. There were bands of cloth at their necks and wrists—suggestive of shackles—and a strange sort of hat, reminiscent of a rabbit's ears. And that was *all*.

I found myself staring at these lovely apparitions until Annastashia kicked me, quite painfully, in the shin.

Conrad didn't bother to sit as cool beer was placed before us. He simply downed his mug with a single pull, said, "To the showers!" and went out the inn's backdoor.

"Can he do something to make it rain?" Natalia asked between gulps of beer.

"No," Krystyana said. "He just means that we should follow him to the bathhouse."

"Oh, good! I've always wanted to take a bath!"

Count Lambert's castle town had a sauna for use in the winter and there was a nearby stream with a swimming hole for use in the summer. But there was no bathhouse. The girls had heard Krystyana's descriptions of the glories of soaking in a hot tub and they scurried eagerly after Conrad.

I, perforce, mounted rear guard and showed admirable foresight in securing a pitcher of beer from the table to take with us. The bathhouse was an establishment separate from the inn, but adjoining it. Conrad did not own the place, but had made special arrangements with it for the convenience of the inn's servants and guests. A brass token from the inn paid our fare.

The baths were of the traditional sort, with men and maids bathing together. There is a fad, prevalent in some of the larger cities, that separates the sexes. An annoying modernism, it spoils the scenery; and how is a man to get his back clean?

As I entered the changing room, Sir Conrad was already walking out, having left his clothes and armor scattered on the floor.

"A wise thought, that," he said, noticing my pitcher. "Boy! Run to the inn and bring back a few more pitchers of beer! And mugs!" He stumbled into the darkened bathroom.

The girls, having seen Conrad scatter his clothing and equipment about the room, naturally assumed that this was the proper way to do things. Soon stockings and embroidered petticoats were scattered atop chain mail and leather.

Now, my arms and armor were worth three hundred times the money in my purse. To treat them in this careless manner was painful to me but I did it, to keep up appearances. As I finished stripping, an old female attendant came in, shook her gray head at the mess, and started folding things. I wanted to tell her to take special care with my armor, but didn't, fearing that she would expect a gratuity.

The bathroom proper had no windows; it was lit by

but two oil lamps and one must needs feel one's way in until the eyes became accustomed.

"Well now," said a voice that I almost recognized. "They seem to let anyone come in here."

"You'd think the place was a common stews," said another almost familiar voice.

"But then, again, it *is* a common stews," said a third voice. "That is to say, it *is* common and we *are* all here up to our necks stewing."

"True," said the first. "And he doesn't seem a truly bad sort."

"Indeed, he comes in the company of five of the truly good sort."

"Unclad ladies must always be considered socially acceptable," agreed the first. "In fact, I move that we make a guild ordinance to that effect."

"Moved, seconded, and passed by general acclaim."

It was still too dark to see who was talking. Straining to see them, I bumped my shin on the rim of one of the two huge half-sunken tubs.

"Tsk. Such a clumsy sort. And his mother was so proud of him. Twenty years of careful upbringing gone to waste."

"Mothers all feel that way. It comes with the fief. But see. He has had the foresight to bring potables. If this wisdom is matched by generosity, he might prove a valued member of our company."

The girls were giggling at the exchange, but I have found that it is not wise to act belligerent when naked. Had I been in armor, my response might have been different, but I attempted humor.

"I brought the pitcher from the table lest it be abandoned. This very night, little Moslem children will be going to bed thirsty, so it's a sin to be wasteful."

"You know," Conrad spoke for the first time. "My mother used to use a similar argument to try to get me to eat my vegetables."

"Mine as well, though she never used it on beer," said a voice. "I always told her to send them to the poor infidels, but she took no heed."

"I did precisely the same," said Conrad. "Do all mothers read the same books?"

"*My* mother can't read at all. Nonetheless, it was wise of Vladimir to bring the beer. Why, it might have fallen into the hands of some intemperate inebriate and thus contributed to all manner of venial sins."

"As well as a few carnal ones."

"Just who are you men?" I shouted.

"He doesn't recognize us. I'm crushed. It must be eyestrain."

"Doubtless brought on by staring at these lovely ladies."

"Dammit!" I said.

"We're the Upper Selesian Drinking and Fighting Men's Guild."

"Dragons slain, treasures liberated, maidens put in distress, and promptly rescued."

"All services performed by true belted knights."

"I never heard of it," I said.

"Reasonable. We only just formed it this afternoon. After all, if the commons can have guilds with all sorts of special privileges, why can't we?"

"Right. We have, for example, declared a guild monopoly on rescuing fair maidens in distress. Now you, young lady, you look to be in need of rescuing."

"But I'm not in distress!" Natalia said.

"Easily arranged. Gregor here can do it."

"Gregor!" I shouted. "You are my cousin Gregor!"

"A slow lad, but he comes through in the end."

"And that's *second* cousin. You must allow us some dregs of pride," his brother Wiktor said.

"Nonetheless, we *are* family, Vladimir," my cousin Wojciech added. "So get in the tub, share out the beer, and introduce us to your attractive friends."

I got in. The room had lightened enough for me to see reasonably well. "Have some beer, if you need it badly enough to beg. Unfortunately, I can not introduce you three to my friends. You see, they must maintain *their* standards, which would be irretrievably lowered by social contact with the less fortunate members of—"

"Come off it, Vladimir. They played a good joke on you. Don't rub it back on them. Gentlemen, I am Sir Conrad Stargard."

"And I am Sir Gregor Banki. These are my brothers Sir Wiktor and Sir Wojciech."

"*Sir* Wojciech! What fool finally knighted *you*?" I asked, but was ignored.

"You are *the* Sir Conrad Stargard? I should have known by your size," Wiktor said.

"You are the warrior who singlehandedly destroyed Sir Rheinburg's outlaws? The warlock who is doing all those strange things in Okoitz?"

"Gentlemen, if you want to stay friends, I'll ask you to forget that word 'warlock.' I've built a textile factory at Okoitz and I have a few windmills going up. As to the rest, well, it just sort of happened," Conrad said.

A waitress from the inn brought a tray of beer and mugs. Despite the fact that we had five lovely and nude young ladies in the tub with us, all male eyes followed her around the room as she served.

As she left, Wiktor said, "Sir Conrad, how do you go about training them to walk that way? I mean, the way her, uh, *derrière* moves..."

"It's not training. It's the shoes. Walking on high heels requires more hip action."

"I've *got* to get one of those outfits!" Yawalda whispered.

Conrad laughed. "Gentlemen, let me complete the introductions. These are Lady Krystyana, Lady Annastashia, Lady Natalia, Lady Yawalda, and Lady Janina."

"We are honored, ladies," Gregor said. "You must forgive me. I had assumed that since Sir Conrad just came from Okoitz, you must be some of Count Lambert's famous ladies-in-waiting."

"Well, they are," Conrad said. "Or were. But since I seem to be their guardian, I've just promoted them to the nobility."

"Can you do that?" Wiktor asked.

"Are you saying that I can't?" Conrad said.

"Sir Conrad, considering the stories that we've heard of your sword, I'd say that you can do just about anything you want." Gregor laughed.

"Then it's settled," Conrad said. "I think I've soaked enough to loosen the dirt. Krystyana, if you'd get a brush and some soap going on my back, I'll return the favor shortly."

As soon as Krystyana went to work, Annastashia claimed proprietorship of my own back. After a few moments of reciprocal grinning between my cousins and the other girls, there was shortly a great deal of scrubbing going on. A very great deal. In fact, the waitress returned to freshen our mugs and was hardly noticed.

Things became increasingly boisterous, which was just as well. The mood of the company was such that things had to fall out either to sport or to sex and I wouldn't like my aunts to hear that I was involved in a public orgy!

Soon people were bumping into people, Natalia splashed Gregor, he retaliated, and in moments the room exploded with soapy water as everyone joined in.

As the water settled, Conrad vaulted from the tub and went to the clean-water tub for a hot soak. The old bath attendant, having finished with our clothes, came in, shook her tired gray head and picked up a mop. She dried the floor, muttering under her breath. The waitress returned with fresh mugs of beer, as the old ones were half filled with soapy water.

The others followed Conrad to the clean tub, but Annastashia motioned for me to stay behind with her.

"What Sir Conrad said," she whispered, "about how we were all ladies, now. Is that real? I mean, would your parents..."

I shook my head. "It means that you will be treated with great courtesies at the inn and on Sir Conrad's lands. But my parents, especially my mother—she'd look down on anyone whose great-grandfather was a commoner."

After the bath, my cousins accepted Sir Conrad's invitation to supper. We returned to the inn to find the table ready for us and fairly groaning with food and drink. We did justice to a slab of smoked sheatfish, a joint of lamb, and an entire goose. Gallons of wine and buckets of beer washed down mounds of bread and cheese. I think only my Uncle Felix sets a better table than Conrad's innkeeper.

Further, we did not have to go to the market to purchase these things so that the inn could prepare them, as is the usual arrangement with inns, but the inn provided the service, not only to us but to all as a matter of custom. The innkeeper told me that this innovation of Sir Conrad's was partly responsible for the profitability of the inn, for by buying in vast quantities he was able to get the best at very low prices.

"Further," Tadeusz continued, "I need only prepare a half dozen items a day to satisfy my guests, saving the cooks much effort."

"But how do you know how much to cook?" Krystyana asked.

"My lady, we know about how much of what our guests will eat. True, sometimes the pigs are fed better than they deserve, but not often. Also, our waitresses have become adept at persuading our customers to purchase that which we have in excess."

I laughed. "I think those girls could have a man eating dog meat without his noticing!"

"Hmm...an interesting suggestion, my lord. But I'm afraid that Sir Conrad would not approve."

"No, Sir Conrad would not approve," Sir Conrad said. "And you're feeding surplus food to the pigs? That's not good. Tomorrow, talk to Father Thomas and see what can be done about giving it to the deserving poor. Don't give them anything you wouldn't eat yourself, but, well, there are hungry people out there."

I drifted off in private words with Annastashia and so lost the thread of the conversation. When I returned, Sir Conrad was reading from a list.

"...two dozen carpenter's hammers, two dozen mason's hammers, three dozen wood chisels, assorted, one dozen wheelbarrows, two dozen..."

"Sir Conrad," I said, "what are you talking about? And what is a wheelbarrow?"

"A wheelbarrow is a sort of pushcart with only one wheel."

"One wheel? Then why doesn't it fall over?"

"It would, except that a man holds it up."

"That makes no sense at all."

"When you see one you'll understand. Come take a

look at this list of tools I need to buy. Tell me if I've forgotten anything."

"Tools? Why buy tools?" I asked. "If you hire workmen, they'll have their own tools."

"Really? I didn't know that."

"Then there is perhaps another thing you don't know, Sir Conrad," my cousin Gregor said. "And that's that a workman with tools costs half again more than one without. If you project work of any size . . ."

"We have a town to build, with a wall and a mine to redig, and—"

"Then you will save by providing the tools yourself. Also, your tools would doubtless be made hard by this cementation process of yours that we have been hearing about."

"Of course."

"Then they will be better tools than any a workman would have. Times have not been good in Cieszyn. In the last year, not a workman in the city has spent a penny on anything but food, and little enough on that."

"That rough, huh?"

"It saddens a man to look at them, the men ragged and hungry, the women worse."

"And the children?" Conrad asked.

"The children? They're aren't many of them. Mostly they die very young. But what can one do? My own peasants are well enough fed and we support our own poor but that is all. I have no great store of wealth with which to feed all the wretches in the city."

"But surely something can be done."

"If you would be a benefactor, Sir Conrad, hire more men than you need. You'll get them cheap enough. And build on a lavish scale."

"A good thought, Sir Gregor. I'll act on it."

# Chapter Four

FROM THE DIARY OF CONRAD SCHWARTZ

It soon became obvious that I couldn't simply hire a construction company and go to Three Walls. I would have to hire individuals and form them into a unit myself.

Furthermore, most workmen *didn't* have their own tools. They had sold them to feed their families. What few tools were in the men's hands were in very poor shape and were often poorly designed in the first place.

Nor could I go to a store and buy tools, not in the quantities I required. I had to contract to have them made and if I was going to do that, I might as well see that they were designed properly. I set up my drawing board and went to work.

I started drawing pliers and was astounded to discover that I knew the designs for more than ninety sorts of pliers. I spent two days drawing them and then realized that most of them would be useless in construction work.

I had to stop and think out exactly what we would need, because if we later discovered some lack, we'd be hard-pressed to supply it.

I only had to put up some buildings fourteen miles away, yet my situation was almost like that of a nineteenth-century explorer going into the jungle. If we didn't bring it, we wouldn't have it.

The usefulness of many tools often depends on subtle properties. At first glance, you normally wouldn't notice much or any difference between a crosscut saw and a ripsaw, but in use the difference is huge. One cuts much better against the grain of the wood and the other with it. The difference has to do with the angle of the teeth and it took some experimentation to get it right.

When I was sure of a design and the quantities required, I put it up for bids by nailing a notice to the church door. I know that sounds sacrilegious, but that's how these people posted a public notice.

Bidding for work was not the usual way of doing things and many blacksmiths objected. It was contrary to guild rules. They were working men, not merchants. It was unheard of.

I listened to their objections and then told them that if they wanted my work they would have to bid on it. In the end, they did it my way and for a reasonable price, but it is sad that a good socialist would have to do such things.

All of this took time, and two whole months went by before we could leave for Three Walls.

One morning, I was having dinner with the Banki brothers, and mentioned that I had run into a German knight on the trail in the High Tatras Mountains who had given me a bash on the head. And a month after that, I'd been attacked on Count Lambert's trail by another German. And the day after that I was attacked by a whole band of Germans!

"It's like there was an invasion of damned Germans!" I said.

"You must be careful with that sort of talk," Sir Gregor said. "Did you know, for example, that Duke Henryk's paternal grandmother was a German princess? That his mother was a German princess? That his wife was a German princess? And that young Henryk's wife is a German princess?"

"No I didn't. Why on Earth did they all marry Germans?"

"I couldn't say exactly, of course, but I suppose the

fact that a German princess often comes with a dowry that is ten times what any Pole could pay for his daughter has a lot to do with it. So many of their young men go wandering off and getting themselves killed that there's always a surplus of young women. Then, too, in Germany only the oldest son inherits the father's lands and title. The younger sons, with scant prospects in life, aren't the most sought after of marriage partners."

"Then there are the German skilled workmen," Wiktor added. "They know many things that our own people don't. Many of them come to Poland to improve their position and it is the duke's policy to welcome them."

"Well, peaceful or not, it still seems like an invasion to me," I said.

Sir Wojciech said, "Oh, that I should have a hundred skilled workmen and a beautiful German princess and a full sack of gold to go with her! Invade me! Invade me!"

I took a pull of beer from a new pitcher and it was foul. I called Tadeusz over.

"Try that and tell me if it's the beer or only my mood that's bad."

He did and he blanched white. "Forgive me, Sir Conrad. This must be from the new batch. The whole barrel must be bad. We can't serve this to our customers. A pity, but the barrel must be dumped and sulfur burned in it, then filled with boiling water, and soaked before it can be used again."

"So you're saying that you have a bad strain of yeast going. How much beer are we talking about?"

"This was the big barrel, my lord. More than six thousand gallons."

"Ouch! That's a lot of beer. Look—don't dump the barrel. There's something we can do with that beer. It tastes bad, but it still has alcohol in it. There's a process called distillation that will let us save the alcohol."

"This alcohol, my lord. What is it good for?"

"Drinking, mostly, but it has other uses. It's good on cuts and wounds and helps keep them from festering. It's useful in making other things like perfumes and medicines. It's a good preservative and keeps things from rotting. But mostly it's for drinking."

"This sounds wondrous, my lord. And we could do this distillation here at the inn?"

"Here or at the brass works. I'll go over there and see what I can come up with in the way of a still."

We had two big brass kettles that were made for washing wool at Count Lambert's cloth factory, but not yet delivered to him. They each had a tight-fitting lid.

For distillation, you need a container to simmer the mash, or in this case the beer. You contain the vapors and cool them down so that they can liquify. This is traditionally done with a coil of copper tubing, which we didn't have. But the only important thing is to have enough surface area to provide cooling.

I took one of the kettles and set it up over an outdoor fireplace in the inn's courtyard. I found a hefty length of cast brass pipe intended for the washline that was as long as I was tall. I set the second kettle in a washtub that distance from the first. Then I got a smith from the brass works to solder the pipe between the two kettles, near the top.

This involved punching holes in my liege lord's new kettles, but he probably wouldn't notice. If he did, I could probably think up a good reason why I put the holes there on purpose. Engineers all develop a certain skill at snow jobs.

I also had the smith put a hole in each of the lids so we could check the liquid level in the kettles with a stick. Some thick leather made a good enough gasket for the lids. Sandbags held them down tight and wooden plugs took care of the holes in the lids.

By midafternoon, we had a still that any moonshiner would be proud of.

With the help of one of the cooks, I put forty gallons of bad beer in the boiler kettle and got a fire going under it. We filled the washtub around the condenser kettle with cool water and sat back to watch it work. By dark the level in the boiler had gone down about ten percent and I figured that we'd gotten all that we were going to get.

Sure enough, there were about four gallons of clear liquid in the bottom of the condenser. I took a pitcher of it into the inn and told the cook to put the rest into a barrel someplace. What was left in the boiler could be fed to the pigs.

Tadeusz was eagerly awaiting the results of our efforts. The thought of a new drink fascinated him.

You see, there were very few things to drink in the Middle Ages. There was wine that had to be imported. There was beer that was flat for lack of any container that could hold pressure. There was water that often wasn't safe to drink. There was milk that was only available in the spring and summer. And that was all. Nothing else existed with which a person could quench his thirst.

He looked with great anticipation at the pitcher in my hand, and broke out his two best (and only) glass goblets. Glass was rare and fabulously expensive. They were the only bits of glass at the inn, reserved for the bride and groom at wedding feasts. The other guests at the head table had to make do with silver.

I poured two fingers worth into each glass and we drank.

It was raw and rough and rugged. Wicked stuff. I once tried the product of an Appalachian moonshiner and while my results weren't quite as bad as his, I came close.

Tadeusz was literally cross-eyed. I'd heard of people having that reaction, but I'd never seen anyone actually do it before. There were beads of sweat on his forehead and his breathing had stopped. I had to pat him on the back to get it going again.

Once he was something like normal again, he wheezed, "Sir Conrad. Do your people actually drink that?"

"Well, something like it. I think it needs aging."

"God in heaven, but yours must be a tough people."

"Not really," I said. I held the lip of my goblet to the lamp on the table. The dregs burned vigorously and that meant that it was over fifty percent alcohol.

Tadeusz stared aghast at the burning drink, shook his head and walked away.

It took the cook over a month to process the entire six thousand gallons of bad beer. In the end, we had six hundred gallons of white lightning (I couldn't in justice call this stuff whiskey), which was stored in oak barrels in the inn's basement. On rare occasions, some adventurous buck would ask for a mug of it, but I don't think anybody asked twice. I kept a bottle for use as an antiseptic for my medical kit.

Part of my deal with my liege lord Count Lambert was that I was to return to Okoitz once a month to oversee the construction we had going on there. The first month was up and I had to go.

The problem was that the girls naturally wanted to go along and pay a visit to their families and friends. The count had given me the girls, and probably my lands as well, because they had started imitating the manners of the nobility rather than acting like dumb peasants. He felt that it was all my fault and maybe it was.

But he wanted them out of Okoitz before everybody started acting uppity. To bring the girls back would not have been wise. But the girls didn't know that they had been thrown out of their home and I didn't have the heart to tell them.

To make matters worse, Sir Vladimir insisted on coming with me. I had no right to tell him what he could do or not do, and I didn't want to offend the guy. I liked him and I could see where he could be very useful in the future.

Finally, Sir Gregor came to my rescue by suggesting that he and his brothers take the girls on a hunt on my new land before I "ruined" it with a lot of buildings. It only took an hour to talk the girls into it. I mean, I might be the girls' protector, but I wasn't their chaperon. They knew the score. It wasn't as if they were virgins.

## FROM THE AUTOBIOGRAPHY OF SIR VLADIMIR CHARNETSKI

Sir Conrad and I arrived at Okoitz to find Vitold, Count Lambert's carpenter, installing the sails on the windmill that was being constructed in the bailey.

This windmill was a huge affair and the top of the turret was higher than the roof of the church. The blades went much higher and the topmost of the twelve was so tall that I think one could stack ten peasant huts one above another and not reach the height of it.

The windmill was surrounded by a circular workshed and it was on the roof of this that the carpenter worked. Count Lambert and six of his knights were also on the roof watching. Perforce, we climbed up to join them.

"Greetings, Sir Conrad," Count Lambert said. "I see that you have brought the excellent Sir Vladimir with you. You see? It's nearly done."

"There's been more progress that I had expected, my lord," Sir Conrad said.

"My people have worked at little else since they finished spring planting. I'll wager that you think better of them now than you did at the Christmas party."

"No bet, my lord. Not on that subject anyway."

"Yes, there is our wager as to whether or not this mill will work, isn't there? Twenty-three thousand pence, wasn't it? It seems you're gaining on me."

"We'll know soon, my lord. The mill looks about done," Sir Conrad said.

"Only on the outside, my lords," Vitold said. "I don't have the pumps and cams all hooked up yet inside and she's got to be way out of balance."

The last of the sails was on and the great wheel started turning slowly in the breeze.

"You haven't painted the sails with linseed oil the way you were supposed to," Sir Conrad said. "The sails will draw much better if they're not porous."

"We've ordered some linseed oil out of Wroclaw, Sir Conrad, but it hasn't come yet. I just wanted to see how the axle shaft turned before I got to work on the pumps."

"Then I guess you've learned what you wanted to know. It seems to turn easily enough. Like you said, the balance is way off, but you'll have to wait until the pumps are on before you can work on that. Also, I think that the set of the sails could be improved, but that's the last thing you'll want to play with. I guess you can stop it now."

"Now that's something I wanted to talk to you about, Sir Conrad. I understand how to make it go, but you never said anything about how to make it stop."

"What? To stop it?" Count Lambert said. "There's naught to that! Watch!"

I fear that my Count Lambert had scant experience

with the vast power of that huge wheel. He put his arm around the next blade as it came slowly by and attempted to bring it to a halt. The vast wheel heeded his efforts not at all, but continued around.

The count, unused to any disobedience, clung on and was soon swept off the roof of the shed.

Still clutching the windmill blade as it began to rise, he shouted, "You men! Help! Attend me!"

Sir Bodan said, "Right, my lord!" and grabbed onto the next blade as it went by.

Sir Stefan took the blade after and what was I to do? My father's liege lord had bid my attendance in time of his peril. And peril it was indeed, for Count Lambert had now risen halfway to the top and was as high as the church roof with naught but air between him and the ground. Could I show the white feather at such a time?

For the honor of my family, I grabbed the next blade.

With a force that could not have been matched by a team of eight oxen, the great blade lifted me off the roof. I soon found that I could stand on the ropes that held the bottom of the sails and so for a short while was not greatly discomfited.

The other four knights followed those already on the wheel, leaving only Sir Conrad and Vitold on the roof of the shed. By this time, I had risen more than halfway up and my head was lower than my feet. Count Lambert was at the top, completely upside down, saving his life by clutching the blade with arms and legs. I imitated his posture.

Perhaps due to the weight of the men on one side, the wheel was slowing noticeably. As luck would have it, it stopped just when I was hanging upside down at the top.

I did not like it.

I could hear and see everything with that crystal clarity which comes with great danger. Far below, I could hear Sir Conrad and Vitold talking.

"The sails were supposed to be held on with slip knots, like you use on shoelaces," Sir Conrad said. "Then you could stop the mill by pulling the cords as the blades went by."

"I must've missed that part. We didn't use no slip knots," Vitold replied. "I know! We can cut the ropes!"

"It's a little late for that. We have to get these men down. It would probably be best to push it all the way around. That will get Count Lambert off quickest. Get those men up here on the roof."

The whole population of Okoitz had gathered to watch the first turning of the mill, and I heard them shouting to us. Some were praying to God in heaven for our deliverance and some offered bad advice as what would be the best thing to do. No few of them were making wagers on which of us would fall first. The odds of my survival were the lowest of the lot.

But they were all on the ground and it took some time to get them on the roof.

Time was just what I could not spare, for my case was worse than that of the other knights. Not only was I the most vertically oriented, but they were dressed in ordinary clothes where I was just in from the trail and was perforce still in chain mail.

My helmet slipped from my head and fell for a horribly long time before bouncing off the roof of the shed, narrowly missing Sir Conrad. I'd almost killed the man I'd sworn to protect.

Worse, the blade I was clutching was of fresh pine and smoothly planed. I began slipping downward, head first. Count Lambert saw me and called to me to hold tight, but I was already holding with all my might and there was nothing more that I could do to obey him. I continued downward.

At first this frightened me, but I soon reasoned that down was precisely the direction that I wanted to go, could I but do it slowly enough.

Eventually reaching the hub of the wheel, I was able, with considerable difficulty, to remove myself from the blade and stand on the axle.

I was still a great distance in the air, but at least I was now upright and had something beneath my feet. I paused a moment to catch my breath.

By then, Sir Conrad had fifty peasants on the roof and together they were able to turn the stalled wheel. But the first motion took me unawares and I started to fall from the huge axle.

I saved myself by grabbing on to another blade of the

wheel, this time to the one Sir Lestko was on. He was the last man in line, so perforce I was carried again higher, but now with my feet toward the hub.

They turned the wheel sufficiently for Count Lambert to step off, but by this time the force of the wind and the weight of the men was such that the wheel again turned of its own accord. The other knights were able to remove themselves without difficulty as they each came to the bottom, but I was halfway between rim and hub and thus continued around.

Sir Conrad saw my predicament.

"You must slide toward the rim!" he shouted. "If I cut loose the sails now, there's no telling where it will stop. You might end up on top again. Slide down when you are on the bottom half of the cycle and hold tight when you're at the top!"

I could see the wisdom of his suggestion, but the doing of it was no small task. In all, I went around nine times before Sir Conrad and Count Lambert could pick my weary body off the wheel and set me upright.

"Sir Conrad," Sir Stefan said, "your liege lord bid you attend him and you did not! I call you coward!"

There had long been bad blood between Sir Conrad and Sir Stefan. Sir Conrad stared at him for a moment, then shook his head.

"My liege lord asked for help and I gave him help! I got him and the rest of you fools out of the stupid predicament you'd gotten yourselves into. The first rule of safety is that you never touch a piece of moving machinery!"

"That's enough, gentles," Count Lambert said. "Sir Conrad, we thank you for your timely aid.

"Well! That worked up an appetite! Shall we retire to dinner?"

## FROM THE DIARY OF CONRAD SCHWARTZ

On returning to Cieszyn, I continued the work of getting my expedition ready.

I wanted seasoned hickory for the handles of the tools, but I didn't get it. Seasoned wood didn't exist and the idea of using old wood struck the carpenters as being absurd. When they needed wood, they went out and cut down a tree. That's the way that it had always been done and if I wanted it any different, I could wait five years for the wood to season.

You couldn't just buy a wheelbarrow. Nobody had ever heard of a wheelbarrow. You had to design a wheelbarrow and design all the metal parts in a wheelbarrow. Then you had to contract out the metal work, check all the work when it finally got done, and generally reject half of it because the blacksmith had ignored your drawings and instructions. Then you had to get the parts over to the brass works for heat-treating, and once that was done you had to get them to the carpenters who by that time had forgotten what you wanted in the first place.

And once completed, once they got it right, they'd stand around and ask why you wanted such a silly thing in the first place.

I tell you, if the workers hadn't needed work so badly that they were starving, I wouldn't have gotten anything done at all. But the combination of money and hunger is a powerful incentive.

As it was, I ended up spending a quarter of my considerable wealth on a few tons of hand tools.

Then there was the problem of hiring the men who would use the tools to build my facilities at Three Walls.

One of the carpenters, Yashoo, could read and write and was good at following instructions. Furthermore, he was about the only one who picked up reading technical drawings without difficulty. I made him my carpentry foreman and together we picked out his crew.

Many of these people were his close friends and relatives and I suppose that this was nepotism, but in a small medieval city, everybody in a given trade knew each other and many of them were related. Had I made a no-relatives rule, I don't think that there would have been enough carpenters left to fill my table of organization.

Then there were the masons to hire, and the miners. Well, there weren't that many miners available and I hired every one of them. All five.

Then we needed a blacksmith for repairs and a brewer and a baker and leather workers and all sorts of specialists.

I wouldn't bargain on pay. I offered every man a penny a day plus food, take it or leave it. Every man took it.

At long last it all started to come together, but by then it was time to make my monthly visit to Okoitz.

I had asked Count Lambert about the girls. He said that they could visit, but only if they came each in the company of a knight. That way they would be a cut above the peasants, and their upper-class manners wouldn't be so offensive. The Banki brothers were more than willing to visit Okoitz, although after that they had to get back to their estate, their summer holiday over.

So it was a two-day trip for a party of ten to Okoitz, with a stop at Sir Miesko's. A waste of time, but when a bunch of young girls is giving you everything they've got, every night, it's hard to say no.

The mill was working just fine when we finally got there. All of the peripheral equipment wasn't going yet, but a crew was sawing wood in the sawmill and another was pounding flax with the trip hammer. I left my sword with one of the workers, climbed up to the turret of the mill and went to a small turbine in the back.

Well, it was small only by comparison with the thirty-yard diameter of the main wheel. In fact, it was four yards across and was set at right angles to the big one. It was connected with reduction gearing to the turret such that if the big wheel wasn't facing directly into the wind, the small wheel started spinning and turned the turret to face the wind's new direction. It seemed to be working perfectly.

I went into the turret and found that all the pumps were in operation. There were two sets of pumps. One pumped fresh water from a well to a tank at the top of the tower. This was used only for emergencies at present, with a fire hose at the base of the mill. Eventually, I hoped to install pipes for running water throughout the whole complex.

The second set of pumps took water from a tank below ground level up to a tank halfway up the tower. Water running down from this middle tank was working the sawmill down below. This arrangement let work go on even if the wind stopped.

There was only a gentle breeze blowing, but all of the pumps were going full blast. I had seriously underestimated the amount of torque a windmill of this size could generate. Well, better that than having overestimated it. The next model, if there was one, would have bigger pumps.

As I left the turret, I heard a delighted shriek from above. I looked up and saw Sir Wiktor, hanging upside down from the top of the highest turning blade. It seems that he had heard of Sir Vladimir's adventures on the windmill and had to try it out himself.

In time, this became the standard thing to do for every young buck who visited Okoitz, a regular rite of passage. I had invented the ferris wheel.

Vitold was at work constructing the cloth factory, which surprised me. I'd expected him to be working at the second windmill, the one for threshing and grinding grain.

"It was Count Lambert who told me to build this factory first," Vitold said. "You'll have to talk to him if you want it done different."

I found Lambert out in the fields.

"Sir Conrad, you really must learn to report to a castle's lord as soon as you arrive. Courtesy requires it, and I saw you come in hours ago."

"Yes, my lord." Lambert had his moods and in this one it was best to speak when spoken to.

"Those are some strange plants you gave me. What are these things here?"

"Maize, my lord. Sometimes just called corn. I gave you several varieties and I'm not sure which this is."

"It's growing as high as my chest! What do you do with it?"

"It'll grow taller, my lord. It grows an ear, there's one there, that contains a sort of grain. Some kinds make good animal feed, some are good for human consumption. One kind pops and makes a good snack. It goes well with beer."

"Pops? What do you mean?"

"That's a bit hard to explain, my lord. I'll have to wait and show you in the fall."

"And what's this thing here?"

So I spent the whole afternoon lecturing from my meager knowledge of agriculture.

Before supper, Lambert led our party, his knights, and his current twelve "ladies-in-waiting" for a dip in his new swimming pool, the bottom tank of the new mill.

The bathing suit was thought up by the sick minds of the late Victorian era and of course hadn't been invented yet. It wasn't missed since the nudity taboo hadn't been invented yet, either.

Some of Lambert's ladies were remarkably attractive and skilled at frolicking. Indeed, I frolicked with two of them that night, Krystyana being indisposed.

Yet I was angry at this use of the tank. It was adjacent to the new well and seepage from the tank would get into the well water. We weren't using that well for drinking yet, but I'd planned to.

But all I could get out of Lambert was, "Sir Conrad, you take things too seriously."

Count Lambert never mentioned paying me for having won our wager over the mill, and his mood was such that I thought it best not to bring the subject up.

It was a relief to return to Cieszyn.

# Chapter Five

"KRYSTYANA, GO back to the inn and tell Tadeusz to send out a breakfast for six hundred people. Tell him I know it's impossible, but I want him to do his best. This mess will take hours to sort out."

It was dawn and I almost despaired as I looked over the mob scene outside of Cieszyn's north gate. The three dozen pack mules I had bought were there and the Krakowskis had them loaded with tons of tools fresh from heat-treating, along with all the other supplies I had bought. Sir Vladimir was in full armor and the girls were ready.

And the hundred and forty-odd men I had hired were there, dirty, ragged, and skinny. But they had their wives and children with them, who were equally dirty and ragged, and even skinnier. I hadn't counted on being responsible for so many people.

"Darn it, Yashoo," I said to the carpentry foreman, "I never said that you could bring your families!"

"But what else can we do with them?"

"How should I know? But don't you realize that we are going out into the middle of the woods, where there isn't a single building for miles?"

"It's early summer, Sir Conrad, and these people are tougher than they look. We have the protection of you two good knights. It will work out."

"It will work out, will it? Just what do you plan to

feed them? Pine needles? Because that's all you'll find in that valley!"

"Merchants will come. They always do."

"And I suppose you expect that I will pay them."

"Well, my lord, you did agree to feed us while we worked for you."

"You, yes. But not four-hundred-and-fifty extra people. No, the whole thing's impossible. They'll just have to stay here with relatives or something."

"My lord, look at us. Do we look like the kind of men who would have relatives rich enough to feed our loved ones? If we leave them behind, they will die."

It went on for hours, with the other foremen and Vladimir getting words in. I was being conned and I knew I was being conned. In the end, I gave in, knowing full well that I would end up footing the bill for all the food that six hundred people ate all summer long.

I mean, otherwise I would be sitting there trying to eat my breakfast with starving children staring at me.

But I didn't like it.

By then, Tadeusz's food started arriving and we ate. It looked as if he had scraped the cellar of every inn and bakery in the city, but what the food lacked in quality was compensated for in quantity. There was actually some left over, even after the poor wretches had come back for second and third helpings.

"The best I could do, Sir Conrad," Tadeusz said. "I did it, but I don't know what to charge for it."

"Why don't you just bill me for anything you spent and put the rest down to charity."

"That might be the easiest thing to do." The innkeeper surveyed the crowd. "It would surely be the truth. The charity, I mean. A sad group of wastrels."

It was almost noon before we finally got moving. The going was slow. Some of the people were sick, many of them were unused to traveling, and most of them were lethargic after having eaten their first decent meal in some time.

The girls soon lent their palfreys to some of the worst cases and were walking alongside their horses. I would have done the same, but Sir Vladimir absolutely forbade it.

It seems that we were on guard duty and to be off our horses would be failing in our duty. I had to agree with him, but it felt funny, riding while some poor woman limped along beside me.

Finally, I had two small children riding on Anna's rump, with the understanding that they had to jump off if any trouble happened.

It was dusk when we finally got to Three Walls. Everyone was so tired that they just collapsed where they were on the forest floor. I managed to get my little dome tent set up, the first time I'd used it since the previous fall.

While some of the men were getting horses and mules unloaded, Sir Vladimir came with a sack of flour over his shoulder.

"A good idea, that pavilion. It might rain and some of this food has to be protected from the wet."

Again, I had to agree and in minutes my tiny tent was packed solid with flour and grain and hams. There was nothing for it but sleeping in the open. I opened out my bedroll, stripped off my armor and was lying down under the stars with Krystyana when Vladimir came over again.

"What now?"

"I was wondering if you would start a fire for us. That 'lighter' thing of yours is faster than flint and steel."

"Yeah, okay."

That chore done, I went back to find Krystyana already asleep, which was just as well. It had been a long day.

It was a long night, too. It rained.

We spent the night half dozing in the darkness with the sleeping bag over us and with cold water trickling down all over. You would just be falling asleep when you would become aware that there had been some part of your anatomy which had been dry, but had now been discovered by some minor river. And it was cold.

Not an auspicious beginning.

I woke in the gray dawn to find Sir Vladimir still awake and still in his armor, sitting by a smoking fire with Annastashia asleep by his side.

"Did you stay awake the whole night?" I asked.

"Someone had to do it. There are wolves in these hills

and wild boars. And worse things. I thought you'd have a hard day's work set for you, getting these peasants busy. I wouldn't be much help there."

"Well, thank you." I was embarrassed. I hadn't even considered security.

The woods of twentieth-century Poland are mostly friendly places, and nature itself is regarded as charming. Most people see nature through their television tubes, with cute little animals doing cute little things while a narrator tries to make them seem as anthropomorphic as possible. They do this as they sit in their air-conditioned houses, without a wolf or a bear or a poisonous snake within hundreds of miles. They walk through carefully manicured gardens and tell each other that nature is wonderful! Or they go out and really rough it, staying at a public "wilderness park" at nicely prepared campsites, with park rangers to stop anything rude from occurring.

Oh, they all say that they love nature, but they would sing a different tune if hungry wolves stalked their front yards!

In the thirteenth century, nature was the enemy.

Nature was wolves, wild boars, and bears that would kill you and eat you if ever they got the chance. Nature was the cold wind that froze you solid in the winter, the blinding heat that fried you in the summer, the poisonous plants and snakes that would quickly end your life if you were not vigilant. Nature was hunger and thirst that could only be fought back by the endless toil of mankind. It was the domain of the devil.

"Your thanks are accepted. Have someone wake me when food is cooked." And with that Vladimir lay back and was asleep in seconds, still in his armor.

Shouting, I got the mob awake and busy. I put Janina and Natalia in charge of issuing tools.

"These are my tools," I shouted, "and they are going to stay my tools. But I'm going to issue them to some of you, and you're going to be responsible for them. If you lose them, it comes out of your pay! You got that?" They looked like they took me seriously.

Then I assigned tasks. Some I sent to bring water from the old mine shaft. Some I sent for firewood and four more to digging latrines. I put Krystyana in charge of the kitchen and Yashoo in charge of building some temporary shelters, the understanding being that if there weren't enough up by nightfall, the carpenters would sleep outside again.

The masons went to work on an oven for cooking bread and I said that if it wasn't big enough, they wouldn't eat. In short order, everybody was running around, looking busy.

I found a comfortable spot and sat back. About every ten seconds, somebody would run up with a question that he should have figured out himself, but I suppose that that is what management is all about.

I sometimes chose at random between alternative answers. The truth is that when a subordinate comes to you for a decision, he has already debated the pros and cons of the matter and they are pretty much equal. If one way or the other was obviously better, he would have felt justified in making the decision by himself. Since one way has as much chance of being right as the other, a random guess is as good as anything else, and it gets things moving. Thus do they call you wise.

What with Lambert's changeable moods, I'd decided not to risk sending him the big kettles I'd damaged to make that still. I'd brought them along and ordered new ones made for the cloth factory.

Krystyana put the old ones to use for cooking. By ten, some food was actually ready. Just kasha, a boiled, cracked-grain dish, but filling and plentiful. And only water to drink. I made a mental note to buy some milk cows and told the carpenters that after the shelters were up, they should start on a brewhouse. No argument on that one.

I forgot to send some food to Vladimir, but of course Annastashia didn't. He just got up, ate and sacked out again. An earthy fellow, but a decent and useful one, within his limitations.

Another meal was served at six, just kasha again, with mushrooms and wild vegetables thrown in. Nobody complained about the poor fare, which was good. Despite my considerable wealth, I was worried about my ability to feed six hundred people. If I had to maintain the standards of Lambert's table, I never would have made it.

It was weeks before I discovered that the people thought that the food was wonderful! They actually got enough to eat!

Keeping track of so many people was beyond my ability, so at supper I called Natalia aside. She had very good handwriting and was one of those compulsively neat people who make good secretaries and clerks.

"Natalia, I have a special job for you. I want records kept on everybody here. I want a separate sheet of parchment for every man. Put down his name and the names of his parents and his grandparents and as far back as he knows. Put down his wife's name and her ancestor's names and their children's names. I want to know everybody's age, when and where they were born and married and when we hired them. And write small, because we'll be adding things later."

"All *that*? Why do you want to write such things down? If you need to know, why not ask them yourself?"

"Because I don't have time to, and I couldn't remember it all anyway."

"Why should *anybody* have to remember all that?"

"Pay records, for one thing. How can I remember how much I owe each man?"

"Pay them every night or every week and then you don't *have* to remember it."

"That would be very time-consuming. Everyone would have to stand in line for an hour every day. I am talking about permanent records. It is important that we know everything about our people."

"We *can't* know everything. Only God in heaven knows everything."

I tried two or three other lines of argument, and always ran up against the same unshakable logic. But there are more ways than logic to get your way.

"Natalia, would you please do this for me as a favor?"

"Why, of *course*, Sir Conrad! You know I'd do *anything* for *you*."

So Natalia became our records-keeper and eventually my secretary, but she still thought records were a silly waste of parchment. But these would be permanent records and records are important. Aren't they?

By nightfall, the camp had some semblance of order. I had a hut of my own, thatched with pine boughs. There was one for Vladimir and a third for our spare ladies. I'd told them to make two latrines and they'd assumed that I meant one for nobility and one for commoners, rather than one for men and one for women. But there was no point in arguing about it.

Everyone else had at least room under a roof. All told, I was pleased with our accomplishments, considering that we had started out with nothing but a mob of wretched, underfed people without enough sleep.

In the morning, I left with Yawalda and one of the men for Sir Miesko's manor to buy food. I bought grain, eggs, and veggies and made arrangements for my man to come by three times a week for more supplies. I also bought a milk cow, the only one available, which was a mistake.

It was dark before we got the silly animal back to camp and we had to stop and squirt the milk on the ground because we didn't have a bucket with us and I refused to lend my helmet for the purpose. At that, we were lucky, since Yawalda knew how to milk a cow and neither of us men did. I didn't even know why it was bawling and refusing to move. The joys of the pastoral life.

By the end of the next day, they had built a complete, if rustic village. The blacksmith was set up and making barrel hoops for the brewery and the masons were cutting a huge millstone that would be turned by two mules. Carpenters were at work making a gross of beehives. There was a hut for every family and all the outbuildings we needed for storage, cooking, and eating. We even had tables and benches, made from split logs, under the dining pavilion and enough new bowls, trenchers (a sort of board you ate off of), and spoons to go around. It is amazing how much six hundred people can accomplish when they're motivated.

There were splinters in everything, of course, and enough wood chips to pave the place, which was exactly what we used them for.

The next day was Sunday, and that afternoon Sir

Miesko's village priest showed up and said mass under the dining pavilion.

Anna watched the mass intently and came closer to listen to the sermon. Thereafter, each week she became more interested and was soon kneeling, sitting, and standing with the faithful.

The priest was obviously disconcerted, but didn't know how to bring up the subject of a church-going horse.

Just as well, because I didn't have any answers.

# Interlude One

I HIT the STOP button.

"Tom, that horse is one of your critters, isn't it?"

"She's an intelligent bioengineered creation of my labs, if that's what you mean."

"Then what's an old atheist like you doing designing religious animals?"

"In the first place, Anna's not an animal in the sense you're using the word. She's intelligent. In the second, I didn't design her. That sort of thing takes a big staff a long time to do. And in the third place, it was as big a surprise to me as it was to you."

"It was?"

"Those horses are very literal-minded. They will always take every word that an authority figure says as the absolute truth. Nobody ever thought that one of them would be told deliberate lies."

"Tom, you're an old heathen!"

"I'm also your boss and your father. Now shut up."

He hit the START button.

# Chapter Six

FROM THE DIARY OF CONRAD SCHWARTZ

I hadn't thought to pay anybody, so none of the people had any money. The collection basket came back empty. To cover the embarrassment, I paid the priest. This set another precedent. Conrad pays the priest.

Now we could get down to real work, building permanent housing and getting the valley productive. I put the masons and the miners to enlarging the old mine shaft. Medieval miners cut shafts that were barely crawlspaces. I wanted the shaft big enough for a man to work in and there had to be room for a steam suction pump.

Thus far, I'd let the carpenters build whatever they liked, since it was all only temporary. But I had some definite ideas about what I wanted for the permanent buildings.

The valley had about a square kilometer of flat land and was surrounded by a sloping wall that eventually became quite steep. The only entrance was between two cliffs about two hundred yards apart. The obvious structure to build was a combination apartment house and defensive wall between them, about six stories tall. It would have to be of wood, of course, good enough against animals and thieves but worthless against Mongols. But the cliffs were more than two hundred meters long and the land sloped down considerably as the cliffs fanned out. We could build now at the narrowest point and later build another wall, or several walls, that were taller and made of masonry.

I knew we had coal and limestone and that meant that we could make mortar with existing technology. I was confident that with clay and sand and much higher temperatures, we could make cement and with that we had concrete!

Enough concrete will stop anybody.

The valley was filled with huge trees. Oh, nothing like what you would find on the west cost of America, but hundreds of them were well over two yards thick at the base. Poland had many such trees at the time and for a very good reason.

It was extremely difficult to fell a really big tree with only axes. Once you did have it down, without machinery it was very hard to move. For the small groups of woodcutters common at the time, it was impossible.

And then, what could you do with it? Medieval Poles made boards by splitting logs and then planing the wood smooth. That doesn't work on a log that is as big around as you are tall.

For many centuries, they left the big trees alone and took only the small ones.

I'd had a dozen steel crosscut saws and ripsaws made, some of them four yards long. We had big timber, and fasteners were very expensive. The price of nails was absurd. But the bigger the parts, the fewer the fasteners. My plans called for the floors, doors, and shutters to be made with wood slabs a yard wide and the outer walls of boards a yard wide and a half-yard thick with the bark left on. It would be good insulation and indestructible except by fire.

Eventually I was to regret this plan. With no civil engineering experience, I had no idea how much a big piece of green wood can shrink. Every winter, a crew had to caulk the walls; I don't think that a single door ever fit right. It would have helped if I had laid the outside slabs sideways, in the manner of a traditional log cabin. But, no, I had to put them all vertically because it looked better structurally.

Furthermore, it doesn't matter how well your walls

are insulated if you have to open a window to the wind when you want to see. In the winter, without artificial lights or window glass either you are cold or you are blind. I began to see why architects are such a conservative bunch. But I get ahead of myself.

The carpenters objected and were vocal about it. But not one of them mentioned the shrinkage problem and I chalked up their complaints to stick-in-the-mud conservatism. I paid the bills and got my way. As the old capitalist saw goes, "Him what pays, says."

It's remarkable, some of the things you have to do to build socialism.

They objected even more to the climbing spikes. These are the things that strap to a man's legs and feet and let him, with a sturdy leather belt, quickly climb a tree to cut the top off. A big tree has to be topped, otherwise it will shatter when it falls.

But my people were lumberjacks who had never left the ground. They thought being fifty yards off the ground was *scary*.

Of course, they were right. Hanging fifteen stories up while trying to saw through the tree you're hanging from *is* scary. But I couldn't let *them* think that, or we'd never get the place built.

When the first of the teams flatly refused to climb more than ten yards up a tree, I called them down.

"Come on down, you cowards!" I shouted, tossing my sword to a bystander. "Yashoo, let's show these little boys how to do their job."

The foreman came to me and whispered, "My lord, I've never, I mean I *can't*! I've never done anything like this before!"

"I'll let you in on a secret," I whispered back. "I haven't either."

"Then how—"

"If these people can't do the job, I'll have to send the lot of you back to Cieszyn and find another batch. But if *you* do it and *I* do it then *they'll* have to do it. Now, what say we both go up there and pretend like we have more courage than brains?"

He thought a few seconds. "If I die, you'll take care of my wife?"

With the rig we were using, if one of us came down, the other would come with him. But Yashoo needed assurance, not logic.

"On my honor."

"Then let's go."

It was a huge tree and even fifty yards up it would take two men to pull a saw through it.

With a two-man rig, each has spikes strapped to his legs and feet. Each has a hefty belt around his waist, and a long, thick belt goes across each back, around both men and the tree. The long belt fastens to each personal belt twice, with sturdy loops. It's really two shorter belts end-to-end, with a buckle by each right hand. The big belt has to be shortened periodically as the tree is climbed.

Technology is not a single thing. It's a lot of little things that add up. Things as simple as a new way to climb a tree, something we've been doing since before we were human.

I'd watched men topping trees at a lumberjacks' festival and I'd thought out how it had to go. The men had to work as a close team, taking two steps in unison and hitching the big belt up together.

To make matters worse, they had to be on opposite sides of the tree, where they couldn't see one another. If either moved without the other, they'd come down. Maybe not the whole way, since you shorten the belt as you go up. If the belt is too short to let you slide all way down the tapering trunk to the ground, you just might get to live.

But the least you got was a faceful of bark and a bellyful of slivers.

Seeing something and thinking about it is a far cry from actually having done it. Having to do something dangerous the first time in front of an audience doesn't help much either.

As we strapped on our gear, with the thick new leather squeaking about us, we rehearsed our moves and discussed each step. Yashoo's hand was shaking, but I figured he'd steady down once he was actually up the tree.

"I'm frightened, Sir Conrad," he said desperately, as we passed the belt around the tree.

"Of *course* you're frightened. Only a fool wouldn't be. But a man does his job for all of that." I took a few steps up. It wasn't bad. Sort of like climbing a ladder.

Yashoo made an elaborate sign of the cross, which ruined the effect I was trying to create, started up, and then seemed to slow down.

"Come on, Yashoo! Just like a dance! Stomp your spikes right into the tree. Left foot, right foot, raise the belt! Left foot, right foot, raise the belt!"

"But I can't dance either, my lord!"

"What 'either'? You're climbing! And I bet Krystyana could teach you how to dance." We were maybe ten yards up. "Maybe I could ask her. What do you think about throwing a dance Saturday night? Do we have any musicians?"

"Please don't talk about dancing. I fell down on a dance floor, too." He talked like a coward, but he was keeping right up with me.

"*Cut that out*! We're almost there."

The saw was tied to my belt by a measured length of rope. When it started lifting, we were high enough. I leaned around to where I could see my partner. He was white, bone white.

"Yashoo, I think there's enough of a breeze blowing so we won't have to take a wedge out. We'll do a back cut on my left first."

Yashoo didn't answer, but I could hear him praying. He took his end of the saw and did his part. We worked in silence, getting the feel of each other's rhythm. After the blade started binding, we cut from the other side.

When we were most of the way through, the tree parted with an explosive *crack*! It leaned way over as the top came crashing past us, then snapped back like a released bow.

It was like being on the end of a whip half the length of a football field that was snapping back and forth fifteen stories in the air. The trunk now came only to our waist and I could see Yashoo digging his white fingertips into the bark. Mine were pretty white, too.

My mother told me I should have gone to the beach.

"Well, Yashoo, what do you think? Should we walk

down, or shall we have the men saw down the tree so we can ride?"

He stared at me but didn't answer.

After we got down he said, "Do I have to do that again?"

"Not today. Go back to supervising. I'm going to see how the masons are doing." I swaggered away, stopped at a latrine and vomited my guts out.

Eventually, we had four good topmen. They considered themselves to be something of an elite, strutting around and wearing their spikes constantly, even to church.

# Chapter Seven

AFTER THE first few days, I put myself on a schedule which I have tried to stick to ever since. Mornings, I played manager and was available to anyone with a problem. Afternoons, I was a designer and your troubles had to be serious before I was bothered. Natalia did a good job keeping me from interruptions.

I had my drawing board set up in my hut and went through parchment by the bundle, drawing the buildings and making detail drawings of every sort of board in them, a job made easier because I used a lot of standard parts. That is to say, many parts were identical and the same design could be used over and over.

I had a few dozen sticks cut to exactly the same length and as long as I remembered Lambert's yard to be. These became our standard of measurement. A lot of the men had difficulty with the concept of standards. They were used to cutting each piece to fit as they went along and all this measuring and looking at plans struck them as a stupid waste of time.

As the weeks went on, there was a growing pile of finished parts, but that was not as satisfying as watching the buildings going up.

I delayed assembly of the buildings for a good reason. Wood set directly on the ground rots and I wanted our buildings to have masonry foundations and basements. We couldn't do masonry construction without mortar and we couldn't make mortar without coal.

There was coal in the mine, but the mine was still full of water. Parts for the steam pump were arriving regularly from the Krakowski brothers, and the pump functioned well enough after some reworking, or TLC as the Americans call it, but it all took time.

Oh, we could have used charcoal to make mortar, but that would have been time-consuming, too, and the coal would be there soon.

Getting my way was rarely an easy task. I had to talk and persuade and cajole. I shouted and screamed and pretended to throw temper tantrums. But what helped most was when I dug out my bible and read them the description of the building of Solomon's Temple. It put God on my side, which generally helps.

Piotr Kulczynski, my accountant, was commuting regularly between Cieszyn and Three Walls, keeping the books on our operations here as well as on the Pink Dragon Inn and the Krakowski Bros. Brass Works. He was a very efficient young fellow except when he was looking wistfully at Krystyana, which, it seemed, was most of the time.

The poor kid was obviously smitten, and just as obviously, she wouldn't have anything to do with him. It wasn't any of my business. I just don't like to see anybody in that much pain. They were both about fifteen, and that can be a very rough time of life.

I supposed that a certain amount of opposition to my plans from the workers was inevitable, but I never expected Vladimir and Piotr to be against my building plans. I had my drawings unrolled before us.

"I tell you that these indoor garderobes are a bad idea," Vladimir said. "I've seen them in some of the big stone castles. They make sense if you have to stand a siege. But that's the only time they use them, during a siege when you can't do anything else. The rest of the time, they use an outdoor privy just like everybody else.

"Shit stinks and you don't want it in your house! In the second place, wood buildings can't stand a siege. They're too easy to burn down. So there's no sense in putting in a garderobe in the first place."

"I agree with everything you've said, but you've

never seen indoor plumbing. It's completely clean and sanitary. No smells at all. And this will be more than a garderobe. Besides the flush toilets, there's a washroom and a shower room. We'll be able to clean ourselves and our clothes even in the wintertime. We'll have hot water, too. There's a big hot-water heater built above the kitchen stove. I tell you that a hot shower on a cold winter morning is a glorious thing."

"What happens to the shit?"

"It's flushed down these brass pipes until it leaves the building. Then it goes by clay pipes to these septic tanks and finally to this tile field."

"I'll believe it when I see it," Vladimir said.

"Sir Conrad, what troubles me is the expense of all this," Piotr said. "I have calculated that for what you are spending on cast brass pipes and all these pottery toilets and washbowls and the valves and all, you could hire twenty chambermaids for fifty years!"

"That's a pretty ugly job, isn't it? Hauling away someone else's chamber pots?"

"There are many who would take it, sir, and be thankful."

"I'll allow that it'll be pretty impressive, if it works," Vladimir said. "But if you must have these gimcracks, why share them with the peasants? Put in a smaller bunch of fixtures for yourself and your high-born guests."

"Someday, everybody is going to have indoor plumbing. We might as well start here. I'm not going to deprive my people of something that basic."

"Your people would be far happier if you took what this cost and divided the money among them."

"Probably. But I'm still going to put in the indoor plumbing."

"It's your castle," Vladimir sighed. "These firewalls take a vast amount of stone and mortar. If you used that amount of material on the outside wall, it could be entirely of masonry, adding greatly to your defenses."

"I'm more worried about a fire than a war, at least in the next few years. We have over six hundred people here and the next settlement is eight miles away. If this building burns down entirely next winter, we might not survive it. With the firewalls where they are, it's likely that we wouldn't lose more than a fifth of our housing and we could live through that."

"You are lord here," Vladimir said. "Another problem with this plan is the gate. It's too big. Six knights could ride abreast through that thing. Reduce it by half, at least. It'll be a lot easier to defend."

"At this point, I'm not worried about defending against anything but thieves and wild animals. As you said, a wooden building can't stand a siege anyway. In later years, we'll build other walls, farther out, of bricks or stone. But even they'll need big gates. Remind me to tell you about railroads."

"Now what in hell is a railroad?"

The days rolled by. We set up a saw pit, an arrangement whereby a log was rolled over a deep pit; then one man stood in the hole and another on top of the log, working a saw between them. It was a miserable job, with the man below eating sawdust and the man above breaking his back. They often traded jobs, but never decided which was worse.

And it was slow. I did some time studies and calculated that, even with all of our ripsaws going constantly, the snow would be flying before the place was half done.

Something Vladimir once said gave me an idea and we built a walking-beam sawmill. We made a huge teeter-totter out of a halved log that was fifty yards long. At each end, ropes and pulleys connected it to a long ripsaw, each two of our longest welded together. Wooden troughs, running downhill, guided a huge log into each blade.

A railing ran around the teeter-totter's edges, and sixty men walked back and forth, working the thing. You walked uphill until the high end came down, then you turned around and walked uphill again until the high end came down, then . . .

Not exactly intellectually stimulating, but then very few of these people were intellectuals. It cut wood.

What's more, the strange, Rube Goldberg monster worked right the first time we tried it, and it was fast enough. The only problem was that sixty men was half our workforce.

But why did they have to be men? A man's arms are stronger than a woman's, but this machine was worked by the legs, walking. A woman's legs are as strong as a man's. Why not?

I put it to the women one night, during supper and got a lot of cold stares. Finally, I asked why. One woman got up and talked on and on about her hardships for the longest time until it dawned on me that she was assuming that I was not going to pay for this extra work.

When I shut her up and said that I planned to pay for what I got, she turned right around and gushed so enthusiastically that I had to shut her up again.

It was the men who were against it. They'd been starving when I'd hired them and now they didn't want their wives earning extra money. Ridiculous! Finally, I got together with the foremen and we worked out a deal.

The women would each work a half day, some before noon and some after. (A half day at this time of year was almost eight hours.) They would receive half pay and their money would be paid to their husbands. Stupid, but that's the way they wanted it. And some of the bigger children could work if they wanted to, being paid by the pound.

Loading the logs into the sawmill was a job for all our men and horses, despite all the ropes and pulleys we had going. But this could usually be done in a few minutes first thing in the morning and again just after dinner. After that the ladies could work without assistance for half a day.

It had been an exhausting day, and I hoped whoever I found in my hut wasn't expecting much. Except for Annastashia, who was regarded as Vladimir's property (or vice-versa), the ladies-in-waiting had apparently decided to share me equally, with Krystyana somehow being more equal than the other three. I never had anything to do with it and I never knew who I'd be sleeping with that night. But I never asked questions because when you're in pig heaven, you don't want to make waves in the mud.

A few mornings later, there was a lot of shouting by the trail, so I went down to see.

Sir Vladimir, in full armor, was on his horse and leading two others that I recognized as being my own pack animals. Loaded on them were a lot of my steel tools and two dead bodies, former workers of mine.

I ran over to his left side. "Vladimir! What happened?"

"They stole your horses and property. I went to get them," he said in a quiet, strained way.

I was suddenly furious. "God damn you for a murderous bastard! You killed two men over a couple of lousy tools?"

He stared at me, his face white and strained.

"No. I killed them for putting an axe into my side. Now help me down."

He leaned toward me and I caught him around the waist. My hand was bloody and there was blood running down his right leg, filling his boot.

I eased him down on the ground and started shouting at people. "You! Run and get my medical kit. One of the ladies can show you where it is.

"You! I need a bucket of clean water.

"You! Get Krystyana. Tell her to bring all her clean napkins."

"Stupid of me," Vladimir said. "I didn't realize that there were two of them. I had the one at swordpoint when the other struck me down before I knew he was there. He struck me from behind, the bastard, but then I suppose you can't expect honor among thieves."

"We're going to have to get that armor off you. I think I should cut it off."

"Cut my armor? Not bloody likely! It's worth a fortune! My father had to save to buy it. Here! You peasants! Sit me up."

We had to pull his hauberk off over his head and lifting his right arm must have caused him a lot of pain. I saw his eyes bulge and his jaws tighten, but he never cried out, or even publicly acknowledged the agony.

The leather gambezon laced up the front and was easier to remove. Under it was a remarkably feminine-looking embroidered shirt.

"Annastashia's work. A pretty thing. I'm afraid I've ruined it," he said, referring to the blood.

The medical kit arrived and I went to work, washing

down both the wound and my hands. It contained a bottle of white lightning, my only antiseptic.

"This is going to hurt a bit, Vlad. Would you like a shot of this stuff before I pour it on the wound? It might dull the pain a bit."

"Do what you must, Sir Conrad. As to drinking that devil's brew of yours, well, I tried it once and I would prefer the pain of the wound to the pain of the medicine."

The crowd was getting bigger and pushing in on us. "Yashoo, get these people out of here. And do something about that," I said, gesturing toward the horses, tools, and dead bodies.

I had the wound clean by the time Krystyana got there. Annastashia was with her, almost hysterical but keeping it in.

"Krystyana, your sewing is better than mine. Why don't you stitch him up? Two of his floating ribs are broken and the wound is pretty deep, but it didn't cut an artery and I don't think it penetrated to the stomach cavity.

"Annastashia, why don't you hold his head up? He looks uncomfortable."

So our gallant ladies took over, and I stood back.

After sewing him up, Krystyana put a hefty pad of peat-bog moss over the wound. The girls swore the stuff had antiseptic properties, and their mothers agreed with them. I'd long since used up everything in my original first-aid kit, so falling back on folk medicine was the only thing I could do. I suppose there was some truth to their beliefs, since we rarely had problems with infections.

This was not the brown peat moss that is sold in modern garden supply shops, but the green plant itself, cut while alive and dried. Peat-bog moss was remarkably absorbent, more so than a paper towel, and it absorbed odors as well as moisture. Besides using it to bandage wounds, the ladies used it as a disposable diaper as well as for menstrual pads.

Thinking about it, peat-bog moss doesn't rot. That's why you get peat bogs in the first place. The new generations just grow on top of the old. Maybe killing off decay organisms with some natural antiseptic leaves more nutrients available to the young. Anyway, it worked.

Yashoo came up.

"The horses are taken care of, the tools are in the shed, and Sir Vladimir's property is back in his hut except for his byrnie. I took that to the blacksmith for repair. But what do I do with two dead bodies?"

"Bury them, I suppose. I guess we should get the priest."

"For a couple of thieves who tried to murder good Sir Vladimir? Why, no priest would let them be buried on hallowed ground, even if there was any around here."

"What about their families?" I asked.

"Those two were bachelors. Never heard them mention any kin."

"Then get twelve men, take the bodies far into the woods and bury them. Best do it now."

"Yes, sir. We won't mark the graves either."

That evening, I was still feeling guilty about shouting at Sir Vladimir when he was wounded. When I visited him, all of the ladies were tending him in a style that Count Lambert would have envied.

"Sir Conrad, have you set a guard for the night?"

"Yes, there will be two men with axes awake all night. Look, about what I said when you rode in this morning—"

"Think nothing of it, Sir Conrad. You had a perfect right to be angry."

"I did?"

"Of course. Not only had I killed two of your men without your permission, but in so doing, to a certain extent I had usurped your right to justice. In truth, I only defended myself, but you couldn't know that at the time."

"Well, thank you for forgiving me."

"I said it's nothing. But if you want to do something in return, I ask a favor."

"Name it."

"Listen to my advice and heed it. I haven't said anything so far because these are your lands and you are lord here. Your ways are strange and eldritch, but that's your business. But what you've been doing with these peasants is so stupid that I just have to speak out!"

"But—what have I done to the workers?"

"Nothing! That's the problem! It is one thing to hire

work done in a city or on another lord's lands. That's common and proper. But you have taken whole families onto your lands and worked them and promised them nothing but money!

"Can you wonder why those two men this morning felt no loyalty toward you? You'd given them no place here! You treated them like lackeys to be hired for a job and then to be cast off.

"All these buildings you are putting up. Who is going to live in them?"

"Well, I figured I'd hire—"

"You'd hire. What's wrong with the men you've already got?"

"Well, nothing. But what should I do?"

"Do? Why, swear them to you, of course!"

"To me? You think they would?" I was flustered.

"They'd be damn fools not to. Your other subjects at your inn and your brass works are all becoming rich and these people know it. That and they know you're a soft hand. Why, you haven't whipped a man since we got here!"

"You think I should swear in everybody here?"

"Well, I can't swear to you, of course. I'm already sworn to my father. But everyone else, yes."

"Very well, Sir Vladimir. I'll bring it up with them at tomorrow's dinner."

"You'll do that only if you swear these ladies to secrecy! Without that, every man in the valley will be crowding you at first daylight."

And that's just the way it happened. At dawn, Yashoo came to me and asked if he might swear to me and be my man. Tomas, the masonry foreman, was on his heels with the same request. Within minutes, the whole population was crowding around me. It really touched me and I had trouble keeping the tears back.

One at a time, they raised their arms to the sun as I did by their side. They swore to serve me honestly for the rest of their lives and I swore to protect them for the rest of mine. Once all the men were sworn in, I surprised them by asking their wives if they wanted to swear as well.

Every one of them did. It meant that I would be responsible for them even in the event of their husband's death.

Krystyana was staring at me earnestly.

"Sir Conrad, do you think— I mean could we—"

"You ladies want to swear as well?"

"Oh, yes!" came all five voices at once.

"Then we'll do it."

There wasn't a dry eye in the place.

Dinner was two hours late, but somehow they got a lot more done than on any day before. Now they were on their own land, building their own homes. It showed in the way they worked and in the way they walked.

# Chapter Eight

I MADE my monthly trip to Okoitz alone. Anna can run like the wind and it took less than an hour, whereas with the girls and their slow, docile palfreys, the trip would take all day.

The count was still being taciturn with me, and still wouldn't mention our wager. One of the knights told me that he suspected that Count Lambert was having some sort of financial problems with his wife in Hungary. I supposed that could be the reason for both the count's tightness with money and his unusually rude behavior. But I could do nothing but try to live with it.

Vitold the carpenter and Angelo the dyer had everything going smoothly. The factory was almost finished and a hundred wheelbarrows had been built to speed the harvest. Mostly, I spent my two days talking with the farmers about the new plants I'd given them.

Most were growing well enough, but how did you harvest them? Could this sort last through the winter? How do you cook this thing? And most often, what part of it do you eat?

The flowers were doing beautifully, and everybody was astounded at the size and numbers of the blossoms. Particularly popular were the sunflowers, which were three yards tall and had flowers that moved in the course of the day so as to always face the sun.

There was a wedding that day, and the bride proudly

carried a single sunflower as her bridal bouquet. I was getting ready to object to this, since that bouquet cost one-twelfth of the world's known supply of sunflower seeds. But I couldn't interrupt the ceremony, so I waited.

When it came time to throw the bouquet to the bride's maids, the bride gave it a healthy toss over her shoulder. The sunflower, which must have weighed three pounds, caught one of the girls in the face, knocking her to the ground and giving her a fat lip.

I walked away. Nobody was going to waste another sunflower. Not *that* way, at least.

I left at dusk of the second day, and we made the run home in the night. I swear Anna can see in the dark.

Vladimir was up and around in a week, so tough was his constitution. And a week after that, he took to spending his mornings hunting with Annastashia. She turned out to be a good bowman, nothing like my old friend Tadaos the boatman, but good enough to bag her share.

I was delighted, since it put meat in the pot. Our diet was too heavy on grains and way too light on everything else.

One morning, they came back with a woebegone individual walking in front of them.

"What have we here, Sir Vladimir."

"A squatter on your lands, Sir Conrad. It didn't seem right to kill him out of hand, so I brought him to you."

"I'm glad you didn't kill him. What do you mean, a squatter?"

"He has a hut hidden on your property. He's been farming your land and hunting your forest."

"Nothing to get upset about," I said. "Well, fellow. Would you like to leave peacefully, or would you like to swear to me and stay on your land?"

"I could stay?"

"Certainly. You'd have to give me a share of your produce, of course. Say, one-fourth of what your fields yield and one-half of any game you bag."

"I could even hunt? Oh, yes my lord!"

So I swore him in and had Natalia open up a file on

him. After he left, Vladimir was looking grumbly. I asked him why.

"First, that man was probably an outlaw."

"Well, I can't condemn a man on a 'probably.' Anyway, maybe he's ready to rejoin society."

"Then there is the fact that the usual terms would be half his produce and he wouldn't be allowed to hunt."

"I know, but I didn't want to lean on him too hard. As for hunting, well, there's plenty of game out there and there's no point in letting it go to waste. Half of something is better than all of nothing. Look, he won't cost us anything, and if he works out, well, we have a lot of mouths to feed around here."

"The decision is yours, Sir Conrad, but the other lords won't love you for charging less than they do."

The squatter came back two days later with six deer, a wild boar, and a bison. He had with him his wife, three children, and eight of his friends, squatters who also wanted to swear to me.

They were rough, sturdy-looking fellows and each carried an axe in addition to his belt knife. The axe was a Slavic peasant's universal tool. With it he would build his house, slaughter his pig, and defend his land. It was just the right length to double as a cane, and the single-bladed axe head was shaped to be a convenient handle. They carried them everywhere, even on dress occasions. They even danced with them, at least in some of the men-only dances. It made a formidable weapon.

Once, in a museum, I saw an ancient Egyptian axe of almost exactly the same design. Oh, the Egyptian one was made for a prince, and was covered with gold decoration, but the basic shape was identical. Some things are hard to improve on.

By the end of the month, a total of twenty-six squatters were turned into yeomen. I never stopped buying food, but they sure helped.

Of course, my relationship with the yeomen wasn't all one way. I invited them regularly to Three Walls for holidays and less formal social events. There weren't any serious problems in the first few years, but if there had been, I would have had to do something about it. The only time-consuming thing I had to do was visit them all once a year. That took an entire week.

Vladimir said that I ought to have a bailiff or foreman for so many men, and thinking about it, he was right. I contacted one of the yeomen and told him to get together with his friends and elect a leader. The yeomen were delighted with my faith in them. Vladimir was scandalized.

By this time the miners and masons enlarging the old mine were down to the water level. The pumps were working around the clock, but the rock around the shaft was porous and completely soaked. We not only had to pump out the mine, we had to pump out the mountain as well. We were gaining on it, but the miners alone could not keep up with our progress.

I put six of the masons to cutting grindstones from a nearby sandstone outcropping. We'd been sending our supply mules back empty, so transportation out was essentially free. There wasn't much profit in grindstones, but there was some.

The rest of the masons went to work cutting limestone blocks for the foundations, basements, and firewalls of our main building. Limestone isn't the best material to use for a firewall. Fire will eventually ruin it. But it will hold for a while and that was all we needed. Anyway, we had a lot of limestone and we were short on sandstone, which would be needed for the blast furnaces.

Things were settling down and starting to run smoothly. Even the brewery was doing well. With little else to drink, people in the Middle Ages drank an awesome amount of beer. Per capita consumption at Three Walls was over a gallon a day, and that's counting women and small children as well as the men. We went through three huge thousand-gallon barrels a week. Oh, it was weak and flat, but the volumes involved were still frightening.

Nothing I could do about it, though. These people wouldn't mind if I whipped them, and giving me free use of their daughters was just the expected thing. But if I had reduced their beer supply, I would have had a revolution on my hands. I'm just glad that I didn't have to pay a liquor tax on what we made.

Next Sunday evening, I announced that we would be

throwing a dance on the following Saturday night. We'd be inviting the yeomen, and anyone who could play a musical instrument could take an hour off each evening for practice.

I soon had to retract that last offer. Over half of the people there could play some sort of instrument. After a lot of haggling and argument, we eventually settled on a band master. He was to choose twelve people and they could have the hour off, but I couldn't have half the workforce gone every afternoon.

They mostly had to make their own instruments, and I noticed some of my old parchment drawings turn up as drumheads. At first the band was pretty heavy on percussion and woodwinds, but in time they became a fairly professional outfit.

I held my first formal court just before the dance, since the yeomen were there and Sir Vladimir had been after me to do it for some time. He wasn't happy with my usual informal ways of doing things, and I suppose that there is something in the human animal that wants formality since we act that way so often.

We moved a few tables together under the dining pavilion and put a chair on top of them. My throne.

I got into one of my best outfits, asked Natalia to bring her records and take notes, and asked Sir Vladimir to run the show, since he knew the procedure.

He showed up in full armor, and carried a lance in lieu of a halberd, as though he was a royal guard. He shouted in fine theatrical style.

"Oyez! Oyez! The honorable court of your liege lord, Sir Conrad Stargard, Lord of Three Walls, is now in session. Any who have need of his advice or consent should now come forward!"

Two of the yeomen had an argument over a pig, which they brought along as evidence. They both had a pig run away on the same day, and only one pig had been caught, which they both claimed as theirs. I let them both go on for quite a while, since much of the reason for a court of law is to provide a place where social tensions can be drained off.

As they droned on, I noticed that Natalia was sitting at the table below me, which gave me a pleasant shot down the front of her dress. I didn't know why that should be interesting when I'd seen her naked a thousand times, but somehow it was.

It was soon obvious to me and to everyone else that both men thought they were right, and that one pig looks much like another.

I said that the facts were now clear and that I had reached my decision. I told the first man that the pig was his, and that he could take it home. Then I told the other guy that the pig was his, and he could take it home. Then I charged them each a half a pig as court costs, and said that they should do the butchering away from camp. This way they could each take home half a pig.

One of the men asked how would I get my court costs. I said that both of my halves were running around in the woods some place, and should he see them, he should return them to me. I thought I was telling a joke.

He nodded very seriously and said, "Of course, my lord."

Two weeks later, the yeomen showed up again, each carrying half a pig, which they had found wandering about in the woods, still stuck together. They returned my property to me and both thought that my justice was excellent.

It takes all kinds. My father told me that.

The only other item on the agenda was the formal request of two of my subjects to be married.

As lord, I had the right to demand that the bride spend a night with me before she went to her husband, or to accept a bribe from the groom to not touch her. I didn't like the custom. Either the girl was in love with her prospective husband, in which case she wouldn't want me, or she was pregnant, in which case I'd worry about harming the child, or both.

I always waived my rights to the bride. Heck, I had trouble enough satisfying the volunteers.

Naturally, I always gave my permission to marry, but they liked me to go through a certain amount of rigmarole. I asked the father of the bride if he gave his blessings on the proposed marriage. He did. Did the father of the groom bless this marriage? He did. Did anyone present see any reason why these two should not be married?

Nobody said anything. I nodded to Sir Vladimir.

"Know you that the proposed wedding between Maria Sklodowska, daughter of Tomas Sklodowski, and Mikolaj Kopernik, son of..."

I nearly fell off my chair on the table. Maria Sklodowska was the maiden name of a woman scientist known as Madam Curie, after she married a Frenchman. And Mikolaj Kopernik was better known by his Latinized name, Copernicus. He was responsible for starting the entire modern scientific revolution!

And they were getting married?

It was a moment before my historical sense caught up with me. Copernicus was born in the fifteenth century, Madam Curie was born in the nineteenth century, and I was stuck in the thirteenth century. The names were obviously just a coincidence.

Obviously.

But I had Natalia make a note in the file that I should get yearly progress reports on any kids they had. There might be a genius coming along.

The dance went off pretty well. Krystyana and I showed them the polka and the mazurka, which instantly became popular. Perhaps it was the fact that here was a way that you could hold a woman who wasn't your wife, and do it in public in a socially acceptable way.

The yeomen did a vigorous, all-male number that involved huge leaps and clashing their axes together. It was something between a dance, a contest, and a military training exercise. It was vaguely reminiscent of a group of karate students running through a *kata*. Not as polished as the National Ballet, but impressive for all of that.

During a break in the dancing, I had a wooden framework I'd had made brought out. This had two small upright logs about two yards long set up so that we could adjust the distance between them.

I announced a contest. I would give six silver pennies to the man who could squirm through the smallest crack.

This was an unusual contest, but six pence was a whole week's pay. The competition was spirited. Little Piotr Kulczynski won, but Krystyana wasn't impressed.

"Good," I announced, "I was worried about a thief

being able to crawl into our new building. Now I know how wide to make the windows!"

It was a successful event, and we agreed to throw a dance every two weeks from then on. Eventually, we even got a wooden dance floor.

I was getting ready to make the trip to Okoitz one more time when there was a commotion on the trail.

Friar Roman Makowski came in riding a mule with his cassock up almost to his waist. As he dismounted, I could see that the insides of his thighs were worn raw. Overexcited and limping, he rushed over to Sir Vladimir and me.

"Sir Conrad! Thank *God* I've found you!"

"Slow down, kid. What's the problem?"

"It's Tadaos, the boatman! They're going to *kill* him!"

"You'd better start from the beginning."

"You remember the boatman we rode with on our way to Cracow? Well, this spring you wrote him a letter bearing Count Lambert's seal that was sent through my monastery. Since I knew the man, I delivered it to him. He had to leave for Sacz immediately, but he said that he would reply on his return to Cracow.

"You remember the deer he shot by the River Dunajec last fall? Well, he shot another one in the very same place two weeks ago.

"Except this time it wasn't a real deer, but only a dummy. As he got out of his boat to get his kill, the baron's men arrested him for poaching. They would have hanged him forthwith save that he had the letter from Lambert with him and the baron was loath to offend so great a lord as your liege.

"He threw Tadaos into the donjon and wrote Lambert that unless a fine was paid, Tadaos would be hanged in six weeks! Again the letter came through my monastery and I obtained permission to deliver it directly to Lambert.

"Lambert told me that it was none of his affair, but that you could do as you saw fit. So I came here and had the awfulest time finding you."

"Then there's a month to go before they hang him. We don't have to panic yet," I said. "You have the baron's letter?"

The kid handed it to me and I read it. Medieval letters

were just folded and only sealed shut if the matter was private. The seal on this one dangled from the bottom on a ribbon. They didn't use envelopes, but parchment is pretty tough stuff.

"Baron Przemysl wants *four thousand pence*? For *one lousy deer*?" I gagged.

"And not a *real* deer, at that," Vladimir said. "I've heard of this Tadaos and his poaching is notorious. But Cousin Przemysl is being even more greedy than usual."

"You're related to him?" I asked.

"He's a third cousin, actually. Doesn't like to eat anything but fresh-killed game."

"I hope he gets the gout."

"In fact he is so afflicted. How did you know?"

"A pure meat-and-fat diet can do that to you. I guess I have to go to Sacz right after I do my duty at Okoitz."

"But no, Sir Conrad," Friar Roman said. "Count Lambert said that you could be excused this time if you wished to save Tadaos."

"Sir Conrad! Do you mean to tell me that you actually intend to pay this fabulous sum to save the life of one criminal?" Vladimir said. "Why, knights have been talked into marriage with that as a dowry!"

"I guess I have to. I mean, I know the man, and once I was hungry and he shot a deer and I helped eat it. It's not as if poaching was a mortal sin."

"Mortal enough in this case. But if you mean to go, let's make a lark of it. Let's take Annastashia and perhaps Krystyana and combine duty with pleasure. It's the best time of the year for traveling and I could show you all the sights.

"I know most of the important people in that part of the country and we'd be invited in everywhere. Why, the whole trip shouldn't cost a penny, except you could buy salt at the mines where it's cheap. And I could show Annastashia to my parents."

As soon as Krystyana heard of this one, I'd have no peace until I went along with it. Best to bow to the inevitable as soon as possible. Anyway, things were going smoothly here and I was ready for a vacation. I'd been working hard for almost a year and it was time.

"You talked me into it. We'll leave in the morning.

Friar Roman, do you want to come along?"

"With your permission, I have done certain damage to my privy members and—"

"And you'd better have them rubbed down with goose grease or some such and rest up here for a few days. Riding a hairy mule bareback while wearing nothing but a cassock was a dumb thing to do."

"Yes, my lord. Also, I won't be returning to Cracow for some time. My abbot has asked me to go to Okoitz to learn about your cloth works there. He wants looms of his own at the monastery."

# Chapter Nine

WE GOT a very early start, with the sun still far below the mountains as we rode out. The girls were on their palfreys and each led two of our sturdiest pack mules. Our baggage wasn't all that much, but I wanted to bring back a ton of salt from the mines near Cracow for the winter. Salting was about the only way we had of preserving meat and I had a big hunt in mind come fall. The ladies did the leading, as Vladimir insisted that a knight must not be encumbered, in case of emergency. He and I were in armor and on our war-horses, and Anna seemed to be delighted to be traveling, instead of hauling logs.

Krystyana had insisted that I wear the gaudy gold-and-red velvet surcoat given me after my run-in with the whoremasters guild in Cieszyn and I found Anna in the matching barding. I was surprised to find Krystyana in a matching dress with barding for her own horse. Furthermore, Vladimir and Annastashia were similarly decked out, but in Vladimir's family colors, silver and blue. We even had pennons for our lances, which meant that I had to take a lance along, even though I'm not much good with one.

The girls had to have planned this weeks ago and must have bought the cloth in Cieszyn. I supposed that they had a lot of fun, sneaking around getting it made and that the others had similar garb. I'm sure I had paid for it somehow, but I was on vacation and wasn't going to let little things bother me.

So we made quite a pageant leaving Three Walls and despite the early hour, most of the people came to see us off.

I'd been mostly wearing my grubbies for the last few months and I hadn't much noticed how shabbily my people were dressed. Now, the difference in our dress was so extreme that I started having guilt pangs and I vowed to buy a few dozen huge bolts of cloth next time I was in Okoitz.

We got to Sir Miesko's manor just in time for dinner and by noon were on the road again under a clear blue sky. In a few hours we were on Lambert's trail, heading east and hoping to make Vladimir's home by nightfall.

We were laughing and singing all the way, acting for all the world like a bunch of drunks although none of us had downed more than a few beers in a row in the last month.

We met a caravan coming west, dozens of pack mules and a few guards in the somber garb of the German Teutonic Knights. They were friendly enough and saluted us as we got off the trail to let them by.

After the mules came a long line of prisoners and something hit me as being terribly, horribly wrong. There were maybe six dozen boys chained neck to neck. They were all naked, or nearly so. Their feet were bleeding and there were whip marks on their backs.

Behind them was a line of girls in the same pitiful shape. None of the children had much body hair. They were all adolescent or even younger.

"What—what is all this?" I asked the black-and-white clad knight at my side.

"Why, that's a prime lot of slaves, heathens every one of 'em. My order saves the best ones when we takes a Pruthenian village. We sell 'em to merchants in Constantinople, Jews mostly, who sell 'em to the Moslems far south of there.

"I know they look pretty rough now, but give 'em a bath and a few days to heal, and them Saracen buggers'll snap 'em up. Them girls'll all do harem duty and half the boys'll be castrated, 'cause them buggers're like that."

"But none of those children is old enough to be a criminal." I was flabbergasted.

"Well, who said anything about *criminals*? There's no money in *criminals*! Who'd want to buy one? These are *prime slaves* we're taking to Constantinople."

"You can't do that!"

"Yeah? Who says?"

"I do! These children don't deserve what you have planned for them!"

"And just what do you intend to do about it?"

"I'll show you!" I drew my sword.

## FROM THE AUTOBIOGRAPHY OF SIR VLADIMIR CHARNETSKI

We were in a merry mood, my love and friends and I, as we moved toward my father's manor. Sir Conrad knows a thousand songs and stories and I know a few myself. What with our ladies' jokes and songs, it was truly pastime with good company.

We stopped to let a caravan of goods and slaves go by. I was joking with the ladies as Sir Conrad chatted with one of the Teutonic Knights of Saint Mary's Hospital at Jerusalem, known as the Crossmen, or the Knights of the Cross, from the huge black crosses they all wear on their white surcoats. They were guarding the caravan and owned the slaves.

They are the largest body of fighting men in Poland and are not to be trifled with.

Suddenly, to the surprise of all, Sir Conrad drew his sword and rode down the line of slaves cutting their chains. So incredible is that skinny sword of his that the iron chains parted while hardly jerking the necks of the slaves. They, and everyone else, stood stark still staring at him.

Then one of the knights came to life, shouted a battle cry, and charged with his sword held high. So intent was Sir Conrad that I don't think he noticed.

His horse, so remarkable in other ways, saw the Crossman coming, but perhaps in fear that if she reared up she would spoil Sir Conrad's aim and so injure a slave, she kicked out sideways, breaking the man's thigh. I know that what I say is impossible, that a horse can't kick high sideways, but I tell you I saw it.

Sir Conrad turned as if seeing the man for the first time. The Crossman's sword was still high and Conrad took his hand off between wrist and elbow. The sword went flying with a hand and part of an arm still clutched to it. The armor was still on the arm, for that blade cares nothing for steel or leather or bone.

The six other Crossmen attacked Conrad and I was faced with a moral dilemma, with no time to think it out!

You see, I was vassal to my father who was vassal to Count Lambert who was vassal to Duke Henryk the Bearded. Count Lambert had all of his vassals swear to defend the trail so that it might be safe for merchants. My duty to my father thus required that I aid the Crossmen in subduing Sir Conrad. But the duke had me swear to defend Sir Conrad and by that oath, I was bound to attack the Crossmen in Sir Conrad's aid.

Now, did my oath to the duke, who after all was neither my liege nor my father's, take precedent over my father's oath to Lambert? Or did the fact that the duke was Lambert's liege mean than an oath to him was more important than an oath to his vassal? I could not resolve it in the time I had.

In truth, I have not resolved it yet.

All I could think was that if there were no survivors, no one would hear of Sir Conrad's indiscretions. The matter would never come before any of the liege lords involved and so my dilemma would not require resolution.

I lowered my lance and charged the Crossmen.

"For God and Poland!" I shouted, out of habit. In part, a battle cry is made to warn an opponent that you are coming, so that you won't dishonorably take him unawares. But now the niceties of civilized combat were less important than the fact that all the Crossmen must die. After that, the baggage-tenders and other peasants would be the work of a few moments.

They didn't notice me coming, probably because of those barrel helmets they wear. There were so many of them trying to get at Sir Conrad that they couldn't all fit around him.

One man was hanging back watching the fight as I went by. I caught him square in the throat with a quick side jab of my lance. I saw the blood squirt and the Crossman start to topple. Then I was onto the main crowd of them and my lance tip caught one in the back of the neck just below the helm line. He fell beneath Witchfire's hoofs as we went by, and I knew he was dead.

On my next pass, a Crossman turned to me as I came. I changed targets at the last instant and caught him in the eye slit. A difficult blow, but it went right in!

All the stories always talk about flashing swords and singing swords and every other kind of swords, but I tell you it's good lancework that wins battles.

I was feeling glorious, unbeatable, as I turned again, to see Sir Conrad's sword trailing flecks of blood and a Crossman's body sitting headless on its horse.

The remaining two Crossmen, seeing five of their number dead without injury to Sir Conrad or myself, promptly turned and fled. I raced after them. We ran a mile or so, with Witchfire glorying in the race as much as I did in the fighting. Then they stopped and saw that the two of them were being ignominiously chased by a lone knight. Their pride got the best of them.

They turned and they charged.

They came at me together and passed one at either side of me. I managed to parry both their lances at the same time with my shield—no easy feat! Try it in your next battle!—but my lance got only a glancing blow off the helm of the Crossman to my left.

We all three of us turned and went at it again. Something Sir Conrad once said occurred to me, that when faced with a problem, one should be wary of thinking in ruts.

Knights always pass on the right because they carry their shields on their left arms and their lances in their right hand. So they're used to striking another knight on their left, as I had done on the last pass.

This time I started out as usual, but switched opponents at the last instant and skewered my man right fair in the gut! He hadn't thought to cover his belly on that side. More, my brilliant tactic so startled both of them that they both missed me entirely.

I turned to see the last Crossman riding for the horizon. Watching all six of his comrades die was just too much for him. We chased after him but to no avail. After two miles he was still drawing ahead of us. In hindsight, I blame this on the barding Witchfire wore. It was a warm day and I think it overheated him.

I turned back with an enviable fighting record, but having ultimately failed. That Crossman didn't look likely to stop this side of Torun and once he was there all the forces of hell would break loose.

But we are all in the hands of God. A man can only do what is right and hope for the best.

For myself, why, I had killed four full knights in a single afternoon. Crossmen who are less than noble wear a "T" on their surcoats rather than a cross and none of these had done so.

My God! That meant that I had won four full sets of arms and armor! And four war-horses besides! For the first time in my life, I was rich! I could buy things and have spending money and—I wondered if Sir Conrad would sell me a plot of land where I could build a small manor for Annastashia, so even if my father didn't bless our union—but no. She deserved a true husband and an honorable marriage.

Then there was the rest of the caravan. All those mules and their cargo. Did I have a share of that? It had to be valuable to be worth sending all the way to Constantinople. And the slaves, what was a slave worth? Whatever it was, a gross of them must be worth a great sum.

So my thoughts were pleasant as I came to the Crossman I had gutted. The poor wretch was still alive, but with a stomach wound, a man is dead even if it takes a week. I had nothing against him, even if he had charged me two against one.

"Well, sir, with that wound you know you're as good as dead and a festering belly is a bad thing to die of. Would you like a bit of mercy?" I drew my misericord, the usual instrument for such things.

He answered me in German, a language I don't speak.

I pantomimed his stomach blowing up and he nodded yes, he understood. I gestured at cutting his throat, but he shook his head and repeatedly made the sign of the cross.

He wanted to be shrived and I nodded yes and loaded him up on his horse, tying him into the saddle. Conrad insists on using a silly low saddle, but a waist-high warkak has its advantages. The high bow and cantle can keep a man in place even if he's unconscious.

With his weapons slung over my saddle bow, we went slowly back to the others. Four victories and not a spot on my new outfit!

## FROM THE DIARY OF CONRAD SCHWARTZ

Looking back, I'm sure that I handled the whole thing wrong, but at the same time, I don't know what I could have done differently. I couldn't have possibly let those children be abused any longer. No decent man could. My admittedly harebrained idea was that if I could free enough of the kids, the guards might chase after them, rather than coming after me. Once I had all of them running loose, the guards could never catch but a few of them and those few might be rescued later. I never for a moment thought I could take on all seven of the guards and win, even with Vladimir's help. And he can be unpredictable.

As it was, the boys had been too stunned to run away! The guards had all piled on me before I could cut more than three of the slaves loose and the kids had just stood there. If Vladimir hadn't joined in, I know they would have killed me. His absolutely murderous charges killed three of the guards and chased off two more. I wounded one man and had to kill another, but we were alive and a hundred forty-two children were safe and that's the way I wanted it.

Yet as soon as the fight was over, Vladimir rode off down the trail like a madman! I swore I'd never figure the fellow out.

After the fight, I looked over the mess we'd made. Four men were dead, but the man I had quite literally disarmed was still alive. He was the same one I had been talking with earlier. I got a tourniquet on the stump of his forearm and called for my medical kit.

I was getting quite good at this sort of thing and had the arteries tied off and the stump sewn mostly up, leaving it open enough to drain, by the time the man regained consciousness. Besides being thirsty, the fellow was surprised that he was alive and that I was patching him up.

"It won't help you none, you know. After what you've done, the Order will get you even if you do fix me up."

"I'm not doing it to win any gratitude. I wouldn't want gratitude from the likes of you, or your kind. You enslaved children! You brutalized them. You were selling them into an absolutely ugly life. Why should I want your friendship?" I finished bandaging his arm.

"Then why're you doing this?"

"I don't really know. Maybe it's just that there's no real reason for you to die right now. I'm not your judge. Maybe it's just Christian charity."

"You're a strange man."

"I've been told that. Let's move you back into the shade." He cried out when I started to drag him away. I soon discovered that his leg was broken.

"How in the world did you do that to yourself? Well, let's get your pants off and a splint on it."

An hour after the battle, I had the group into some sort of order. Anna had taken it onto herself to round up all the stray horses, mules, and ex-slaves, plus the dozen-odd mule skinners who had accompanied the caravan.

I put the men to cleaning up the mess, stowing the bodies on their horses and making a litter for the surviving guard.

The Pruthenian children spoke a language that was just beyond the edge of intelligibility. It was a little like the Kashubian tongue spoken by a minority group in modern Poland. But not quite.

Two knights approached. "Sir Vladimir!" I shouted. "Welcome back. Where have you been?"

"I was trying to get the last two, but I only bagged one, and he needs a priest. You are ready? I think we should go back to Sir Miesko's manor."

The guard next to Vladimir was in the saddle but unconscious. His stomach had been ripped open and contents of his small intestine was dribbling down his leg, mixed with blood. There was nothing I could do for the poor bastard. Even with a competent doctor and a modern hospital, it would be touch and go.

"Yes, Sir Miesko's would be best. Mount up! We're going west!" I cried.

We left the gutted guard in the saddle, since taking him down would be doing him no favor. He needed speed, for there was no comfort. The girls had been silent, frightened since the fight started. As we went slowly back, they stationed themselves on either side of the gutted guard, keeping him upright and soiling their dresses with his blood.

I went to Vladimir's side. "You saved my life, Sir Vladimir. I'm grateful."

"Think nothing of it. But tell me, all these arms and armor and goods. Do we own that now?"

"I don't know. Maybe. We'll ask Sir Miesko. He was once a clerk and knows something of the law.

"Please don't think that I'm criticizing, but why did you go after those last two guards? They were running away and wouldn't have hurt us."

"Why? To kill them, of course! Had I gotten the last one, perhaps no one would hear of this bit of work. We could have dispatched the peasants and taken the caravan to Constantinople ourselves, with no one the wiser. As matters stand, if Count Lambert doesn't hang us, the Knights of the Cross will.

"Incidentally, why didn't you come to my aid with those last two Crossmen? Your horse can outrace a windstorm. We could have gotten the last one and wouldn't be outlaws. But perhaps we can sell much of this loot quickly and go to France. I've heard lovely things about France.

"And another point. Whatever prompted you to loot this caravan? Aren't you wealthy enough already?"

This whole line of thinking was absolutely foreign to me.

"Wait a minute. I'm not an outlaw. I haven't done anything wrong!"

"You haven't done anything wrong? Attacking a caravan on your liege lord's land wasn't wrong? Killing a half dozen peaceful guards wasn't wrong? Putting me into this awkward situation wasn't wrong?"

"I'm sorry I got you into this and I'd be dead without your help, but the fact is that I never asked for it. You charged in of your own free will. I'm glad that you did, but I'm not responsible.

"As to the caravan and guards, they were abusing innocent children, whom we rescued. I am not ashamed of doing that."

"Children? You mean the slaves?"

"Ex-slaves," I said. "And I am not going to run off to France or any place else."

"You mean to stay? After breaking your oath to Count Lambert?"

"I never broke my oath! I swore to protect the people on Lambert's lands. Well, those children are people. They are on Lambert's land and they certainly needed protection. I did what was right."

He stared down and shook his head. "Oh, my. The cat's been at the yarn with this one!"

That evening at supper, we talked of the day's adventures with Sir Miesko and his wife.

When we finished, Lady Richeza had tears in her eyes.

"Sir Conrad, we were so close! In another few years, the schools would all be running and . . ." She got up and ran out of the room.

Sir Miesko was shaking his head.

"Sir Conrad, if ever a man fell down an open garderobe, you've done it. You have affronted your liege lord, attacked the merchants, and declared personal war on the most powerful military force within a thousand miles. While you were at it, why didn't you pee on the Pope? Then you'd have everybody at your hanging!"

"No, I think we did a thorough job of it," Sir Vladimir said. "After all, the Crossmen are a religious order with a papal sanction."

I ignored him.

"I still say that Sir Vladimir and I did no wrong."

"In Sir Vladimir's case, you're probably right. He's

likely in the clear, unless the Crossmen decide to get really vindictive, which they always might.

"It's the doctrine of implied vassalage. See here. None of us present is liege to one another. But you are eating at my table and under my roof. If I were attacked at this moment, you would be obligated to come to my aid as though you were my vassals.

"Furthermore, as my vassals, you would not be responsible for any of my actions. Now, as I understand it, Sir Vladimir has been traveling with you for some months, at your expense, so I would suppose that implied vassalage would apply."

"This implied vassalage is new to me," Vladimir said, "but it takes a weight off my mind. Tell me, does an implied vassal have a share of any booty?"

"Yes," Miesko replied, "he does. But in this case there may or may not be booty. Sir Conrad argues that the Crossmen were performing a criminal act, abusing children. In that case, the property of the criminals would be his, subject to his liege lord's share.

"But the Crossmen will claim that Sir Conrad is the criminal, a highwayman who attacked a caravan, in which case a thief has no right to the property he stole.

"While you were washing up, I looked over that caravan, since it's in my barns. The mules belong to the farriers, and don't enter into this, but the cargo belongs to the Crossmen and it's rich. There are fourteen muleloads of prime northern furs and three of amber. Those slaves are worth six hundred pence each, and the arms, armor, and war-horses are all of the first quality. All told, it could easily be worth more than the booty Sir Conrad won last fall."

"Be that as it may," I said, "I didn't do it for the money. I did it to save those children and I'm not sure what is to become of them. Can they be sent home?"

"Impossible. They no longer have homes or families. When the Crossmen take a heathen village, they kill every man, woman, and child, except for those few that might have value as slaves."

"Brutal bastards. They remind me of another bunch of Germans I can think of. If I can't send the kids home, I guess I'll just have to take care of them myself. Sir

Miesko, can you make arrangements for them to be sent to Three Walls?"

"Gladly. I wasn't looking forward to feeding them. You understand that they are not to leave your lands until the whole matter is settled, though. You had best write a letter of explanation to your intendant, explaining matters."

"Yes," I said. "I'll have to write one to Lambert as well."

"What? You're not going to him directly?"

"If I did that, he might throw me in jail. Then who will go and get Tadaos out of that donjon?"

"Please understand that Lambert is my liege as well. I can't let you leave without some surety."

"Lambert already has surety from me. Most of my money is in his vault."

"Hmmm. True. Well, go then and come back quickly."

"First thing in the morning. One last item. Can you recommend a good lawyer?"

"Lawyer? You don't need a lawyer. Your case will never come before any court. Any human court, anyway."

"What? Then what was all that legal talk about a while ago?"

"Oh, that was just my old clerkish training coming out again. See here, if you and I had a dispute, we could gather our arguments and take them before Count Lambert for settlement.

"Likewise, a dispute between Lambert and his brother could be taken before the duke. But Duke Henryk is vassal to no man and the Crossmen are not vassal to him. So there is no human court before which this dispute can come. It must be settled before God."

"You mean an ecclesiastical court?"

"Of course not! I mean a trial by combat. The Crossmen will send their best champion against you, and I'm afraid that you don't have the slightest chance of winning."

Wonderful.

Much later, I sat alone by a smoky oil lamp with a

sharpened goose-quill pen, a ram's horn of ink, and some sheepskin parchment.

Dear Yashoo,

This letter should be delivered to you along with the children that Sir Vladimir and I rescued today.

These poor victims of misfortune have been very badly treated. Their homes have been destroyed, their families murdered, and themselves enslaved by a band of foreigners called the Crossmen. They have been whipped and marched for hundreds of miles, with bleeding feet and bloody backs. They were to be sold far to the south to satisfy the unnatural lusts of the infidel Moslems, the same heathens who now hold the Holy Lands against all true Christians.

It is our Christian duty to care for these poor unfortunates. It will not be easy. They do not speak Polish, and have never had the chance to learn of Christ's pure teaching. We must adopt them, bring them into our homes, and give them the benefit of our religion and our love.

I ask each family to adopt at least one of these children, and treat them just as if they were their own flesh and blood.

They are to eat, with everyone else, at my expense.

They need clothing. I am writing my liege lord, Count Lambert, for cloth sufficient to clothe not only the children, but every man, woman, and child at Three Walls. This too will be at my own cost. There should be enough for two complete sets of clothes for everyone, one of linen and one of wool, for the winter. When it arrives, see that it is distributed free to the ladies and put any surpluses in storage.

Read this letter to all the people at supper every evening for three days. I know that I can count on the good Christians of Three Walls to do their duty.

I give you all my love,
Conrad.

P.S. The affair with the Crossmen is not over. There may be some legal tricks that they may try, but don't worry. We can not fail because God is on our side.

I read the letter over. It appealed to duty, family, and pity, as well as to religion and greed. If my ploy didn't work, I'd demand my money back from that course in persuasive writing I once took. Next chance I got.

On to my Liege Lord Lambert, Count of Okoitz, on this Second day of August, 1232

My Lord, Know that on this date I found one hundred forty-two very young people being severely oppressed on your lands.

They were chained neck to neck, whipped, and marched barefoot and naked for hundreds of miles by foreigners. Out of Christian pity and my oath to you, whereby I vowed to protect all the people on your lands, I rescued these oppressed people with Sir Vladimir's valiant aid.

Polish arms were victorious, for God was on our side. We two of your vassals dispatched four of the foreign knights, wounded two more, perhaps unto death and sent a seventh knight fleeing for the horizon.

Vast booty was taken, which Sir Miesko estimates to be as large as that taken last fall, when by the grace of God I cleaned your lands of the brigand, Sir Rheinburg. This booty is now at Sir Miesko's manor, awaiting future division, including your rightful share.

The people rescued will be sent to my lands, to be cared for at my expense and, once healed of their sad wounds, to be put to some useful work, if they will it.

They are all quite young and most of the ladies are not yet budding, but they were all carefully selected to serve the lechery of Moorish princes and are remarkably comely. I think perhaps that in a year or two you might find dalliance at Three Walls to be profitable. Or perhaps some might want employment in the cloth mill, which I am building for you.

They were all naked when rescued, or nearly so and thus I have need of cloth for them, as well as for the other people on my lands. As a favor to me, could you please send wool cloth sufficient to clothe eight hundred people, and a like amount of linen, to Three Walls? Take whatever amount you deem fair for the cloth and transport from my coffer that is in your vault.

I wish that I could come to you at this time but a friend is in danger in Sacz and will die if I do not go immediately to his aid.

Sir Miesko says that there will be some legal problems as a result of my actions, but I hold that slavery is an offense against God and that I did no wrong this day. I shall return to you in a few weeks and place all my wealth as surety for that return.

I remain your loyal and trusting vassal,<br>Conrad

P.S. By this time, the beehives I showed your carpenter the way of making should have attracted some bees. You might want to have your beekeeper survey all the hives and count those hives that are populated, to see how well I have served you in this manner. Please give my regards to all the fair ladies at the mill.

*Conrad*

On rereading the letter, I could see that I was troweling it on pretty thick, but then Lambert wasn't all that sophisticated. I'd put myself in the best possible light without actually telling a lie, I had reminded him of all my past services and appealed to his pride in arms (considerable), his greed (such of it that there was), his lechery (vast, but of a friendly sort), and even his sweet tooth.

Asking him to set his own price for the cloth was more flattery and was in fact the best way to get a low price out of him.

If words could get me out of this•one, this letter

should do it. I just might get myself out of the mess without a fight.

Yet I wasn't really worried, though I didn't know why. Maybe it was because the whole thing was so unreal. In the twentieth century, if I had rescued a hundred forty-two children, I'd be a big hero! I'd be in all the papers and on television and the president would pin a medal on me. Here, they were going to try and kill me. I just couldn't take the whole thing seriously.

But I was tired when I finally stumbled off to bed.

# Chapter Ten

EARLY THE next morning, I read my letters to my party and to Sir Miesko's family, since it was important that our stories were reasonably consistent.

Vladimir felt that I should add a bit more about his victories, so I added a few paragraphs in the margins praising his lancework and horsemanship to the skies. Let him take all the glory. He deserved it and it didn't mean much to me. All I cared about was getting the kids off safely.

Lambert couldn't read, but Sir Miesko promised to read my letter to him before explaining the other side of the story.

Sir Miesko said, "I've been thinking about this and I've had another look at those children. If somebody did that to my kids, well, they'd have to kill me first.

"Thinking about it, their fathers are all dead, aren't they. Conrad, know that I'm behind you in this mess you've made."

He turned to his horse, but then turned back quickly.

"But don't expect too much! I've got my own family to think of!"

So Sir Miesko left for Okoitz, the children were sent with some trusted men to Three Walls and my original party resumed its journey to Sacz. By noon, we approached the turnoff to Vladimir's folks' place.

"I know I invited you all to my father's manor, but I

wonder now if that would be wise at this time," Sir Vladimir said. "In another hour we could be at Oswiecim, and if we push on till dusk we should arrive at the monastery of Tyniec. I think the monastery might be best."

"Why a monastery?" I asked. "They'd have us sleep with the other men and the girls would be lonely."

"True. But the monastery gives us the protection of the Church, which might be needful. We still don't know how the matter sits with Count Lambert, or what the Crossmen are going to do. Tyniec puts us beyond Lambert's territory and the Crossmen would never violate Church property."

"Never?"

"Of course not. After all, they are a religious order."

"A religious order? You call that bunch of murderers, who massacre villages, enslave children, and trade with the Moslems a religious order?"

"It does seem odd, doesn't it? But they are santioned by the Pope and follow the Order of Saint Benedict, except for the fighting, of course, and the merchandising."

"Painting a wolf brown doesn't make it a cow. They're a bunch of damn murderers even if they do wear crosses on their shirts.

"I still don't see why you don't want to visit your parents. We were all looking forward to it, especially Annastashia. Surely we'd be safe enough there," I said.

"Safe, yes, but the timing isn't right. May I speak frankly? You know that I wish to persuade them to permit my marriage to Annastashia. I want them to be in a good mood when I broach the subject. But just now, I'm under something of a cloud."

"I don't understand that."

"Well, you see, my father is also my liege lord. He swore to keep the trail safe for merchants. By aiding you yesterday, I violated his oath. I dishonored him. He would be well within his rights to have me hanged! Oh, my mother would never let him do it, but he certainly won't be in any mood to grant favors. In fact, I think it best to avoid him entirely until this matter is settled and we are either proved innocent or are dead."

"If you don't want to visit relatives, fine, but the monastery is out. There must be an inn nearby."

"Not a clean one."

I'd been without fleas for months and I suppose the monastery would be an interesting experience for the girls.

As we rode into Cracow the next morning, the guards at the gate stiffened up and saluted. The last time I was there, they had haggled with me and charged me a toll to get in. Obvious wealth and rank have their privileges.

The girls were thrilled. The big city at last! Hundreds of colorful things to see and do. Huge cathedrals, massive stone castles on Wawel Hill, more shops than anything imaginable!

To me, well, take a few dozen historically interesting buildings, put them on a hill with a fine view and populate it with a few hundred gaudily dressed nobles and you have all that was attractive to the eye.

Then surround this with a squalid town of ten thousand uneducated and underfed people and cover it all with a half yard of shit and you have the reality of the situation. With plumbing, sewers, and street cleaners, it would have made a fine tourist trap.

As it was, I preferred the forests.

But the girls deserved a treat after all they'd been through lately. They had done a fine lot of work at Three Walls and they'd seen their first bloody combat, which shook them up a lot more than they wanted to admit. And they were a lot more worried than I was about the upcoming trial, so I worked at keeping them cheered up.

The girls wanted to go shopping and sightseeing and Vladimir felt that it was important to report in at Wawel Castle as soon as possible. I wanted to go see Father Ignacy at the Franciscan monastery. He was the only friend I had in this century who knew that I was from the future. He was my confessor, and I was in need of his services. And there was a certain matter of a Church inquisition into whether I was an instrument of God or an instrument of the devil.

So we compromised. I gave the girls each a handful of silver (their back pay really, but they didn't look at it that way. They were thrilled), had Vladimir take them shopping, and agreed to meet them at the monastery at noon. Then we'd go to the castle.

A monk who had considered me a klutz when I worked here now greeted me effusively, like a combination great lord and long lost friend. The outfit, again. Father Ignacy met me in his cell and he, at least, was unchanged.

"Welcome, Conrad."

"Thank you. Father, you said that you would file a report on me with the proper authorities in the Church. How is that going?"

"Quite well, my son. I wrote my report even within the time you were still here last December, and delivered it to my abbot. He delayed it hardly at all, but dispatched it within the month to the Bishop of Cracow.

"His Excellency acted with surprising speed and tact and within two months sent the letter back to my abbot, suggesting that it would perhaps be better to go through the regular arm of the Church, rather than through the secular one. That is to say, he felt it should go, not through his office, but through the Franciscan home monastery in Italy.

"We were able to find a messenger going to Italy in much less time than you'd think, and by June the report was speeding its way to Italy."

So nine months had gone by and the report hadn't even been delivered. And I'd thought the Russians were screwed up.

"Thank you, Father. A great deal has happened to me since we last met."

"You wish to confess? How long has it been since your last confession?"

"Only about a week, Father. But—I suppose it's wrong to say this, but my confessions since I last saw you haven't felt right. It's almost as though I didn't really confess at all."

"This might be caused by the promise of silence I required of you. You could never tell the whole truth."

"That might be it, Father."

"Well, the reasons for that promise are still valid, so you must live with it. But now I want you to confess since our last meeting."

And so I did. I told him of all the things I'd built, the women I'd had, and the men I'd killed. Confession with Father Ignacy is never the rote affair it is with some priests. He digs into things for hours if need be, but always arrives at the truth of a situation. Once we were through, he looked down and shook his head.

After scolding me about Krystyana and the other ladies-in-waiting, he said, "All this fighting! I hope you realize that I never thought that you would be in such danger when I found you that position with the merchant, Novacek."

"I've never found fault with you, Father."

"You are generous, my son. So. You attained wealth, lands, and power of a scope that most men can only dream about and it seems that two days ago you threw it all away.

"What is this problem you have with the Knights of the Cross? On your first day in this century, you insulted one of them and got your head bashed in the bargain. Now you have attacked one of their caravans and caused the death of five or six of their number. You should know that very few men are truly evil, and certainly there could not be an entire order of them. The Crossmen do valuable service to our country, keeping the Mazovian borders free from invasion."

"They do it by murdering entire villages."

"Then we both know that such an event was probably in retaliation for some atrocity by the Pruthenians."

"Father, I know nothing of the sort."

"Do you think that the northern barbarians are innocent, peaceful dwellers of the forests? They are heathens and worship barbarous gods."

"There must be better ways to convert them."

"One would think so. Many missionaries have tried it over the past three hundred years, but to no avail. Many have died, martyrs to Christ.

"It's not some simple matter of putting a new image in their church. Those people practice human sacrifice! And cannibalism! Those 'innocent children' you 'rescued' have every one of them eaten human flesh!"

"Now *that's* news to me, Father. But I'll make Christians out of them. And no matter what the heathens have done, it doesn't excuse what the Crossmen have done. You don't know their whole history."

"Perhaps you should tell me about them."

"Well, you know that their organization was formed forty years ago in Jerusalem, a German imitation of the Knights Templar. They soon lost interest in the Holy Lands, I suppose because there wasn't much profit in it.

"They tried to set up in Hungary, but King Andrew found out the truth about them in time and threw them out. Duke Conrad of Mazovia wasn't that intelligent. He invited them in—what?—seven years ago?—to guard his northern borders. Their way of doing that has been to murder every non-Christian in sight and to take as much Polish soil as they do Prussian.

"In the future, they will do nothing but grow and many of the most murderous battles of the medieval period—"

"The *what*?"

"Forgive me, Father, but that is what this current period of history will eventually be called. The middle period between the ancient world of the Romans and the Renaissance, or awakening, that led to the modern world."

"Now *that* is a *shock*. I'd always thought of *this* as being the modern world."

"Hmm. Then again, I don't know what generations future to mine will call my own civilization. Perhaps they won't be as polite."

"Some time you must teach me more of your history. But for now, return to your story of the Crossmen."

"Yes, Father. Eventually their murderous ways became so notorious that they were censored by the Pope. This didn't bother them a bit. They simply became a secular order and went on doing as they had been. Many long wars and bloody battles were fought by the kings of Poland against them."

"Then Poland will again have a king?"

"Of course, Father. We're but a century from the time of King Casimir the Great!"

"Praise God! But continue your story."

"Eventually, they were defeated at the Battle of Grunwald or Tannenberg, it's sometimes called. This was—will be—the bloodiest battle fought by Christians in the Middle Ages.

"The surviving Crossmen became vassals of the Polish Crown, as the Duchy of Prussia. By that time they had completely eradicated the Slavic tribe of Prussians, or Pruthenians as they are sometimes called, and had taken that name for themselves, the way a barbaric warrior takes the clothing of his victim.

"But despite their vassalage, they never became Polish. Six hundred years from now, they were instrumental in organizing and dominating all the German states.

"Their spirit was that of another German group, the Nazis, which conquered Poland as well as most of the rest of Europe. Their crimes were so horrible as to be unimaginable. Not far from where we sit, they built a death camp called Auschwitz where they systematically killed four and a half million people. That is half again as many people as there are in all of present-day Poland.

"This was not a matter of the sack and slaughter of a city, done in the heat of passion. This was a matter of Germans going to work each day for four years and killing their quota of men, women, and children.

"And that was not the only camp, and the camps were not the only atrocity. In the end, more than fifty million people died in six years. That's twice as many people as lived in the entire Roman Empire at its peak."

Father Ignacy was silent for a while. "I cannot comprehend the numbers of people you speak of, but I have never known you to lie. You are saying then that this is a great evil that must be fought?"

"Yes, I guess so, Father."

"I take it then that you are not intending to run away, as many men would."

"I don't see how I can. If I did, they'd probably take those children back and sell them to the Moslems. I can't have that on my conscience."

"No, I don't suppose you can. But you are only one man, and they are many thousands."

"I know that I can't lick them alone," I said, my eyes blurring with tears. "But I intend to do everything that one man can. If I die, well, I die. Father, you once told me that I might be an instrument of God, and I didn't believe you. Well, in this matter, I know that I have God on my side." I think I was crying a little.

"Very well, my son. For what small worth it might be, know that in this matter you have me on your side as well. Go with God, my son. I give you no penance for your sins, for I think that you will soon be punished more than you deserve, and more than you can bear."

I had to stop a while in the vestibule to compose myself before I joined the others. It doesn't do to be tear-streaked when your friends are worried about you.

But the others were in a merry mood when I joined them in front of the monastery, and the girls were prattling about all the wondrous sights they'd seen. I leaned back on Anna and soaked up their gaiety. I needed it.

Vladimir informed us that the dinner hour at Wawel Castle would be over by then, and we hadn't eaten lately. I suggested an inn that I had stopped at last fall.

A healthy-looking, well-filled-out young woman took our order, then did a double take at me.

"Oh my God! You're Sir Conrad!"

"Guilty. Then you must be Malenka."

"Oh my God! Zygmunt! Zygmunt! Quickly! Look who's here!"

She ran out of the room to get her husband.

"What was that all about?" asked Annastashia.

"Oh, once I played matchmaker," I said.

The innkeeper came back with his wife, wiping his hands on his apron and smiling. Introductions were made and he announced that the meal was on the house and so were the next five, if we'd come back.

Soon, their other duties called them away and we could eat.

"They certainly were happy with you," Krystyana said. "How did you happen to bring them together?"

"Well, I hired her."

"Hired her?"

"Hired her."

"There's more to the story than you're telling."

"You are right. But that's all of it that you're going to hear. A man deserves some secrets."

They complained, but I wouldn't say another word. Actually, Malenka had been a prostitute and I'd hired her just to keep her from being used by a young friend of mine; it wouldn't have been good for him just then.

She was very young and hungry-looking at the time, and I had to report to a new job. So I told her that she had to do honest work for the innkeeper for the three days that I had hired her. The upshot was that she married the innkeeper, my friend became a monk, and all three of them are very happy. Pretty fair mileage out of three silver pennies.

But to talk about it would only embarass Malenka, so I kept silent.

"They must have a lot of knights to guard all these walls," Annastashia said, as we rode again through the city.

"Not really, love," Sir Vladimir replied. "Down here in the city proper, they don't use knights at all. The castle and Wawel Hill are guarded by the nobility, but in an emergency the outer walls, gates, and towers are all guarded by the commoners."

"They *do* that?" Krystyana was scandalized.

"Most assuredly. That tower over there would be defended by the haberdashers guild, and the gate we came in through was the responsibility of the butchers guild."

"You mean the man that saluted us when we came in was a butcher?" Annastashia asked.

"No, no. I said 'in an emergency.' That fellow was hired by the city council to guard the gate. He and a few dozen others do that for a living. But he wasn't a knight, either. At least I don't think he was. Just a man at arms."

"I thought you had to be a knight to have armor and guard things," Krystyana said.

"Not at all," Sir Vladimir said. "Anyone who can afford it can have it, in Poland anyway. I've heard that in Germany and France it's a little different, but that's the way it is here. That only nobility may stand guard is one of Count Lambert's rules, which only apply at Okoitz. He says that it keeps his knights from getting lazy and supports their rights to all their special privileges."

"*What* special privileges?" Krystyana asked.

"Like not having to do manual labor," I said. There wasn't much point in telling Krystyana that *she* was a special privilege.

"How about that tower over there?" Annastashia asked.

"The brewers guild, I think. Every guild has its tower or section of wall, except for the surgeons and the armorers. They'd have other duties if the city was attacked," Sir Vladimir said.

"But who could possibly attack a city this huge?" Krystyana said.

"Well, nobody for hundreds of years has tried it. But that's because it's ready for war," Sir Vladimir said.

"Not ready enough," I said. "In eight and a half years, the Mongols will come and will burn this city to the ground."

They all looked at me aghast.

"Sir Conrad! Don't *say* things like that!" Krystyana said.

"Yes, Sir Conrad. That's hardly a thing to joke about!" Sir Vladimir added.

"I wish I were joking. But there's nothing we can do about it right now.

"I'm sure Sir Vladimir knows the tale, but have you ladies heard the story about King Krak, who killed the dragon and founded this city?"

"I'd heard it was a monster, but not necessarily a dragon," Sir Vladimir said.

"Then tell it your way."

"I shall."

He launched into a windy telling of the tale that almost got us to the castle gates.

"And it's all true?" Krystyana said. "There *really* was a King Krak?"

"I could show you his burial mound. They named the city after him. What other proof can you need?" He said with a twinkle in his eye. He gave me a quick wink.

There *are* these two huge prehistoric mounds in the area, but nobody ever found anything buried under them. The best guess is that they were used as defensive structures. Poland and the rest of the north European plain have been inhabited, off and on, for at least a hundred eighty thousand years. A lot can happen in that time.

"And Princess Wanda *really* drowned herself in the

river rather than marry the German prince?" Annastashia asked.

"I could show you her mound as well."

"And the monster's cave is *still* under Wawel Hill?"
Krystyana asked.

"It is. But the mouth of it was covered over hundreds
of years ago and no one remembers where it's at."

"Do *you* believe the story, Sir Conrad?" Annastashia
asked.

"The way I heard it, Wanda turned Prince Rytygier
down. He then got mad and invaded her country. Her
armies defeated his, and in thanksgiving, she sacrificed
herself to the gods. But far be it from me to contradict
Sir Vladimir."

"God wouldn't want anybody to do *that*!" Annastashia said.

"This was hundreds of years ago. We were pagans
then. Pagan gods want a lot."

"Thank God we're Christians," Krystyana said.

The last time I was in Cracow, they wouldn't let me
on Wawel Hill. This time the guards saluted us as we
entered. The uniform gets them every time.

As we dismounted, a page ran up to me.

"Sir Conrad? The duke is expecting you. Please come
with me."

This startled me, but I followed the kid. The castle
had little in common with the one I remembered from the
twentieth century. A lot would be torn down in the next
seven hundred years and a whole lot more built. But
every now and then I'd get the déjà vu feeling and realize
I was seeing a familiar landmark from a formerly impossible angle.

Duke Henryk's chambers were straight out of a movie
set, and his bearing and beard were as formidable as
ever. I bowed low.

"Oh, stand up, boy! I'm too old to waste time on that
nonsense. In private, anyway. They still make me do it in
public. Better still, sit down. Now what's this about your
chopping up a Crossmen caravan?"

"They were abusing over a hundred children, your
grace."

"They were transporting a consignment of Pruthenian

slaves to the Greeks so the Greeks could sell them to the Moors. Go on."

I was trying not to sweat. "Yes, your grace. I tried to free the kids and the guards attacked me. Sir Vladimir came to my aid and we won."

"Two of you kicked shit out of seven of them. I like that! How did Sir Vladimir do?"

"He killed three and wounded one more to the death, your grace."

"Ha! I knew that kid had his father's blood in him! Four men in a fair fight!"

"More than fair, your grace. In the end, he was charged twice by two knights at the same time and he still killed one of them."

"What! Two on one? The bastard Crossman never told me about that! Yeah, I've talked to him. He came through yesterday, still scared. Ha! You could smell the shit on his britches. He said you'd killed all six of his comrades. What happened to the last one?"

"He lost his right arm, your grace, but I think I got to him in time. He'll likely live. He's at Sir Miesko's now."

"Ah, Miesko. He used to be my clerk before I knighted him.... Well. Damn good fight, boy. But it's still going to be the death of you.

"If the Pruthenians were on my border, I'd make peasants out of them damn quick, but that sluggard the Duke of Mazovia couldn't handle them, so the damn fool invited in those Crossmen. He invited in the wolves to keep down the foxes!

"Well, I don't like them, but I'm not strong enough to beat them. And that's what it would take for me to get you out of this mess you've made. A war. I can't afford it and I couldn't win it. So I've got to stand back and let them kill you. You hear me, boy? You'll get no real help from me! The best I can do is to delay your trial a few months."

"I'd appreciate that, your grace. Maybe the horse will sing."

"Eh?"

"One of the Aesop's fables, your grace. A man condemned to death asked the king not to kill him because

he was the only man in the world who could teach a
horse to sing. The king was skeptical, but gave the man a
horse and a year to teach it. The man's friends asked him
why he had done such a foolish thing. Nobody could
teach a horse to sing! The man answered, 'True. But a
lot can happen in a year. The king may die. I may die.
And maybe the horse will sing.'"

"I wish I had an education. Damn. A man comes to us
from the far future and we go and kill him."

I was shocked. No one was supposed to know about
that!

"You know, your grace?"

"Yeah. I worked it out of your priest. Don't be hard
on him, though. I can be very persuasive."

"I can believe that, your grace."

"You'd better. Even so, he had a time convincing me.
What finally turned me was when he showed me that
parchment you gave him and I realized the wealth of
your people."

"Parchment, your grace? You mean the paper money
I gave him for a souvenir?"

"No, not the miniature paintings, although that was
pretty impressive, too. Any people who would use
works of art for their currency instead of silver must be
truly cultured! But no, I mean the parchment arsewipes
you gave him."

Once, when we were walking north from Zakopane,
Father Ignacy had gestured that he was going off to the
bushes, presumably to relieve himself. I'd given him
some toilet paper and he'd taken it without comment. I
hadn't thought of it since. It appears that rather than
using it, he'd kept it as a treasure from the future.

"The toilet paper?"

"That's what he called it. People who can afford
parchment to wipe their butts are richer than anyone in
this century!

"Your priest told me why he swore you to secrecy,
and I have to agree with most of his reasons. You can
count on me to keep my mouth shut.

"Look, boy, you don't have much life left, so you get
along and enjoy yourself. Tell the guard to send in the

castellan. I'll have him fix your party up with the best rooms available."

I bowed and the duke waved me out.

Whew! At first I thought the duke himself was going to kill me! And toilet paper is the most impressive arti-fact of modern civilization?

# Chapter Eleven

I RETURNED to the courtyard to find that Sir Vladimir was having problems with the palace grooms. They didn't know how we were to be treated.

"Relax, boys," I said to them, "the duke is giving us the red-carpet treatment."

"Sir? Do you mean red with blood?"

"I mean that he is giving us the best rooms in the palace, and you may assume that he means our mounts to be very well cared for as well.

"Ladies, Sir Vladimir, let's tour a castle."

Sir Vladimir was thrilled that the duke had complimented his prowess and had me recite much of what was said word for word. Then he had me do it again in front of a dozen witnesses.

I played along with it. For a man like Sir Vladimir, peer approval is the most important thing in the world, what money is to Boris Novacek, or the Church is to Father Ignacy. I owed Sir Vladimir my life and a few moments of lip service was a small price to pay.

We were treated with considerable deference by everyone. Even those who outranked us crowded around. Barons and counts seemed eager to make our acquaintance. Word of the duke's approval traveled quickly, and stories about me had been circulating for months. But I think that much of it was the morbid curiosity people have about a condemned man. Finally, one knight simply offered his quite sincere condolences and said that if there was anything he could do for me before the end, or even after it, he would be most happy to oblige.

"Thank you, sir," I said. "But why is everyone so convinced that I'm going to die? We're talking about a trial by combat, not an execution! It's going to be a fair fight in front of witnesses. I've been in three fights in the last year—four, if you count that nonsense with the whoremasters guild in Cieszyn. Most of them were against odds, yet I've hardly been wounded. I'm going to win this trial, I tell you."

The knight looked awkward, but Sir Vladimir said, "Sir Conrad, I'm afraid that you don't seem to understand what you're up against. You'll be fighting a champion! A man who does little else but train for this sort of thing. The Crossmen have two of them, and each has killed more than thirty men in public trials and duels.

"Even so, I'd say you had a chance if the fight were strictly swords. But the rules are 'arm yourself' and he'll come at you with a lance. Sword against lance, you'd have no chance against even a poor lanceman. Lance against lance—Sir Conrad, I've seen your lancework and a plowman could do better. I'm afraid you have no hope at all."

"It's as bad as that?"

"It's worse than that, but I lack the skill to state it more strongly."

Meals were all served formally at Wawel Castle, with every lord seated by his lady in strict order of precedence. This put us pretty far down the line, but not quite at the bottom.

The food was well served and decorative enough, but not at all to my taste, mostly overprepared, overcooked, and overspiced. It was like something done by home-economics students who were trying too hard.

But Sir Vladimir and the girls were happy.

At supper, the duke publicly praised Sir Vladimir's battle skills and insisted on hearing a blow-by-blow account from him. Sir Vladimir gave it in a very animated fashion, shouting battle cries, waving his arms, and prais-

ing himself in a way that would have been in very poor
taste in the twentieth century.

Here it was the proper thing to do, I suppose.

At any rate, Sir Vladimir was the man of the hour and
Annastashia gloried in it.

There was a dance after dinner, and I discovered that
the steps I'd shown people in Okoitz last winter had
reached Cracow before me. Only the dances had become
Conrad's polka and Conrad's mazurka and Conrad's
waltz.

My rather embarrassing thirteenth century bunny
club, bought and set up one night when I was drunk, had
become known as Conrad's Inn, and six different men
asked me if I wouldn't set one up in Cracow.

The girls' riding outfits had full-length skirts with that
sewn-in panel that I had suggested so that they could
ride a man's saddle while maintaining feminine decorum.
The very next day after the ladies of Wawel Hill saw the
things, fully a dozen women were sporting them. How
many seamstresses lost a night's sleep over that, I
couldn't tell you. The new-style dresses were called
"Conrads."

But the serious work I'd done and was rightly proud
of? The windmill I'd designed and the looms and spinning wheels I'd designed and the factory I'd designed?
Oh, they were Lambert's mill and Lambert's looms and
Lambert's wheels. There is very little justice in this
world.

The rooms we got were fabulous by medieval standards, suitable for visiting royalty. That is to say, about
up to the level of an American Holiday Inn, except that
the furniture wasn't as comfortable.

We also got a servant apiece, which was awkward. I'd
never had a personal servant before, and I really didn't
like it. Krystyana was thrilled, though, so I put up with it
until bedtime.

Then I found that the servants expected to sleep in
the same room as us. It seems that one of the reasons for
the drapes hanging around the bed was to give us what
medieval Poles considered to be sufficient privacy, so
that the servants could sleep on the trundle bed next to

us, in case we wanted anything in the middle of the night.

Now, I'd spent the night before celibate in a monastery and I had no intention of staying that way again. But I could hardly make love to my girl with a couple of strangers not a yard away. I tried to send them out, but they didn't want to go. They said that if they went back to the servants' quarters, everybody would think that we'd found fault with them.

The final compromise was that they would sleep in Sir Vladimir and Annastashia's room next door, but they made us promise to beat on the wall if we needed anything in the middle of the night. Exasperating.

With Sir Vladimir a hero and the girls being treated like human beings (Krystyana had taken a terrible snubbing at Cieszyn Castle last spring), leaving the next morning as I had planned was out of the question. In fact we stayed the next three days, with everybody but me having a marvelous time. There were dances and games and a hunt that I managed to duck out of by asking another knight to take Krystyana.

When the others were out hunting, I stayed alone in my room, and it felt marvelous. It was the first time I'd been alone since I'd stood guard duty last winter. Being alone gave me time to think, to order the strange things that fester up in my garbage-pit mind.

When I use the word "socialism," I mean a political system in which the social rights are held to be more important than, say, property rights or rights of inheritance. I mean a system in which every person is born with the same basic rights.

The right to live comes first, and included in that is the right to the minimal food, clothing, and shelter, without which life is impossible. I don't mean luxury, but I do mean enough to keep body and soul together.

I mean the right to an education, paid for by the community, to the extent of the individual's ability.

I mean the right to start out even with everybody else. I think that inherited wealth is a bad idea and is harmful to both the individual and to society.

I believe that democracy is the best possible system

for a nation with an educated, concerned, and reasonable population.

It is not that the people are particularly wise. They aren't. And the larger the number of people involved in a decision, the poorer the decision is likely to be. To find the IQ of a group, take the average IQ of the people involved and divide by the number of people in the group. Anyone who has ever marched troops can verify that a hundred men have the collective intelligence of a centipede. Worse. A centipede doesn't step on its own feet.

No. Democracy is a good system because it is an extremely stable system.

In many parts of South America and Africa, when an individual becomes truly disgruntled, he gets together with six hundred friends, three hundred rifles, and maybe a hundred bullets and starts a revolution. This practice is socially disruptive and results in lost worktime, destroyed property, and dead bodies.

In America, such an individual does not go off to the hills with a gun. He becomes a political candidate. Of course, he knows that, to be effective, he must start at the bottom—say, sewer commissioner.

So he runs against six other social misfits for that office.

If he loses, at least he feels that he has done his best to straighten things out, that if the people don't appreciate him, they don't deserve him. Anyway, an election is so exhausting, physically, financially, and emotionally, that he is likely to be over his initial anger.

If he wins, well, he can't really do much harm. There are engineers to make sure that shit flows downhill. And who knows? Maybe he will turn out to be a *good* sewer commissioner.

In any case, society is the winner. Seven potential troublemakers have been defused, only one of them has to be paid, and they just might get some useful work out of that one.

The eastern bloc nations do not enjoy this social advantage. A single political party approves all candidates for office, assuring their loyalty, but also screening out the obvious mental defectives, at least on the lower levels. In so doing, they increase the amount of social frustration, which causes a lack of the very stability that the approval process was designed to ensure. Still, it's a better system than having the sons of kings warring to see who will be the next king.

Democracy doesn't work well unless the proper level of education *and* the proper institutions both exist. Those things won't happen in thirteenth century Poland for at least one generation and possibly three, no matter what I do.

Capitalism, as practiced in the twentieth century, has some definite advantages. For one thing, companies are allowed to fail and so cease to exist. The physical assets are redistributed, the workers find new jobs, and the poor management which generally caused the problem is put out to pasture.

In a centrally-controlled economy, it is extremely embarrassing or politically impossible for such powers that be to eliminate inefficient managers.

In large organizations, it is hard to be noticed, so it is very difficult to do something that is demonstratively right. It therefore becomes critically important to your career that you never do anything that is demonstratively wrong. Fools may not be fired, but they are rarely promoted, either. To downgrade a subordinate manager seems to imply that one didn't know what one was doing when one promoted him in the first place. Best to leave him alone and hope that nobody notices. It takes something fairly obvious, an exploding atomic power plant for example, to get anything changed. But generally, things just go on as usual.

This results in the same fools making the same mistakes forever. People become demoralized, especially the best, most energetic workers. Useful work slows or even comes to a halt. I don't mean that the workers stop working. They are all furiously active, looking busy. They worry all day long and go home tired. But they are not doing anything useful.

Nor is this problem limited to the centrally controlled economies of eastern Europe. In major American corporations, poor managers are sometimes given "lateral promotions," perhaps to "company historian," but they are rarely removed.

Another advantage to capitalism is that small companies can do astounding things without the matter becoming political. And I mean both astoundingly good and astoundingly stupid. If enough people try enough new things and if there is some mechanism for dumb ideas to be eliminated, better processes will develop and society will benefit.

People will shake their heads or laugh at someone doing something silly with his own money, but they won't try to vote their congressman out of office because of it. But if it is the *goverment's* money being spent, they rightly think it's their money being wasted and the matter becomes political. Consider the way one blown gasket stopped the entire American space program for years.

Progress is impossible without trying new things. New things often don't work. Since large organizations do not permit failure, virtually all progress results from the work of small private companies.

Yet capitalism has a number of serious problems that seem to be intrinsic to it. Private companies are generally founded by productive people, often engineers. But when the founder retires, somehow the accountants always seem to take over, and a button-counter is rarely a good decision-maker. Or, the founder's widow or son-in-law tries to run the company and things are worse.

Such foolishness would be unthinkable in eastern Europe. There, managers are almost always trained engineers. Many are not brilliant but most are competent.

Oh, the worst faults of capitalism, the ones Marx was concerned with, have been patched over with governmental institutions and regulations, at least in America. Monopolies are forbidden or regulated. Surplus workers are not allowed to starve. Vast profits are largely taxed away, although there is still a huge class of people who do nothing productive but are very wealthy.

Yet this very patchwork has problems of its own. In Poland, if your teeth are bad, you go to a dentist and he fixes them. No matter who you are, even if you are not a citizen, if you are human, you have a right to good teeth. Paperwork is minimal.

In America, some people have this right and some don't. Most people don't, so they have a vast number of office workers filling out forms that try to prove that only those with special rights get these special privileges.

I am convinced that it should be possible to design an economic and political system that has the advantages of both capitalism and socialism with the problems of neither. If I can figure it out, thirteenth century Poland is going to be a fine place to live.

By the time Krystyana and the others returned from the hunt, I was feeling much better, having thought a lot of things out of my system. We dressed for another boring supper.

I simply didn't have much in common with the nobles of Wawel Hill. There wasn't much of anything I could say to them and I was eager to get on with our errand and return to Three Walls.

Eventually, by repeatedly painting a sad picture of poor Tadaos in a donjon, not knowing if help was on the way or not, contemplating suicide perhaps, I finally got my party to agree to leave.

# Chapter Twelve

OUR PARTY was in sumptuous attire as we went to the riverfront at Cracow the next morning. Clothing equated with rank in the thirteenth century, and rank equated with services. If you wanted to be treated good, you had to dress good.

At the river landing, we engaged a ferryboat to take us to the northern bank of the Vistula River. This boat—a raft, really—was made of a dozen huge logs that had been split and burned out hollow, then shaped and smoothed on the outside. These half-round dugout canoes were laid lengthwise side by side to let the river flow past easily. Rough planks decked it over and tied the dugouts together.

A dozen men were required to pole and paddle the massive raft across the river. No fare was waiting on the north bank, so the boatmaster sat down to wait.

"You know," I said to him, "I can't help thinking that you are wasting the efforts of all your men."

"What do you mean, my lord?"

"Well, you see that big tree growing upstream there on the south bank?"

"Yes."

"If you tied one end of a long rope around that tree and the other end of it to the left side of your boat, near the bow, the force of the water would push your boat back to the other side. And once you were there, if you tied the rope to the right side of your boat, the river would push you right back to here again."

He thought a while. "Would that really work?"

"Prove it for yourself. Get a small boat and a small rope and try it."

"Hmm. I just might, my lord. I just might."

Sir Vladimir and the ladies were eager to push on so that they could get back to Wawel Castle again, since I had promised a second visit on our return journey. Vladimir planned to take us on a short cut that skirted the Wysoki Beskid Mountains, a part of the Carpathians. That would get us to Sacz in two easy days of travel.

We traveled across the Vistula flood plain with Annastashia and Krystyana chattering constantly about all the wonders they had seen in Cracow. When we started climbing the foothills in the afternoon, the previously perfect weather began to cloud over. In a few hours it began to sprinkle on our expensive clothes.

"I'd thought that we could make it to my Uncle Felix's manor today," Sir Vladimir said. "But we haven't come as far as I'd hoped and I'm loath to get wet in a rainstorm the new finery our ladies made. I know of caves in these hills. I played in them when I was a boy. What would you think of making for one of them?"

"Fine by me," I said. "We have my old backpack with us. I can treat you all to some freeze-dried stew."

Sir Vladimir found a cave in short order. There were bat droppings near the mouth. Bats are common throughout the Carpathian Mountains. They're all harmless insectivores and there are so many of them that you can go for weeks without swatting a bug.

It was a four-yard climb to the cavemouth, but over easy rock, almost a stepladder. We couldn't get the horses inside, but a summer shower wouldn't hurt them. I set up the dome tent and stowed our baggage in it while Sir Vladimir unloaded and hobbled the horses. Anna wouldn't tolerate hobbling, but she was so loyal that there was never any worry about her wandering off.

Annastashia and Krystyana collected a night's supply of firewood and soon we were sitting in a semicircle around the fire, facing outward, waiting for the stew to start bubbling in my aluminum cooking kit. Krystyana was on my left and Annastashia and Sir Vladimir were to my right.

We were settled just in time, for soon lightning and thunder were crashing and rain was coming down in sheets. I've always loved thunderstorms when I don't have to be in them, and the view from our mountain cave was spectacular. But soon the show was over and the rain almost ended.

We started telling stories, a great art form in the Middle Ages but one that has been almost lost in modern times. Krystyana told a hilarious tale about how her uncle bought a pig, but came home with a cow. I rambled on for an hour about nine-fingered Frodo. A modern man may lack storytelling skills, but he sure knows a lot of plotlines.

With dusk the bats rushed out in a clicking, squeaking swirl. The girls, unfamiliar with the harmless creatures, started screaming.

Sir Vladimir took this as the cue for his story, which was about a vampire. His basic story line, that of a man who was of the living dead, who hated sunlight and water, who drank human blood and made his victims into creatures like himself, was much like a modern movie plot.

Vladimir's flashy storytelling style, with many gesticulations and facial expressions, added a lot to the natural setting, for Count Dracula had lived in these same Carpathian Mountains, only farther south.

What's more, Sir Vladimir adamantly claimed that every word of his tale was true and his eye didn't have the wink and twinkle it had when he was fibbing. He actually believed it and had the girls doing so. While I, of course, am above such things, I confess he had my heart thumping.

As he was approaching the climax of the story, he suddenly stopped and looked behind me. The expression on his face was one of pure horror and I remember thinking that in the twentieth century he would have gone to Hollywood.

There was a shuffling noise and I wondered briefly how he had arranged the sound effects. Then I saw that the girls too were horror-stricken and actresses they weren't.

I looked over my right shoulder and made what was perhaps one of the biggest mistakes of my life.

A man was coming toward me, totally naked with skin as white as bone china. Spittle and foam were dribbling from his mouth, his throat was convulsing and his chest was quivering. He was reaching toward me!

I was horrified and frightened. With no rational thought in my head, I drew my sword and with one motion slashed at him.

I cut him entirely in half at the belt line. The two pieces fell to the ground at a crazy angle, the throat twitched a few more times and stopped.

Instantly, a new horror struck me. I had just murdered a man, a crazy hermit perhaps but a fellow human being, for no other reason than that I was scared. I had become so callous in this brutal century that killing had become a reflex.

Sir Vladimir was the first to come to life. He grabbed a piece of firewood, sharpened it frantically with his belt knife and began beating it into the chest of the dead body with a rock.

This desecration of the dead brought me back to my senses.

"For the love of God, Sir Vladimir, stop that!"

"It must be done, Sir Conrad! It's still alive! It still can kill us!" There was more than a hint of panic in his voice.

There was no obvious way of stopping him short of violence. Sir Vladimir was swinging the rock with all his strength but forcing a wooden stick through a human ribcage—expecially one that is open at the bottom—is no easy feat. The intestines and liver were squirted out onto the cave floor, and all of us were splattered with blood.

I stared at the man I had murdered. Slowly something dawned on me. The foam at the mouth. The white skin. The convulsions. "Rabies," I said. "RABIES! Sir Vladimir, get away from that body! That stuff is infected! It's contagious! We could all end up like that poor bastard!"

"Not any more, Sir Conrad. I've done it." He stood

up from his grisly work, a stump of wood projecting brutally below the corpse's left nipple.

"Trust me on this! If ever in your life you take me on faith, do it now! That's a *virus,* a disease, like leprosy or the plague. We must clean this blood and dirt off of us!"

"Just what would you have us do?"

"We've got to get out of here! We've got to get ourselves clean!" I started shoving them toward the cave-mouth.

"Sir Conrad!" Krystyana said, "It's *raining* out there! Our *clothes!*"

"*Damn* your clothes! This rain is a Godsend! Get out there or I'll throw you out! You too, Annastashia! *Move!*"

They scurried out, but Sir Vladimir stood staring at me.

"Sir Vladimir, please!"

He paused a moment, then said, "Right."

I tossed our possessions over the edge and followed them down to the ground. The rain was coming in buckets again and the lightning was flashing. Both were welcome, by me at least. In total darkness and without water, the task would have been impossible. Anna heard the commotion and came running up.

"Back, girl! Rabies!"

She nodded her head and backed off.

"The rest of you, strip!" I shouted above the storm. "Hang your clothes over the bushes where they'll get rinsed out. Wash yourselves. Krystyana, break out my soap!"

I bullied them into sudsing down twice in the bone-chilling rain. Finally, we gave the girls the tent and Sir Vladimir and I hunkered down as best we could under a tree.

"Sir Conrad, was this really necessary?"

"Yes."

"It's some sort of superstition among your people?"

"It's not a superstition. I've told you before, most diseases are caused by germs, tiny animals, smaller than you can see. That poor bastard in the cave was infested with them."

"Sir Conrad, you've also taught me the scientific method, and told me never to believe anything that I could not prove with my own senses. With my own eyes I just saw a vampire. I touched it. I felt it. I smelled it. Can you doubt that this is true?"

"You certainly saw something, but what you saw was the victim of a disease."

"As to these germs, well, to be scientific about it, I've never seen one. If you ever build that microscope that once you talked of, perhaps I will. For now, I know what I saw, I know what I did.

"As to this chilly midnight bathing party, well, you are a stranger here and I was only being polite and going along with your customs as you have so often gone along with ours."

"Okay. Have it your way. Your scientific deductions were satisfied by pounding a stake into the vampire's heart and my superstitions required that we ritually bathe off the devil-viruses.

"That's not what's bothering me.

"What bothers me, Sir Conrad, is sitting here wet and naked in the cold rain, with only male company, when but a short time ago I was most comfortably situated with my love at my side."

"Well, I'm sitting right next to you."

"More's the pity."

We were silent a long while. Then I said, "I think we were both right about the man in the cave. Most legends have some basis in fact. The symptoms of rabies are a lot like the way you described a vampire. The fear of light and water. The white skin. And if one bites you, you'll certainly become one. I think your vampire is my rabies victim. Two names for the same thing."

"If you say so. How long does your ritual require before we can go back to the cave?"

"It's not a ritual and we don't go back, ever."

"Right. It is not a superstition. The cave is merely permanently defiled and unclean."

It was a long night and I spent it soul searching. I suppose I did the man a favor, giving him a quick death. Rabies is a rough way to die. Maybe he would have bitten one of us and maybe I saved one of the others from joining his sad fate. There was nothing I could do to cure the disease.

But this was all rationalization after the fact. In truth, I had murdered a man because he frightened me.

The lands we rode through the next morning were cheerful, despite the depressed mood of our party. The fields were well tended and soon to give a good harvest, the peasant cottages were big and well built and most had brightly painted trim. The people were well fed, half of them were fat, and all were fairly well clothed. And everybody bustled, as if whatever they were doing right then was the most important thing in the world.

That sort of attitude is contagious and we had cheered up some by the time we entered Uncle Felix's manor in our second-best clothes. I had to call him that even though he was Sir Vladimir's uncle and not mine. He was the kind of man who is everybody's uncle. Big, bluff, crude, and wholesome, he radiated good cheer and good wishes.

"That you, Vlad boy? You big enough for girls already? Pretty ones, too! And a giant! You must be Stargard! Welcome! Mama! Go kill a fat calf for supper! We got company! Iwo! Iwo you lazy peasant! Come take care of the horses! Well, you people? Get down!"

A little intimidating at first, but you couldn't help liking him. Soon dozens of people were rushing about, our horses unloaded and put in a barn, and our baggage opened out. Some women *tsk-tsk*ed at our wet finery and took it away, while the four of us were treated to an impromptu dinner for twelve.

Uncle Felix had already eaten, but sat down to join us and ate enough for six men just to be sociable.

"So, boys. You are out adventuring? Have you killed any dragons?"

"No dragons, Uncle Felix," Sir Vladimir said. "But we killed five Crossmen in an open fight and we dispatched a vampire last night."

"Another vampire in my hills, eh? That's the second one this year. I'll have to warn the peasants. Tell me about the Crossmen."

Sir Vladimir launched into his tale, which grew better each time he told it. He never exactly lied, you understand, but the embroidery around the edges got constantly brighter.

"Whew! The duke may like it, but the duke is not your liege lord." He waved a chubby finger at Sir Vladimir. "You know, your papa is not going to be happy about this!"

"I know. I was wondering if you could intercede for me."

"Maybe. But it's too close to harvest for me to leave now. After that, well, maybe the trial will settle everything. But if he's still mad at you at Christmastime, I'll go talk to him.

"Now you, big fellow—I've heard so many things about you that I don't believe that I'm thinking I should have believed some of them after all. Tell me what you know."

"That's quite an order, Uncle Felix—excuse me, I mean Sir Felix."

"Uncle Felix is okay. Everybody calls me that. Never could figure out why. I heard that when you came here, you were walking through the woods with nothing but what you could carry on your back. With no weapons and no armor and living wherever you stopped for the night. And you did this just for sport. That true?"

"Well, yes."

"Then you're either a very brave man or a damn fool."

"I don't think I'm either of those. It's a common sport where I come from. We're mostly city dwellers and you need to get back to nature every now and then. The equipment we use is very lightweight. You can actually carry everything you need."

"But no weapons?"

"Uh . . . weapons are frowned upon. But they're really not needed. Most animals will leave you alone if you don't frighten them."

"Animals, maybe. What about men?"

"What about them? I wasn't looking for any trouble."

"Trouble finds *you* in the woods. What about thieves?"

"There aren't that many of them. Look, I shouldn't be talking about this. I made a vow."

"As you wish, Stargard. What about all these fights you been in?"

"Well, four times I've been attacked by crazy people on the road. I defended myself. What more is there to say?"

There was no question of our proceeding that day. Uncle Felix wouldn't have stood for it. It was raining again and anyway, Sacz was a full day's ride away. It was best to leave in the morning.

I never quite left the table that afternoon. With dinner completed, more beer was brought, with a few snacks: sausages, cheeses, breads, cold pies, preserved meats, smoked fish, puddings, spreads, pickled fish, pickled cabbages, pickled pickles, and a vast pile of *et ceteras*.

It was Tuesday, but somehow a holiday had been declared. Maybe it was the rain and maybe it was the fact of our visit. Or maybe these people always acted that way.

Chessboards and checker sets were broken out, as well as a half dozen board games I'd never seen before. There was Nine Man Morris, which had elements of tic-tac-toe and Chinese checkers. There was Fox and Geese, a chase-and-capture game, and Cows and Leopards, a vastly more complicated variant. There was Goose, a race game.

Furthermore, every game seemed to have a skill variant and a chancy gambling variant. Uncle Felix got me into a game of Byzantine chess, which was played with normal chesspieces but on a circular board. He further insisted that we play it with dice. You had to roll a one to move a pawn, a two to move a knight, and so on.

If none of the moves permitted by the dice was possible by the rules of chess, you lost your turn; if you were in check, you had to roll the right dice to get yourself out of check or you lost your turn. Then your opponent had to roll the right dice to take your king to win. This resulted in some very strange games and I'm glad I wouldn't bet him. Anyway, I think his dice were loaded.

Sitting and playing board games suited my mood, but Sir Vladimir was feeling far more energetic. He had Krystyana, Annastashia, and a half dozen or so of Uncle Felix's ladies playing something called The Last Couple in Hell. I never quite figured out the rules, but it involved a lot of running around and screaming.

People wandered in and out, bringing things, eating things, and taking things. At least three conversations were going on at any one time and the noise never stopped. Children and dogs wandered through and were petted, spanked, or ignored as the case required. Uncle Felix almost never used a proper name. He just pointed and yelled, and things happened.

I never figured out who were family and who were servants; perhaps they weren't too clear about it themselves. When Uncle Felix yelled, people jumped, but not always the same people who jumped last time. The girl who brought in a steaming plate of braised meat promptly sat down with us to help us eat it. Later, Uncle Felix pinched her butt; up till then I'd been sure that he'd been patting his daughters and pinching the servants.

Try to imagine a friendly, loosely organized madhouse with sound effects. Intimidating, but you grew to like it.

After six hours of continuous eating and drinking, Uncle Felix got up, belched, and announced that supper was served.

They really had killed a fatted calf and two men brought it in on a spit. Having already done a full day of heroic trencher duty, the best I could do was dawdle at my food. Uncle Felix looked at me, genuinely hurt.

"There's something wrong with the food?"

We were back in our best clothes, only slightly the worse for wear, the next morning. The sky was gray and we were all still logy from too much to eat and drink the day before, so we were mostly silent on the way to Sacz.

The land and climate around Sacz were identical to Uncle Felix's, but the living was far worse. The leader sets the tone of an organization, and the tone of Sacz was bad. Half the fields were unplanted and I don't just mean those lying fallow. The forests were encroaching on the farmland. Those fields that had been planted were rank with weeds.

The cottages were hovels and the people were listless, lackadaisical, uncaring. You had the feeling that they thought that nothing they could do would improve things, that nothing really mattered. Most of them looked underfed.

In Poland, every man, even a sworn peasant, had the Right of Departure. If things got bad, he could sell out or abandon whatever property he owned and move elsewhere. It was a little like the bankruptcy laws of modern times. Well, around Sacz, anyone with any gumption had already left.

I decided that hunting was so important to Baron Przemysl because he was such a poor manager his lands and people would not produce enough to support him; wild game was the only thing that he had to eat, so he was hard on poachers.

Baron Przemysl was a grimy, gouty, disagreeable person. He produced a Tadaos much whiter and thinner than I remembered. Tadaos was speechless while the baron carefully, publicly counted the ransom money. He shook his head, blinked at the sunlight and rubbed the scabs where the shackles had been on his wrists. Having lived in his own filth for almost a month, he stank monumentally. I stayed upwind of him, but the baron didn't seem to notice the smell.

Once the baron had finished his long, slow count, he turned and limped away without so much as a thank-you or an invitation to supper, and it was late in the day. I decided not to tell him how to cure his gout.

"You came! By God in Heaven, you came!" Tadaos yelled suddenly.

"Yes, I came. Now get on one of the mules and let's get out of this pig's sty."

But once mounted up, he said, "My bow, Sir Conrad, do you think I could get my bow?"

Tadaos's bow was an English longbow and pretty special. He was a fantastic shot with it, and I didn't know how much of that was the man and how much was the equipment. The guard at the gate was a graybeard in rusty armor. After some argument, haggling, and suggestions of violence, he produced bow, quiver, and arrows for eight pence. A bargain, except that the equipment was Tadaos's in the first place.

"And my boat. Sir Conrad, do you suppose that there is any chance of getting back my boat?"

On this point the oldster was adamant. None. The boat had been confiscated along with the cargo, and both had been sold.

"Then I am a boatman without a boat. What is to become of me?"

"I can tell you that," I said. "You're coming along with me. I'm not going to charge you for my traveling expenses and I'm not going to hold you responsible for all the trouble I've gotten into on this trip. But I just shelled out four thousand pence to save your neck and I'm going to get it back, somehow. You once hired me at three pence a day plus food. That's what I'll pay you until you work off your debt."

"You're a hard man, Sir Conrad."

"Huh. That's the first time anyone's ever said that. Well, come along, gang. There's one more stop to be made before we head home."

I had been transported to the thirteenth century while sleeping in the basement of the Red Gate Inn. I didn't know how that was accomplished but the answer just might be in that inn. In all events, I meant to go there.

# Chapter Thirteen

^^^^^^^^^^^^^^^^^^^^^^^^^^^^^^

WE WERE fortunate to find a decent-enough inn that evening. They wouldn't let Tadaos in until he had taken a bath, which I considered to be a good recommendation for the place.

The innkeeper set up a wooden tub in the courtyard, checking the wind with a wet thumb to be sure that Tadaos stayed downwind of the dining room. It was filled with hot water and Tadaos was tossed a bar of brown soap from beyond flea-jumping range.

He was ordered to strip and get in. A servant picked up his old clothes with a long stick and carried them off, the stick pointing carefully downwind, to be burnt. They changed the water three times before poor Tadaos passed muster and was permitted to rejoin humanity. Even then, he was probably aided by the fact that it was getting dark.

I also got a bill for washing down the mule Tadaos rode in on.

One of my outfits fitted Tadaos fairly well, with the cuffs and sleeves rolled up, but I wouldn't let him cut it down permanently, not one of my nifty embroidered outfits!

"It's just as well that Cousin Przemysl didn't invite us in for supper," Sir Vladimir said. "His table is terrible."

I inquired of the innkeeper about the Red Gate Inn and was told that I shouldn't go there. It had been struck by lightning and was inhabited by devils.

Slighting the competition a little was one thing, but

that was ridiculous. When I pressed him further, he assured me that I could get there by staying on the trail we had arrived on. I couldn't possibly miss the place, if I was fool enough to go there.

I couldn't tell my friends why the trip was necessary, and Sir Vladimir was not happy with this extension to our vacation. He wanted to go back and play hero some more at Wawel Castle. Krystyana and Annastashia were solidly on his team. It got to be a nagging contest, three against one.

"Okay. Then don't go to the Red Gate Inn. I'm not sure I wanted you along anyway. Stay right here tomorrow with the girls. I'll take Anna and run up to the Red Gate Inn in the morning. She's fast enough to make it there and back in a single day, where the whole party would take two days easy. Anyway, Anna has been acting like she wants a good run, and we can't do that with you guys along."

Sir Vladimir and the girls gave their grudging approval to the plan, and we called it a night.

The next morning I was saddling Anna when Sir Vladimir came over. "Sir Conrad, I spoke rashly last night. Let me accompany you today."

"Thank you. Apology accepted. But if you go, the girls will insist on going and then with those stupid palfreys, we'd have to move at a crawl. Anyway, we can hardly leave them here unprotected. Anna and I won't have any problems."

"Still, I'd feel better if I went along. And let's bring the ladies. There's no need for undue haste."

"Maybe I need a little time to myself. Anyway, I'm going alone. Don't bother following, you know you can't keep up."

I'd left the horse barding and fancy clothes behind. This was a fact-finding mission and the less attention I attracted, the better.

Anna went like the wind. She could travel as fast with a big armored man on her back as a thoroughbred racehorse can with a little jockey aboard. And she could keep up that speed all day, not for just a single mile.

It was an exhilarating joy to ride her across flat land

and on mountainous trails it was stunt-flying and motor-cycling and a carnival ride all in one. More than those, because we were closer to the ground than any stunt plane ever flew for long and no motorcycle could have maintained our speed over these trails. And on a carnival ride, deep down inside you really know that you are safe. This was reality!

We went for about an hour without passing anyone on the trail. Then we came to a pleasant brook with a nice bit of pasture and we stopped for a while. The cook at the inn had packed me a lunch. In the Middle Ages, it was customary to get up at dawn but eat your first meal at ten in the morning. Dawn, I could take, since without decent lights there wasn't much sense to staying up late. But I've always eaten a big breakfast, and a year in this barbarous time still hadn't changed my desire for that.

We ate. Anna was cropping the lush grass and keeping a sharp lookout.

"Anna, would you come over here, please?"

She trotted over.

"Anna, what's two plus two? Tap it out with your foot."

She tapped her foot four times.

There was once a famous German showhorse called Clever Hans that had everyone, including his trainer, convinced that he could do simple arithmetic. It wasn't until many years later that a psychologist proved that Hans was reading the body language of the person asking him the question. He would start tapping his foot and as he started approaching the right answer, his questioner would involuntarily stiffen up a bit. When he got to the right answer, the trainer would relax a little and Hans would stop tapping his foot.

I had to know if Anna's nodding and shaking her head in response to questions was the Clever Hans sort of thing, or if she really was an intelligent being in the guise of a horse.

"Okay. Now give me three minus one."

She tapped twice.

"Now the square root of nine."

She looked at me inquisitively, sort of tilting her head sideways, the way a dog does.

"Do you know what a square root is?"

She shook her head no.

That tore it. *I* knew what a square root was and if this was the Clever Hans thing, she would have tapped out three. Down deep, I'd been expecting it all along. Anna was an outstanding creature. She was physically, mentally, and morally superior to anything a horse had a right to be.

"Anna, are you really a horse?"

She stared at me for a second, then shook her head no.

"Are you a human being?"

She shook her head.

"Some kind of machine, then?"

No.

"Some sort of alien? From some other planet?"

No and no.

"Are you naturally born? Some sort of mutant?"

Yes and no.

"You were born naturally and are not a mutant?"

Yes.

"Anna, I came to this country in some kind of a time machine, I think. At least it was a strange vault in the subbasement of an old inn. Do you know about time machines?"

Yes and no.

"Let me try again. Are you in any way connected with any individual or group that has anything to do with a time machine?"

Yes.

"Do you know how such a device works?"

No.

"Well, at least that tells me that you're somehow connected with some pretty high technology. Are you the result of some high technology? Bioengineering?"

Yes and yes.

"But you were born naturally . . . oh, of course. Your ancestors were bioengineered."

Yes.

"You're from the future then?"

No.

"The past?"

Yes.

"There was some kind of lost civilization in the distant past?"

Yes and no.

That stumped me for a bit. How could it be there and not there? Technology requires a civilization. Doesn't it?

"You were the product of a civilization?"

Yes.

"Was that civilization in the distant past?"

Yes.

"Then why—okay, it was there but it was not lost."

Yes.

"I guess that figures. If you've got a time machine, there's no way for anything to get lost. Back to you. You're an intelligent bioengineered creation."

Yes and no.

"You're doing that to me again. You, or at least your ancestors, were bioengineered."

Yes.

"And you're intelligent."

Yes and no.

"You're intelligent but not as smart as me?"

Yes.

"If that's true, you're not far behind me. I haven't seen you do anything dumb yet and God knows that I've pulled some boners lately. Anna, you obviously understand Polish. Can you read it?"

Yes.

"Can you write?"

No.

"Anna, if I made up a big sign with all the letters and numbers on it, could you point to them one after the other and spell things out?"

Yes and no.

"You could try but your spelling isn't very good."

Yes.

"Good enough. We're going to have that sign made up as soon as we get back to Three Walls.

"Anna, you're too intelligent to be treated as an animal. As far as I'm concerned, you are people. I don't own you, but I'd like to stay your friend. Is that okay with you?"

Yes.

"Would you like to work for me, doing just what you have been doing all along?"

Yes.

"I pay most of the men back at Three Walls a penny a day. Is that all right with you?"

Yes.

"Fine. We'll make it retroactive to the time I met you in Cracow. That means that you have about three hundred pence in back pay coming. I might as well hold your money for you, but if there's anything you want to buy, let me know. Okay?"

Yes.

"Would you like to swear to me, just like all the other people have?"

Yes, vigorously.

"Then we'll do it. But to do it right, we ought to have witnesses, so I suppose we should wait until we get back to Three Walls. Okay?"

Yes.

That was one of the best moves I ever made.

Getting ready to go again, I said, "Anna, we need more words than just yes and no. How about if shaking your tail means you don't care one way or the other and that yes-no thing you've been doing means that I haven't asked the right question?"

Yes-no.

"I guess I deserved that. Are the above two communication symbols acceptable to you?"

Yes.

She was as literal-minded as a computer. "Eventually, we're going to have some long talks, but for now, is there anything that you are unhappy with that I can do something about?"

Yes.

It took another round of "twenty questions," but I found out what it was. She thought the food was fine and she didn't mind the work. People treated her well enough and she liked traveling. She didn't mind a saddle but the bridle annoyed the hell out of her. Would I please take the damn thing off?

"Happy to, my friend. Of course, you never paid much attention to it anyway."

We continued south, and higher into the High Tatras, a part of the Carpathians. Some purists claim that Tatras are part of the Beskids and the Beskids are part of the Carpathians, but call them what you will, they're half again higher than anything in New England. To me, they are the most beautiful mountains in the world, and I have loved them ever since my father took me up there when I was a little boy.

It was a bright day with clear mountain skies and clean highland air. Anna was making good speed and many Slavic songs were written to be sung on horse-back, to the rhythm of the horse's hooves. I was singing "The Polish Patrol" and in a fine mood when I came across the most dejected-looking man I'd ever seen. He was sitting by the road with his arms on his knees and his head on his arms.

I brought Anna to a halt. Actually, I just thought about stopping, and Anna picked it up from the way I must have changed my body position on her back.

"I know you, don't I?" I said.

He looked up at me, but no hint of recollection lit in his eyes.

"Of course I know you," I said as I dismounted. "You are Ivan Targ. You let me in your home last winter when I was lost in the cold."

"Yes, now I remember. You were the giant with the priest." His head dropped back down to his arms.

"Tell me, my friend, why do you look so sad? What is this terrible thing that has happened?" I sat down beside him.

"That." He pointed to a field. It took me a moment to realize what was wrong with it. It was common to plant two types of grain in the same field at the same time, in that case wheat and rye. If the weather conditions weren't right for wheat, maybe the rye would do well, and vice versa. Most Polish breads are made from mixed-grain flour, so there was never any need to separate the grains after harvest. But in his field, every stalk of grain had been flattened to the ground.

"The rains did that?" I asked.

"Hail. Last night we had a hailstorm."

"A pity. That will cost you a great deal of money."

"That will cost me my life. Mine and my family's."

"Surely your other fields will carry you through."

"That is my only field. That is all the land we have been able to clear in two years' hard work. This crop was all I had. If it had ripened, I could have fed my family through the winter and had extra to sell to the merchants. Now, I have nothing, my family has nothing."

"This is a disaster, but it doesn't have to cost your life. Surely your lord will help you through the winter."

"*I have no lord!* Don't you see! I came to these mountains to be done with lords! I was sick of paying half of what I grew just to keep a fat man in his big house from having to work! I came here to be free, and now I will die for it."

He was serious. This was not the wailing of a businessman over lost profits. This was a man who was looking death in the face.

"Once you let me in from the cold, and gave me a spot by your family's fire. Without you, I might have frozen to death." I got out my pouch and poured about five hundred pence into my hand. It was a trifling amount for me, but enough to feed him and his family until spring. "You didn't know it at the time, but you were throwing bread onto the waters."

Ivan stared at the money, then he stared at me. He was literally speechless. In a single morning, he had gone out expecting to find his field ripening, his plans prospering. He had found instead absolute disaster. And then, just as he had accepted the ultimate tragedy, a man he barely knew had come along and saved everything. His mind was not up to handling it all, and I had the feeling that he would continue sitting there for hours.

"It is not a big thing," I said, "I've been lucky this last year. If you ever want to pay me back, I am Sir Conrad Stargard, and I live at Three Walls, near Cieszyn. If you ever decide that you want a lord again, you can come see me about that, too."

He nodded dumbly. I mounted up and rode off, feeling

good inside. One of the nicest things about wealth is that sometimes you can do some good in the world.

In under an hour, we were approaching the inn, or at least where I had remembered the inn to be. What I found was a hole in the ground. A blast crater more than two hundred yards across. I was dumbfounded as we climbed the rim and looked down into it. Anna stirred uneasily.

There was the clean smell of a thundershower in the air, and this was a sunny day. The not-unpleasant smell of sparking relay contacts. Ozone.

"*Ozone!* Radiation! Anna, get us out of here! This place has been hit with an atomic bomb!"

# Interlude Two

I HIT the red STOP button. Movement on the screen froze in mid-action.

"Oh Jesus Christ, Tom! *You nuked the inn?*" I said. "For the love of God, *why?*"

"Sit down, son. I didn't bomb that place, and neither did anybody else. It was an accident."

*"An accidental nuclear explosion in the thirteenth century?"*

"It wasn't *all* nuclear. More than half the energy in that blast was kinetic, and most of the rest was chemical."

"Even so—"

"You know how our temporal transporters work. A canister arriving from another time has to arrive in a precisely defined volume of hard vacuum. If there's anything at all in that volume, you have two sets of atoms coexisting in the same space. A small percentage of the nuclei will be close enough to fuse, giving you some damn strange isotopes. Some of those are radioactive, and that caused the ionizing radiation that caused the ozone that my cousin smelled. I got quite a dose myself, once, in the early days when we were first working on time travel.

"Many of the electrons interact with the electrons of other atoms, producing a lot of strange chemicals. Some of those chemicals are explosive. Some are poisonous.

All of the atoms repel each other vigorously, and that caused the bulk of the explosion, sixty-nine percent of it, anyway.

"A canister arriving at the inn three months after Conrad's first visit apparently emerged into solid rock, over eighteen feet out of registration."

"Wow. Some sort of failure in the controls?"

"I wish it had been that simple. We knew the explosion occurred, and site investigation showed a typical reemergence explosion. You know we use the reemergence effect under controlled conditions to generate all of our power and most of our basic materials. We understand the process completely, so there couldn't be any doubt about what happened.

"The only trouble was that none of our canisters was missing.

"Weirder things started happening. The investigation team we sent from Hungary came back twice. Two identical teams of men returned, one a few days after the other. And the men in each team claimed that those in the other were imposters.

"Also at that point, I had just returned from 1241, and had met Conrad at the Battle of Chmielnick, which, contrary to written history, the Poles won."

"But that can't be—time is a single linear continuum. Our people have made millions of temporal transfers, and we know that it's all in one straight line. There are no branches. The same battle can't have been both won and lost."

"I'm glad you're so positive of that. Because you're wrong. The correct statement is that everybody *knew* that branching is impossible. They don't know it anymore. Cousin Conrad, damn his soul, has done the impossible and kicked the underpinnings out from under everything just when I was getting ready to retire."

"But how—?"

"How, I don't know. The theory people have been in conniptions for months. No telling when they'll settle down. Maybe never.

"But we have the where and the when down pat. The split didn't start when Conrad first got to the Middle Ages. It happened a month after that, when Conrad had to make a difficult decision. For good and sufficient reasons, his employer ordered him to abandon a baby in a snowstorm. Conrad *both saved and abandoned* that child.

"In our timeline, he obeyed orders. On arriving at Okoitz, however, Count Lambert's ladies didn't treat him like a hero. By their lights, anybody who would allow a kid to freeze to death was a bum, and unworthy of their services. Those are my feelings as well.

"Their influence on Lambert was such that he was not much impressed with Conrad, either. Conrad left Okoitz with his employer, but soon argued with him. They split up and Conrad continued, alone, westward to Wroclaw.

"There he was promptly robbed of his booty, and had a rough time of it for many years. He eventually got involved in copper mining but never really amounted to much. When we tracked him down, he jumped at the chance to return to the twentieth century."

I was still trying to absorb just *what* a split in the timeline meant.

"Everything was doubled? Where did it all come from? What about the conservation of mass and energy?"

"It's right out the window! Along with just about every other law of physics. When Conrad kicked out the supports, he didn't mess around!"

I was so flustered that I didn't notice the naked wench who announced lunch. Tom took me by the hand and led me from the screening room.

In an hour we were back at the documentary.

# Chapter Fourteen

WITHOUT STOPPING we rode to the inn we had left in the morning. The innkeeper gave me an artificial smile. "Did you find the Red Gate Inn, Sir Conrad?"

"You know what I found. A hole in the ground."

"Is *that* what's there? The merchants who reported it to me were very unclear. Does it have devils?"

"Worse devils than you'll ever imagine. You're a bastard for not telling me about it, but keep on warning people away from that hole. People can die just from looking at it."

My party was eager to head back to Cracow, and it was still early in the afternoon, but Sir Vladimir talked us out of leaving until the next morning. It seems that there wasn't another decent inn within six hours; if we left then, we'd have to camp out again, and considering our last experience with camping, we weren't eager. Leaving in the morning, we could easily reach Uncle Felix's by the afternoon.

Uncle Felix didn't have time to kill another fatted calf, so he had to make do with a slab of beef, three geese, a suckling pig, and a whole lamb, plus the usual tons of extras.

He protested vigorously when I insisted on leaving first thing in the morning, but I wanted to get to the salt mines at Wieliczka as early as possible. We got there that afternoon, with Tadaos complaining the whole way about having to ride an unsaddled mule.

In the twentieth century, the salt mines are a tourist attraction *par excellence*: fifty generations of miners have cut nine hundred miles of tunnels, passageways, galleries, and chambers. And what does a salt miner do on his day off? He mines salt, of course. Only he gets artistic about it. Down there the miners have hollowed out two churches plus a "chapel" as big as a cathedral, each encrusted with statuary and carvings ranging in style from the romanesque to the modern. The annual miner's ball takes place on a dance floor that can accommodate thousands. *Tennis tournaments* are held in a chamber more than forty stories underground.

There are natural wonders besides. There is a briny lake down there, and the "growths" in the Crystal Grotto are a natural phenomenon without equal anywhere else in the world.

There are even species of plants and animals that have adapted themselves to living underground. They have a museum to show it all to you.

In the thirteenth century, they had a ways to go, but even then the miners had been at work for at least three hundred years; the caverns were already pretty impressive.

Not that Annastashia and Krystyana were all that impressed. They wanted to get to Cracow, and Sir Vladimir had been to the mines before. But it was my vacation and I was footing the bills.

We were watching a walking-beam pump, a device similar to that which we built at Three Walls to saw wood. But for pumping water, my condensing steam engine was far more efficient. I called the works manager over and started to explain my pump to him.

He cut me off with, "What? You're a miner?"

"Well, not exactly, but—"

"Well I am. And my father was a miner, and his father before him. We've been miners for over four hundred years."

"That's very nice, but about my pump—"

"I know everything there is to know about mining. I don't need to know about your foolish ideas."

"But it's not just some pipe dream! I have one running at Three Walls!"

"Three Walls? I never heard of a mine at any 'Three Walls.'" And he turned and walked away. Arrogant bastard.

The price of salt was about equal to the cost of chopping it out and hauling it to the surface, pretty cheap. By loading down the mules, slinging sacks across the backs of all four horses, and letting Tadaos walk, we were able to take a ton and a half back with us—about two kilos per capita, probably enough to last us until spring. These people ate a lot of salt, maybe because of all the beer they drank.

We had been gone from Cracow for less than a week, but there was a major change in the Vistula waterfront. The ferrymaster had taken my suggestion about using river power to move his ferryboat. A long sturdy rope ran from his boat to the tree I'd suggested, and he'd come up with an efficient block-and-tackle system that let him effectively move the rope from one side of the boat to the other with only the power of his own arms.

He let us ride it free, in thanks for my suggestion, but he was still getting full fare from everyone else. Business had been better than ever, with many people riding it just for the novelty of moving in a boat without oarsmen.

He no longer had to pay a dozen men, and eventually someone would see his vast profits, go into competition with him and drive his fares down. But just then he was in heaven.

I, too, was very pleased. Think of it. Because of an idea of mine and the few minutes it had taken to explain it, twelve men were released from the drudgery of paddling that boat back and forth across the river. Twelve men had been given their whole lives to do more productive, more enjoyable work.

Actually, it was far more than twelve, for there must be many ferryboats operating on the Vistula. Word of the improvement would get around quickly. And there were many other rivers. And it wasn't just those men, but their children and grandchildren had also been set free.

As we rode toward the city gates, I was patting myself on the back for a job well done. Then a rock the size of my fist slammed into the side of my helmet. I was stunned, tried briefly to stay in the saddle, then fell to the ground.

I wasn't quite unconscious, and could hear the shouting around me. Krystyana and Annastashia were holding my head up, and vision was starting to return. Tadaos had strung his bow and had shot two men through the arm, pinning them to a tree. Sir Vladimir and Anna were out rounding up the rest of our assailants. It was all over by the time I had regained my feet.

"Sir Vladimir, what was that all about?"

"Those are the men who once worked the ferryboat. They say that they did you no harm, but that you have deprived them of their livelihoods, and now they will starve, along with their families. I think they might have justice on their side, though perhaps their anger might better have been directed at the boatmaster, for you only talked about harming them, but the boatmaster actually carried the deed out."

"I didn't hurt anybody. I just—oh hell. Bring them here."

Sir Vladimir herded over a very bashed group of men. Most were bleeding from wounds or contusions.

"You were sort of rough on them," I said.

"I killed none and thought myself lenient," Sir Vladimir said.

"I suppose you did. You men! Why did you attack us?"

One of them was nudged forward by the others. "You was the one what told the boatmaster to build that thing! Now no one will ever hire a ferryboat man. Not ever again!"

"That's only to be expected," I said. "Technology often causes slight social and economic readjustments. But the net results will be very beneficial for this city and for our country."

"Whatever you said, I still don't have no food in the house! Before you opened your mouth, things were going good for me, and for these men here!" There were nods and gestures of agreement from the other men.

"Then find some other line of work. There must be hundreds of things that need doing in Cracow."

"There is if you have an uncle who's a master in a guild! But there ain't no guilds on the river, and there's no way they'll let us work in Cracow."

"Are you telling me that you have all tried to get honest work in the city and you've all been rejected?"

"Not all of us. Some of us are smart enough to know what'd happen. But a lot of us have tried, for all the good it's done us."

"All right, then. There's plenty of work to be done at Three Walls. It's about two days walk west of here. Take Count Lambert's trail to Sir Miesko's manor. He'll give you directions from there. Tell Yashoo that I said that ferryboat men are to be hired at the usual rate."

They still looked disgruntled, but the crowd broke up. Before the end of the year, I ended up hiring twenty-six ferryboat men. Or men who said that they were ferryboat men. It wasn't as though there were any records that I could check. More mouths to feed.

Sir Vladimir wanted to proceed directly to Wawel Castle and I told him to take the girls there. I'd be along later. I had to go see Father Ignacy at the Franciscan monastery. There was a little matter of my confession concerning the man I had murdered in the cave in the Beskids.

Four days went by before I could get our party back on the road. At that, it took a direct summons from Count Lambert to get them moving. I suppose that I could have been more assertive, but I wasn't looking forward to facing my liege lord.

Sir Vladimir insisted on taking an alternate trail back, one that was slightly longer, but had the advantage that the Crossmen rarely used it. Until the judicial combat was agreed upon, there was no telling just what they might do. It was best to avoid them.

This route took us by one of the strangest terrain features in Poland. In the midst of the wet, north European Plain, there is a desert.

The Bledowska Desert is about twenty square miles of shifting, windblown sand, and blistering hot in the summer. Fortunately, our route only skirted one corner of it, but even so it was a trial.

"What *makes* it like this?" Annastashia said.

"Some trick of the winds, I suppose, my love. Sir Conrad, do you know anything of it?" Sir Vladimir said.

"Your guess is as good as mine. Maybe something about the way the hills around here are shaped. This area gets very little rainfall."

"They say it never rains here at all!"

"I can believe it."

"Why would God *make* such a horrid place?" Krystyana asked.

"How should I know why God does anything? Even so, this area could be useful. It would make a good place to store grain," I said.

"I think it's a *waste of space*," Krystyana answered.

That evening, we stayed at the manor of Sir Vladimir's cousin Sir Augustyn, and his wife. They were a quiet, phlegmatic couple who talked little and went to bed early. A relief after Cracow.

The next day we were in Okoitz.

Count Lambert wasn't as angry as I had expected him to be. His reaction was more of the "my child, how could you have gone so wrong" sort of thing, which was even harder to take.

"You know that by your actions, you have killed yourself. All the things we'd planned together will come to nothing. All these mills and factories will halt without your guiding hand. And the mission that brought you to Poland at the bequest of Prester John, that too must end in failure."

Count Lambert had become convinced that I was an emissary from the mythical king Prester John. My oath to Father Ignacy was such that I couldn't talk about my origins, so I couldn't set him straight.

"It's not as bad as all that, my lord. Even if I do get killed, what we've started here will continue to grow. Vitold understands the mill as well as I do, and the Florentine knows more about cloth than me."

"Perhaps, Sir Conrad, but you are the fire behind all of them. Even if we do prosper without you, it won't last. If you're right about the Mongols' coming, and you've been right about everything else, this town and the rest of Poland will be burned to the ground in eight years. With all the people dead, what use are factories and mills?"

"The Mongols are a problem, my lord, but at least now you have been warned. Something can still be done —Anyway, I'm not going to lose the trial with the Crossman. I'm going to win. I've won every fight I've been through in this land, and I see no reason why I should stop doing that."

"Your confidence only exposes your ignorance, Sir Conrad. Killing highwaymen and unsuspecting guards is one thing. Going up against a professional killer is quite another. Truth is, you won't even make a good showing. I've seen your inept lancework.

"You've never seen a champion in action, and perhaps you should. A trial by combat is to be held on the first of next month at Bytom, a day north of here. It's just over an inheritance, so it won't be to the death, but it'll give you an idea of what you're up against."

"Very well, my lord, I'll go."

"Good. Sometimes you can get one of the champions to give you some lessons, for a price. Speaking of which, I have some new orders for you. Sir Vladimir seems to have attached himself to you, and he's one of the best lancemen in Little Poland. From today onward, until your trial, you will work out with him every day for at least three hours. That's on horseback and with the lance. You'll never become good enough to win, but at least you won't die in quite so embarrassing a manner."

Little Poland is the hilly area around Cracow, as opposed to Big Poland, the plains area farther north and west.

"As you wish, my lord. I'd intended to practice for the fight. But tell me, was the cloth I requested sent to Three Walls?"

"It was, and I haven't taken payment for it yet. I wanted to discuss the matter with you. We made a wager on whether or not your windmill would work. Well, you won. And you weren't interested in betting double or nothing on your second windmill."

"My lord, would you want Duke Henryk to be owing you a vast sum of money?"

"Hmmm. I can see your point. It would be awkward,

wouldn't it. Very well. What say you to taking that cloth as payment for my debt?"

"If you think the price is fair, it's fine by me, my lord."

"Hmmm. Well. Then how if I threw in twelve more bolts?"

The bolts of cloth were huge, a yard high and two yards wide. And cloth was very expensive in the thirteenth century. "I would think that you were being very generous, my lord."

"Then we'll call the matter settled. Pick out the cloth you want and have it sent to your lands on my mules. And perhaps I'm not really being so generous. After all, I am your liege lord and you have no heir. Once you're dead, all of your property escheats to me. Then too, even though I've sent my vassals their half of the fabric in return for their wool and flax, I have more cloth than I can sell, now that your factory is working."

"Haven't merchants been coming around to buy it, my lord?"

"Not as many as I had hoped. Many come looking to buy wool and go away with their mules unloaded. But few come to buy cloth."

"Perhaps you should consider setting up a sales organization."

"A what? Well, no matter. We can discuss it in the evening. For now, I want to tour the factory with you."

Count Lambert had about a hundred fifty knights, most of whom had manors of their own. To "man" his factory, he had asked each of his knights to send him a peasant girl or two, and each of the girls was to be paid for her work in cloth, giving her a full hope chest.

The knights, knowing their lord's preferences with regards to attractive young ladies, had each sent the loveliest women available, usually the prettiest unmarried girl in a whole village. For a girl to be unmarried in that culture, she had to be in her very early teens.

And rather than risk embarrassment for the lady and annoyance for their liege lord, they had all explained the customs of Okoitz to the girls to be sent, so that any not so inclined could bow out gracefully and another sent in her place.

It was a hot day and there was no nudity taboo in thirteenth century Poland. Many of the girls were scantily clothed and no few of them were completely nude. That factory was like a scene from an Italian science fiction movie.

It was hard to keep my mind on the machinery. It was hard to keep my mind at all, let alone even notice the machinery.

Count Lambert was wallowing in all the beauty like a pig in mud. He wandered around, patting a butt here, pinching a tit there and smiling and flirting all the while. The girls seemed thrilled by all the attention from so high a personage, and many were actually competing for their share of caresses.

Once Count Lambert made it known that I was the favored vassal responsible for the factory and mill, I got my share of the attention, too. Distracting, but vastly enjoyable!

There were a dozen looms on the factory's third floor. Each was set up to make a different sort of cloth, from heavy tweed to a very fine linen. Vitold had outdone himself with the fine-linen loom, taking wooden machinery farther than I would have thought possible.

It was sort of the way the printing done by Gutenberg was some of the best ever done, and the way the machining on a prototype is often so much better than that on a production item. When a craftsman knows that he is breaking new ground, he puts his soul into his work. And it shows.

The cloth that loom turned out was pretty impressive as well. It was strong and light and looked like thin nylon even though it was really linen.

"This stuff is incredible!" I said. The naked operators stopped their work and crowded around. It was hot on the third floor, but I suspect that the real reason for their nudity was that they got more petting that way. I couldn't resist putting an arm around a redhead.

"It is good, isn't it," Count Lambert said with a girl in each arm and a young breast in each hand.

"Good? It's so sheer that you could make a kite out of it!"

"And what might a kite be?"

"A kite, my lord? Well, it's a thing made out of sticks and, I suppose, this cloth. It flies."

Count Lambert suddenly lost all interest in the ladies he'd been fondling. The sparkle faded from their eyes. "You mean that it were possible for a man to build a thing that flies?"

"Of course, my lord. I could make you a kite this very afternoon. I simply never thought that you would want such a thing. And there are many things that fly. Aircraft, balloons, helicopters, rockets, dirigibles, and what not."

"These others we must discuss, but later. For now I want you to immediately build me this kite thing."

"Yes, my lord. Uh, there is the matter of the fighting practice you ordered."

"Forget about that for now. After all, you're going to die anyway, and I want as many of your devices saved as possible."

So on that cheery note, I went out and flew a kite.

Vitold was pulled from supervising the construction of the second windmill to give me "every possible assistance." I told him to lend me a junior carpenter and sent him back to work.

I took a yard of the fine linen cloth and put Krystyana and Annastashia, good seamstresses both, to work cutting and sewing. It was done in an hour, and we gave it a thin coating of linseed oil. We set the finished kite up in the sun to polymerize the oil, then had a few rounds of beer.

It was a simple, traditional diamond-shaped kite, and there was enough of a breeze to fly it right out of the bailey. I no sooner had it airborne than Count Lambert was there. By the time twenty yards of string was out, he'd taken it out of my hands like an impetuous child, and was playing with it himself.

"That a man could build a thing that could fly!"

"Of course, my lord. You saw us make it. It's a simple enough thing. This is probably the simplest design, though there are many others."

"Then I must have them! Sir Conrad, could you stay on a bit past your usual two days?"

"If you wish, my lord.

"Earlier today, you mentioned the cloth I was to have. Do you suppose that I could have a few tons of thread and yarn as well? I'd like my people to have knitted underwear as well as decent top clothes."

"What?" The count was clearly distracted. "Oh, yes. Those marvelous knots you showed my ladies last winter. Take six tons, a dozen tons if you want it."

I took it. In fact, I sent it along with the cloth to Three Walls within the hour. This forced the muleteers to camp out that night, but that was better than to give Count Lambert the chance to regret his generosity.

In making and flying that kite, it was as though I had created the wonder of the world. People who had been indifferent to my mills and factories were astounded by a simple child's toy. In the course of the next week, I made box kites, Rondalero kites, French war kites, and even a monstrous Chinese dragon kite.

Kite-flying became the big game on campus, and grown men, professional warriors and leaders, were soon ignoring their hawks and hunts and flying kites. The fad spread across Poland—within a year across Europe—and the mill couldn't keep up with the demand for Count Lambert's Finest. Prices on that linen cloth soared, and merchants who came to buy it often bought other varieties of fabric as well. By spring, the factory was selling every yard it could make, all because of a silly kite-flying fad.

At least they didn't name it after me.

That night at dinner, Count Lambert was glorying in a thick slice of watermelon. I was sure that watermelon didn't come from the New World, but somehow no one from Poland had ever heard of it. "And to think, Sir Conrad, you gave *this* marvelous stuff to a peasant!"

"Yes, my lord. Just be sure and save the seeds, and next year there'll be more than enough for everybody."

"To be sure, to be sure. You've explained over and over again that there is no reason why all these different sorts of melons you brought can't soon be enjoyed by everyone. It simply seems that they are too good to waste on a peasant! Still, nothing's to be done for it, I suppose."

I'd given the count all those types of plants whose

seeds might be eaten, since I was worried that a hungry peasant might eat, say, our entire supply of hybrid wheat the first winter. Actually, I almost had that problem with him. I'd decided it was good PR to show the cook what to do with sweet corn, and, to get enough acreage the next year to plant all the seed we'd grown, sacrificed one ear out of the twenty-seven that were growing so the count could try it.

The count fell in love with sweet corn. I think that if I hadn't physically stopped him, he would have gone out and personally picked and eaten the entire crop that evening. And there were no more seeds to be had in the century, at least on this side of the Atlantic.

Count Lambert was generous with his vast new supply of young ladies. He had even asked them to see that I was well taken care of. Krystyana found herself sort of whisked aside, and two most attractive young women joined me in bed that night. It would have been a great erotic fantasy come true, except that after an hour of fondling and fumbling, they both admitted that they didn't know what to do. The count, thinking to do me a huge favor, had sent in two virgins.

Now, one virgin is a monumental undertaking, if you're going to do it right. But a clumsy man can turn what could have been a fine lover into a frigid bitch. Two at the same time, when I hardly knew either one of them, seemed impossible. Yet the ladies were there and expecting something wonderful to happen. It turned into something of an all-night tutorial session.

In the end, I did the job reasonably well, and I think the girls were pleased. The truth is that I really preferred an experienced bed partner. This business of two virgins a night was ridiculous, and moderation was in order.

Say, one a week.

# Chapter Fifteen

FROM THE AUTOBIOGRAPHY OF SIR VLADIMIR
CHARNETSKI

When finally we left Okoitz, it was with a certain relief to all our party. Sir Conrad seemed almost haggard
from his overindulgence in Count Lambert's vast supply
of ladies, and Krystyana was not amused. Both Annastashia and Krystyana were not pleased with the change
in character of what was, after all, their home town.

For mine own self, I had stayed true to my love,
though it was a strain. The ladies of the mill were eager
for the services of any true belted knight. Indeed, some
would do almost anything to get a new belt in their
notch.

Upon our arrival, we found the people at Three Walls
far better dressed than before. Every person seemed to
sport at least one new article of clothing, and the former
slaves were properly clothed. I could see that in a few
months, the women would have everyone in fully embroidered peasant garb.

On arriving, Sir Conrad did a very strange thing. He
called his people about him and announced to them that
his horse, Anna, was human, or close to it. She had been
created by some band of wizards from the distant past,
or perhaps she had been transmuted into the form of a

horse. Sir Conrad's explanation was not at all clear to me.

In all events, he had freed her from his ownership of her and proposed to swear her to him in the exact same manner as he had sworn the rest of them.

All of Sir Conrad's people loved him and most also felt a little fear in his regard. Certainly, none objected to this latest strange thing. We had all heard fireside stories about Persian princes who acted oddly with regards to their horses, even keeping them in their houses and tents. Some later speculated that Sir Conrad had come from Persia.

He also swore Tadaos the former boatman, now called the bowman, and eight men, some with wives and children, who had been ferrymen on the Vistula. Then he made a speech, saying that all these people were now full citizens of Three Walls, and could enjoy our entertainments and our church as well as anyone, thus giving official sanction to Anna's church-going habits.

The next day, after our morning's fighting practice, Sir Conrad left for Cieszyn, saying that he wished to discuss some expansion of the Pink Dragon Inn with the innkeeper. Frenchizing, I think he called it, though it involved building a second inn in Cracow, and not at all in France.

He began to make many such quick side trips, and though I was loath to let him go unprotected, due to my oath to the duke, the truth was that I simply couldn't keep up with him. That horse of his was magic.

And my oath required me not only to protect Sir Conrad, but to spy upon him as well, a thing I was loath to think of. It weighed on my mind and dirtied my soul. I was left to look after things, an easy task since Yashoo was well trained in his duties, and Tadaos stood the night guard.

Not long after his departure, some small boys raised a commotion. It seems that they had been playing in the bushes below the mineshaft, and had found another mine or cave. Being young boys, they had of course explored it, and had come out very frightened. One said that the Ghost of the Mines had stolen his belt knife and the other said that the rocks were "sticky," in some frightening manner.

There is in the countryside about Count Lambert's domain an old legend about a Ghost of the Mines. His name is said to have been Skarbnik, once a rich miser who must forever do penance for his sins. They say that he is the guardian of mineshafts, underground treasures, and even the souls of dead miners. He is wicked and mischievous and often wreaks misfortune on those underground.

Usually he appears as a white-bearded old man, but sometimes as a mouse or a black cat, and when he does, it is a sign that fire will break out underground.

And Skarbnik hates noise.

I, of course, am a civilized, *modern* man and don't believe in such old wives' tales. The tasks of a true knight are many and varied, but the protection of the people is always high on the list. There might be some harmful animal in there, or even a thief, so there was nothing for it but to investigate the cave myself.

The mouth of the tunnel was very small. I had to leave my sword outside—there would have been no room to swing it in any event—and crawled into the cave. So tight was it that my mail-clad shoulders brushed the walls and my helmet scraped the ceiling. I pushed a small oil lamp before me and had my dagger in my hand.

I hope you will not think me unmanly when I say that I do not like small confined places, with their stale airs and dank smells. The thought of the many tons of rock above me was oppressive in the extreme. Yet I pressed on, for a knight must do his duty even if his forehead may sweat and his hand may shake.

I came to the end of the tunnel and could see that I was alone. No real dangers were obvious. Then I saw the boy's knife against the end wall and thought to return it to him, for his father would doubtless beat him for losing so valuable a tool. But as I approached it, my own dagger *leaped* from my hand of its own accord and fastened itself to the black rock on the end wall of the tunnel. It was not stuck in the rock, mind you, but laying on it as though it were on a table. Only it was *laying on a wall*! Hanging, with nothing to support it!

Then I was also being drawn to that infernal wall, or at least my chain mail was. And my helmet was pulled from my head, joining my knife on the wall.

At that point, the lamp went out, extinguished perhaps by a drop of sweat, or maybe I bumped it. Or maybe whoever or whatever was pulling at my arms and armor saw fit to do his further work in darkness.

I did not cry out, for a true knight never calls out save as a battle cry. My silence had nothing to do with that silly old legend.

In all events, I could see no use to my remaining. I could accomplish nothing, and whatever was attacking me, its surcease was beyond the abilities of a mere knight. Let some wizard handle it, or perhaps Sir Conrad.

I crawled quickly, and perforce backward, out of the tunnel.

## FROM THE DIARY OF CONRAD SCHWARTZ

Tadeusz the innkeeper was enthused with the idea of opening another inn in Cracow. Several times in the past, he had asked me for permission to enlarge the present inn, since it was so profitable. I always turned him down because we already had most of the business in Cieszyn. The other inns in town handled little but our overflow. When you are already satisfying your entire market, there is no point in investing in further plant and equipment.

But Cracow had three or four times the population of Cieszyn, and a much larger Pink Dragon Inn there would make sense. To Tadeusz, going to Cracow was like a modern ballerina's going to the Bolshoi. The big time!

Tadeusz had six sons working for him, most of them adults. Our plan was to leave the oldest boy in charge of the inn in Cieszyn. Tadeusz would take the rest of his family and, later, one half of his staff and go to Cracow.

There they would buy—if necessary build—a suitable building. The guilds in Cracow wouldn't allow me to handle any construction work, which was just as well. I had my hands full as it was. Tadeusz had definite ideas about what he wanted—something similar to our present facilities only larger and plusher.

After that, I wanted a small inn at Three Walls, and if the Cracow inn was a success, we might expand to Wroclaw and Sandomierz. After that, who knew? Perhaps each of his sons would be an innkeeper.

Tadeusz, his wife, and five of their sons left for Cracow the next morning as I was leaving for Three Walls. But of course they couldn't keep up with Anna.

A mile from Three Walls, I overtook Boris Novacek and a knight heading in the same direction that I was. For a few days last fall, I had worked for the man, and most of my wealth had been gained while in his employ. He had been treated rather shabbily by Count Lambert, to my profit, and I had always felt guilty about it.

"Boris! I haven't seen you since last Christmas. Are your ventures profiting you?" I said as the horses walked slowly down the trail.

"As well as can be expected, Sir Conrad. I thought I would visit your new lands and see what wonders you were working there. This is my new companion, Sir Kazimierz, who now has your old job."

"A pleasure, Sir Kazimierz. I hope you last longer at it than I did." I turned back to my old boss. "You'll always be welcome at my table, Boris. But the truth is that there isn't much to see yet at Three Walls. We're just getting it built. I'm pretty proud of the mill and factory I designed at Okoitz, though. You should visit there."

"I've thought on it, but I fear that Count Lambert would decide that I wanted to gift him with all I own as a birthday present, so I have avoided the place."

"He was pretty rough on you last winter. Nonetheless, he now has a cloth factory and more cloth than he can sell. You once said that you wanted to get into the cloth trade. You might strike a good bargain there.

"Another thing. I now own a brassworks in Cieszyn. They've been selling all the brass they can pour, and are having a hard time getting enough copper. The price of copper in Cieszyn has doubled since last spring."

"An interesting thought, Sir Conrad. To buy cloth at Okoitz, sell it in Hungary, and return with copper for Cieszyn. I think that would be profitable. The truth is that I have no goods just now but plenty of money.

"Quite a bit of money, in fact. You remember that German who attacked us on the road just out of Cracow last winter? Not Sir Rheinburg, the other German the day before."

How could I forget? He was the first man I had ever killed. "Yes."

"Then you will recall that I mentioned that if he had really purchased my debt from Schweiburger the cloth merchant, and if he had no heirs, I would be forgiven that debt of twenty-two thousand pence.

"Well, that very thing has come to pass, and I am now richer because of it. I never had to pay the debt and I even recovered my amber from Schweiburger."

"You mean that man was an honest creditor?"

"A creditor, yes. Honest? Do honest men pull knives on others on the highway? He tried to kill me, and then you as well. Anyway, my debt was not in arrears at the time. He had no right to accost us like that."

"Still, it troubles me."

"Well, it shouldn't. You did no wrong, and now there is a bit of gold for you with which to salve your conscience."

"What do you mean, Boris?"

"I mean that I said at the time that if he really had a deed of transfer, you would get half of my profits. I've never gone back on my word yet, and I won't start now. Eleven thousand pence in those sacks is for you."

"You have traveled three days to pay me a huge sum of money that I would never have known about if you hadn't told me?"

"Yes, Sir Conrad. I suppose that's a true statement."

"I've never heard of such honesty. Especially after Count Lambert took the much larger booty we won from Sir Rheinburg and gave most of it to me, even though you actually found the treasure in Rheinburg's camp. I was so concerned about that baby that I stepped right over the treasure chest without noticing it. I hate to speak ill of my liege lord, but I've always thought that you were robbed."

"I wasn't pleased with Count Lambert either. But his actions as regards the second booty have nothing to do with my word as regards the first."

"Boris, you still amaze me. But there's no way that I can accept that money. It simply wouldn't be fair. If Count Lambert hears about the business, well, it was all a legal matter in Cracow, and so is none of his business.

If he doesn't hear about it, so much the better."

"Now it is my turn to be amazed, Sir Conrad. No other knight in Christendom would have forgiven me this debt."

"Let's just say that we're two honest crazy people who like each other."

"Done. But tell me, is there something that you need? Something that I can do for you?"

"You know, maybe there is. You travel all over eastern Europe. You meet a lot of different people. I want to hire a special kind of a man.

"The truth is that I know very little about practical chemistry. I know quite a bit about theoretical chemistry, but all of it was using packaged and bottled chemicals that were bought from a supply house. Such places aren't available in this land, and I wouldn't know bauxite from phosphate rock. But there must be somebody who knows how to take rocks and sulfur and what not and make acids and bases and salts out of them. I think you would call such a man an alchemist."

"I don't understand much of what you said, but I have heard of alchemists. I will spread the word that you want one. But most of those men are frauds and liars. How could I possibly know a good one from an imposter?"

"I recall that the Moslems had—have—better alchemists than we do, so he might be a Moor. And if he knows how to make the three strong acids, if he can show you a liquid that can dissolve gold, *aqua regia* it's called, then he's my man."

"I will search for you, Sir Conrad. I cannot promise what I'll find."

"Thank you, Boris. Tell me, what became of the amber you recovered from Schweiburger?"

"I sold it at a good price to a caravan of Crossmen."

On arriving at Three Walls, I had to spend a few hours playing manager. The mining foreman reported that they had found a seam of clay in the mine. This was expected, since clay is usually found in association with coal. Still it was good news, for now we *knew* that we could manufacture bricks and clay pipes efficiently.

Then a rather shamefaced Sir Vladimir told me about the second tunnel and "sticky rocks." I had to hear his jumbled tale twice before I could figure out what he was talking about. Then I felt a very pleasant glow.

I changed into my work clothes and went to the boys' tunnel. A crowd of people gathered who should have been working, but I decided that they should be in on this one, since it would affect all of their lives.

I crawled in almost on my belly, so tiny was that shaft. From the position of the shaft and the way it angled upward, it was obvious that it had been dug with the intention of draining the mineshaft above. If I could accurately measure the angles and distances involved, I should be able to compute the distance we would have to pump to reach the coal.

But more important was what stopped the old miners from their digging. Once I reached it, there could be no doubt. The knives and Sir Vladimir's helmet were held magnetically to the ore seam. There's only one magnetic rock that I know of, and that's magnetite, sometimes called lodestone. It's one of the best iron ores.

The old miners had dug that far and had then been scared off by something that they couldn't comprehend. It was probably why the valley had been abandoned fifty years ago.

I really had to yank to get the knives and helmet away from the ore seam, but it seemed important that I do so. Sir Vladimir was glad at the return of his equipment, but from that day on his helmet was magnetized and collected iron filings the way a boy collects dirt.

"Did you find the Ghost of the Mines?" a dirty boy asked me as I returned his knife.

"No, but I found a treasure he was guarding!"

This caused a lot of mumbling in the crowd, so I climbed a bit up the hill so they could all hear me.

"There is a kind of magnetic ore called magnetite that has the property of sticking to iron and steel. We have a seam of it in that shaft. It's perfectly natural and nothing to be afraid of. It's a good ore, and with it we can make iron and steel.

"Do you realize that in this one small valley, God has seen fit to give us every major mineral that we need? We have coal and iron ore and clay and limestone! With that

we can make mortar and bricks and concrete! We can
make iron and steel! We even have sandstone to line our
furnaces and to make grinding wheels! I tell you that
whatever else happens, the success of this valley is assured!"

That got a cheer out of them, even though they didn't
realize all the work that would be involved.

# Interlude Three

I HIT the STOP button.

"Tom, I can't believe that many minerals all in one spot. Was that your doing?"

"It was not. Except for the limestone, which is a common mineral throughout the Carpathians, those were all small deposits. None of them would have been commercially exploitable in the twentieth century, when volumes were large and transportation cheap. Small deposits like that are common in Europe. Conrad just lucked out, having them all so close together.

"Anyway, stop interrupting."

He pressed the START button.

# Chapter Sixteen

SIR VLADIMIR and I had just spent another grueling three-hour session of fighting practice, trying to teach me how to put a lance through a quintain, an old plywood shield with a small hole in the center of it. The glues used were inferior to the modern ones, and the thin strips of wood had started to delaminate. It wasn't quite like modern plywood. The plies were at sixty-degree angles rather than ninety.

The shield was fixed to one end of a crossbar that was mounted to a swiveling post. At the other end of the crossbar hung a hefty sandbag. You charged the thing at a full gallop and tried to put your lance through the hole. If you missed the hole, as I usually did, you hit the shield, spun the post around, and the sandbag hit you in the back of the head. This generally knocked you off your horse.

Sir Vladimir considered even that arrangement to be rather effeminate. He wanted to replace the sandbag with a rock.

I simply couldn't master it. After two weeks of steady bruising, I was just as bad at it as when I started.

"I'm beginning to lose faith, Sir Conrad. I fear you'll never be a lanceman. But see here, it isn't all that bad. Death must come to all men eventually, and at least yours will be in the glory of combat, with your friends looking on. We'll give you a beautiful funeral, and I'll light a candle in the church for you every Christmas and Easter." He really meant it.

It didn't help at all that Sir Vladimir never missed with a lance. He was supposed to be instructing me, but in fact he didn't see how it was possible for anybody to miss so easy a target. He could hit the hole sideways! I mean that he could set the quintain at right angles to its normal position, charge it at a full gallop, and while passing three yards from it thrust his lance out to the side and skewer the hole every time.

It was becoming obvious that if I was going to win the coming trial, I was going to need special weapons, or tactics, or help. Preferably all three. "Sir Vladimir, let's go over the rules again. You said the code was 'arm yourself.' What if I brought in a cannon?"

"What is a cannon, Sir Conrad?"

"That's sort of hard to explain. What if I was a bowman like Tadaos?"

"A bow is hardly a knightly weapon. No true belted knight would use one in honorable combat. The bow is for peasants and women."

"Why is that? It seems a strange prejudice."

"Well, if everybody used them in a battle, who would know who killed whom? Where would be the glory in just going out and getting shot? The best men would fall as easily as the worst! What a horrible situation! No. A true knight would never use a bow or fire a *trébuchet* or anything of the sort."

"So projectile weapons are out?"

"Of course, Sir Conrad."

"I guess that scuttles my cannon idea. I probably couldn't develop gunpowder in the time available, anyway. How about armor? I noticed that you knights never armor your horses."

"There would be no point to it. Striking another knight's mount would be a foul. At your trial, four crossbowmen will be at the ready to kill the man that does a foul deed."

"I didn't realize that. How about weapons? I can use my own sword, can't I, and not one of the heavy choppers you guys use?"

"Your own sword is legal, as are any daggers, maces,

axes, mauls, war hammers, or anything else that is not thrown. A weapon must stay in your hand."

"How about body armor? Do I have to wear chain mail?"

"No, but you'd be a damn fool not to. You ought to have a coat of plates made as well."

"A coat of plates?"

"Yes. I should have mentioned it sooner, but there's still plenty of time. It's sort of a leather vest with iron plates sewn inside. You wear it either over or under your mail.

"You might want to get a great helm as well. They fit over your regular helmet, and you wear them for the first few charges, until the lances are broken. After that, if it comes to swordwork, you can take it off, to see better."

"So anything I come up with in the way of armor is fair?"

"Anything at all. But I hope you don't plan something stupidly heavy. Anything that slows you down will earn you a blade in the eye slit."

"What I'm going to build is going to be as light as chain mail."

The blacksmith I'd hired was good enough to handle general repair work, but I needed a real master. The best man I knew was Count Lambert's blacksmith, Ilya. The man was rude, crude, and obstreperous, but he had the skill.

I left for Okoitz within the hour.

Ilya was willing, indeed eager to come to Three Walls. It seems that he wasn't getting along well with the wife Count Lambert saddled him with.

"You understand that this is only temporary," I said. "I won't be a part of permanently separating a man from his family."

"You don't have four kids screaming in the room when you're trying to relax. Somebody else's kids at that."

"If you didn't want the woman and her children, you shouldn't have married her."

"Count Lambert wanted me to. You go argue with him if you want to."

"It's not my problem."

Count Lambert was willing to lend me Ilya providing I found a replacement. The harvest season was in full swing and it was vital to have someone who could repair broken tools.

I loaded Ilya behind me on Anna's rump, and we made it to Cieszyn before dark. I gave Ilya a sack of money and told him to hire four assistants, plus one more man for Count Lambert.

He was to buy his weight in iron bars and whatever tools he might need, and bring them to Three Walls in two days, along with a ton of charcoal.

I introduced him to the innkeeper and to the Krakowski brothers, and told them to give him every possible assistance.

Then I was back at Three Walls in the early dawn for more fighting practice. After that I limped back to my hut and started cutting out little pieces of parchment.

It took the girls and me three days to get it right, but we made a full suit of articulated plate armor, the kind you've seen in museums. We made it out of parchment, with buttons sewn on where the rivets had to go.

By the time Ilya had his forge set up, we had a complete set of patterns for him to work from. He thought it was crazy, but he thought everything I did was crazy. I let him bitch, just so long as my armor got built.

When you think about it, a blade is an energy-concentrating device. A sword takes all the force in your arm and concentrates it on the tiny area of the sharp edge. That's why a sharp blade cuts better. It has a smaller area.

And a sword not only concentrates energy in space, it also concentrates it in time. It might take a few seconds to swing a sword, but the whole energy of the swing is delivered in *milli*seconds at impact, multiplying the instantaneous force by a factor of hundreds. This is why it's easier to down a tree by swinging the axe, rather than just by pushing it at the tree.

Armor is an energy-*distributing* device. The padding under the steel compresses, delivering the energy of the blow over a longer period of time. The thicker the padding, the longer the time, the lower the force felt by the wearer.

And armor distributes the energy of a blow in space. If the blade can't cut the steel, it must push it forward. The bigger the plate of armor, the wider the area, the lower the force felt by the wearer. With chain mail, the area under each link is small and while it's a big improvement over bare skin, it can't compare with a solid metal plate.

Of course, there are practical limitations on how thick the padding can be and how big you can make the plates. You have to be able to move in the stuff.

But what I was going to wear would be two hundred years more advanced than what my opponent would have, and that just might make the difference. In combat, high technology means higher than your opponent's.

And while all the practice and armor-making was going on, work continued at Three Walls. In addition to the wall—apartment house, the church, the inn, the barn, the icehouse, the smokehouse (which was to double as a sauna), and the factory, we now needed a coke oven and a blast furnace.

The blast furnace would have to wait a bit, but I had to know if our coal could be turned into coke. Not all types of coal can be made into coke in an old-style beehive oven. Building a modern coke oven was well beyond our capabilities.

The boys' cave had to be enlarged and the iron ore extracted using bronze picks and shovels that I was having made up.

And we still hadn't struck coal yet. The masons finally got sufficiently frustrated that they built a big wood fire and threw on all the limestone rubble that they had been generating in the course of making blocks. They kept adding wood and limestone for a week, and when the fire was out, they had quick lime, calcium oxide. Adding water and sand to it made mortar.

When I asked them why they hadn't told me that you could make lime with a wood fire, they said I hadn't asked. That night at supper, I made a speech about how it was important to keep me informed about that sort of thing, but I don't think that it sank in very deep. One of the men said that they saw me doing so many crazy things that if they told me about every one of them, they wouldn't have any time left to work.

Someday, I'd make believers out of them.

Soon, foundations were being laid and people could see signs of progress. I think they had been starting to worry about being stuck in the woods for the winter with only our temporary shelters, because the laying of the foundations made them all look more confident.

The Pruthenian children had mostly fit right in. Looking at them, you couldn't tell the difference between them and the Polish children we had of the same age. Their accents were thick as a millstone, but even there progress was being made. At least we could understand them. To give them religious instruction, the priest had begun staying over until Monday afternoons, and many of them were already baptized. Most of them were starting to learn the trades of their adopted parents. But sometimes, when they thought you weren't looking at them, you could see written on their faces the horror of all that they had been through. That increased my resolve; those children were not going to go back into slavery.

Then there was Anna. I'd kept my promises to her and made a big sign with all the letters on it so she could spell things out. She was still attending church regularly, and the priest was growing increasingly scandalized. He finally broached the subject.

I'd known that it was coming, and had my response ready. I said that Anna was a full citizen of Three Walls, she was smarter than half my workers, and if she wanted to live a moral, Christian life, I certainly wasn't going to stop her. I said it in a straight, deadpan way. Father Stanislaw just shook his head and walked away. And Anna continued to go to church.

Vladimir was growing increasingly depressed as winter approached. For one thing, his brother visited him and said that their father was still violently angry with him, and his family meant a lot to Vladimir. I think there was even more to his depression than that, but I couldn't find out what it was. He wasn't pleasant company anymore, and I found myself looking forward to my trips alone.

I timed my next visit to Okoitz so that I could see the trial by combat at Bytom before returning to Three Walls.

The harvest was in full swing at Okoitz.

In a medieval farming community, the harvest was the busiest time of the year. They had six or eight weeks to bring in all the food they would eat throughout the year, and everything else done in the year was mere preparation for this event. And despite the cloth factory and other improvements I'd made, Okoitz was still predominately a farming community.

Everyone got up with the first, false dawn and worked almost nonstop until it was too dark to see, often falling asleep still in their work clothes. Working eighteen hours a day, these people consumed a huge amount of food, more than six loaves of bread *per capita per diem*, plus other food.

I think that much of the Slavic temperament must be the result of a long-term adaptation to the weather and farming conditions of the north European plain. When the need arises, we are capable of working for months on end with only a little sleep, doing incredible amounts of work, three or four times what people from gentler climates could do. Incredible, that is, to any outsider. To us, it seems only normal.

But when the need is not there, as happens during the long northern winter, we become lethargic, food consumption drops, and spending twenty hours a day in bed seems like a pleasant thing. Having someone to help you keep warm is nice, too, and that also is a part of the Slavic temperament.

In a desert country, the cutting edge of nature is that there is sometimes not enough water. When it is in short supply, and there is not enough for everyone, every man becomes the competitor, the natural enemy of every other man. That is reflected in the temperament of the desert peoples, and by Polish standards they become harsh, ruthless, and cruel.

But when the great killer is not the lack of food or water, but the cold of a five-month winter, every person about you is one more source of heat! The more your friends, the larger your family, the greater your chances of surviving the winter. Good interpersonal skills, concern for others, and *love* have high survival value. So does a strong sense of group loyalty.

During the long winter, there is little to do much of the time but talk, and any subject of conversation is welcome. Things are debated at length, and there is time for everyone to have his say. Decisions are made by eventual consensus.

But when it's time to work, there is no more time for talk. Things must be done, and soon, or winter will close in again without enough food stored up. At such times, we Slavs work well as a group, without argument, and with a solidarity that an Arab couldn't conceive of.

A hundred wheelbarrows had been made to my specifications, and they stayed in steady use. Split logs had been laid along the paths to make pushing them easier.

Everyone was friendly, but busy, so I was left to look things over myself. The seeds I had brought in were doing fairly well. There were small patches of corn, beans, winter squash, and pumpkins that could be left until the more critical crops—the grains—were in. The tiny patches of hybrid grains had been harvested and carefully been kept separate from the standard crops. In fact, Count Lambert had them stored in his own bedroom, to make sure that they wouldn't be eaten by mistake. He showed them to me that night.

"Look at this, Sir Conrad!" He held open a sack with a few pounds of rye in it. "All that grew from the one tiny handful of seed you brought!"

It looked normal enough. "What of it, my lord?"

"What of it? Why, that must be a return of fifty to one! Don't you realize that five to one is considered excellent, and three to one is normal?"

"No, my lord, I guess I didn't. You mean that each year, you people have to take one-third of your grain and replant it, just to get next year's harvest?"

"That's exactly what I mean. Do you mean to tell me that returns of fifty to one are considered normal among your people?"

"I'm not sure, my lord. I wasn't a farmer. But my impression was that the amount of seed required was small. Usually, a farmer didn't replant his own grain. He bought seed from someone who specialized in producing it."

"Those specialists did damn well! I only hope we can do as good. Be assured that every seed of these grains will be carefully hoarded and planted next spring. Now, with most of your crops, the seeds are obvious, but what do we do about the root crops?"

"The important ones are the potatoes and the sugar beets, my lord. The potatoes, I know how to grow. It's unusual to grow them from seeds, as we did this year. Normally, you cut the potato so that each piece has one of the eyes on it and plant the pieces. The sugar beets worry me. I don't know how to make them go to seed."

"Well, if they're like any other beet, they seed in the second year. Some kinds you just leave in the ground. Some you bury in a deep hole, then replant in the spring. Some you store in a basement."

"I think it might be best to try all three, my lord. One way might work."

"We'll do that. Think! A beet that's as big as a man's head!"

"It's not just the size, my lord. Those beets are about one-sixth sugar. Once we have enough of them, I'll work on the manufacturing processes to extract that sugar, and you will have a very valuable cash crop."

"Well, we can but try. But it is late, and I'm minded to retire. Good night, Sir Conrad."

I'd taken the precaution of renewing my friendship with one of the girls from the cloth factory, so it was indeed a good night.

The next day I had a talk with Krystyana's father. This might have been an awkward confrontation, since I was sleeping with his daughter but didn't intend to marry her. It wasn't. He treated the relationship as one only to be expected. He was more concerned about the rose bushes.

Last Christmas, I'd given Krystyana a package of seeds for Japanese roses, and she had planted them in front of her parents' home. They were doing entirely too well, and already they were inconveniently large. He wanted me to ask her if he could uproot them. Of course, as her father, he didn't *need* her permission to do anything, but the wise man keeps peace in his household.

I asked that instead of tearing the bushes out, he simply prune them, and plant the cuttings to see if they wouldn't grow roots. Japanese roses might be too big for his front yard, but they would make a very good fence in the fields. He liked the idea and agreed to try it right after the harvest was in. If they didn't take, he'd try again in the spring, and if the bushes wouldn't grow from cuttings, they'd certainly grow from seed.

This was the second good year in a row, and last year he hadn't been able to get the last of his barley in before the fall rains ruined it. This year, he had a wheelbarrow, and that had made all the difference. With it, he could carry three times as much in a day, and he was actually ahead of schedule. Now he was worried that he might not be able to store it all. I guess a farmer has to worry about *something*.

The next morning, I was with Anna, making the run north to Bytom. We arrived hours before noon, and I was soon talking to a junior herald who didn't seem to have much else to do.

"Less than a hundred people," he said. "Usually the crowd is much larger."

"I suppose having it during the middle of the harvest keeps most people away," I said.

"True, my lord, but it had to be fought now since it will determine the ownership of the harvest of these fields. Also keeping down the crowd is the fact that the trial is not to the death. Only an inheritance is at issue. There is no truly injured party, so it need be fought only to first blood."

"What's the fight about?"

"It's simple enough. A man died without male issue. His wife and daughter would have inherited, but a male cousin of the deceased claimed that they would not be able to do the military duty due on the land, and so claimed that he was honor-bound to challenge the ownership of it. Many women would have compromised with him, yielding a portion of the property in return for the cousin's doing the military duty.

"But Lady Maria is made of tougher stuff. She's hired a champion to defend her, and now the cousin is doubtless regretting his earlier greed. He has no choice but to go through with it, and he hasn't a chance of winning. Rumor has it that he has bribed the champion, Sir Boleslaw, to go easy on him, though the truth of that isn't for me to say."

"So the outcome is preordained and probably fixed. No wonder it hasn't drawn much of a crowd," I said. "I've heard that it's possible to get a fighting lesson or two from a champion. How do I go about doing that?"

"You talk to one of his squires, my lord. They're the ones over there in the gray-and-brown livery, good heraldic colors in Poland, though they aren't used in western Europe. You'll have to pay six or twelve pence for the privilege of a lesson, of course. By definition, a professional is one who does it for money."

I took his advice, talked to the squire, and found that the price was twelve pence the lesson. Twelve pence was two weeks pay for a workingman, but a bargain if I could learn something that might save my life. The lesson was to be held right after the combat. Certainly the squire had no doubts about whether his master would be in shape to teach after fighting.

At high noon or thereabouts, a trumpeter played something to get everyone's attention, a priest said a prayer, and the challenger and champion waited with their helmets off before the crowd. The champion was a quiet man in his thirties. The challenger was much younger, with a smile and flashing eyes. He had very smooth and regular features, was handsome almost to the point of being effeminate, and someone told me that his nickname was Pretty Johnnie.

A herald read two proclamations, one from each party in the dispute, which said what they were fighting about. Some peasants had set up benches, and I paid for a seat right on the fifty-yard line, with Anna watching over my shoulder.

Two armored men charged each other from opposite ends of the field, the champion somberly dressed in gray and brown. The challenger was more gaily clad in yellow and blue, his family colors.

As they met, the champion raised his heavy lance, and at first I thought he meant to give the first round to his opponent. Pretty Johnnie's lance slid off the champion's shield, and Sir Boleslaw brought his lance straight down, like a club, on the helmet of the challenger passing by.

I could hear the *bonk* from the sidelines.

The crowd gave a polite round of applause as the challenger slumped in his saddle and then fell from his horse. The champion waved to the crowd to acknowledge the cheer, then dismounted to see if the challenger would get up.

He did, so the champion unsheathed his sword and walked over to him. He politely waited a few minutes until the challenger stopped staggering, then said, "Defend yourself!"

The challenger tried to do that, but made a poor showing. After a few swipes that the champion contemptuously brushed aside, the champion gave him a backhanded blow that caved in the front of his barrel-style helmet. He fell in a heap.

The champion took off his own helmet, raised his sword, and proclaimed that God had upheld the right, and that henceforth Lady Maria's right and title of her lands would go unquestioned. He then bowed and returned to his tent.

Several people came out to tend the unfortunate challenger and found that they could not remove his helmet. It was bashed in so badly that they had to pick the man up and carry him over to the blacksmith's anvil. Getting that helmet off attracted more interest than the fight itself had, and a crowd gathered to watch the smith go at it with crowbars and hammers. Somebody shouted that they should heat the helmet in the forge to make it easier to bend, and everybody but the challenger laughed.

When they finally got his headgear off, the challenger's face was a red ruin. His nose was smashed flat and all of his front teeth were knocked out. Medieval dentistry being nonexistent, he was maimed for life. Pretty Johnnie wasn't pretty anymore.

# Chapter Seventeen

As arranged, I went for my lesson to the champion's pavilion, a large circular tent, big enough for a man to ride through on horseback. He used it at tournaments, where it was considered classy not to show yourself until ready to fight.

"You'll forgive me if I don't rise," the champion said. "Sometimes an old knee injury of mine acts up. I take it that you're the fellow my squire talked to. From your height, I'd guess you are the Sir Conrad Stargard everybody's been talking about."

"Guilty," I said. "That was quite a beating you gave Pretty Johnnie. I thought you were supposed to go easy on him, Sir Boleslaw."

"You heard about that, huh? Well, before you go thinking ill of me, just remember that I do this sort of thing for a living, my expenses are high, and the widow couldn't afford to pay me much. What she paid me didn't cover my overhead and expenses getting here. But it is the off-season, her cause was just, and my overhead would have gone on anyway, so I took the job. Can you really blame me for taking almost three times as much from the challenger, not to throw the fight—I wouldn't have done that for any money—but just to not hurt him badly?"

"But you maimed him for life!"

"True. My employer hated him and wanted it that

way. A professional often has to walk a thin line to try to satisfy everybody. As I set it up, my employer is satisfied, and the challenger has no legitimate complaint. After all, he could have stayed knocked out after that blow I gave him to the head, the fight would have been declared over, and he wouldn't have been seriously hurt."

"Then why did he get up and fight? He must have known that he couldn't win."

"He got up because he was too angry to think straight. You saw what I did to him. A Florentine Flick to brush off his lance, and then I took him down with the Club of Hercules. I wouldn't have dared try those on another pro, and by using them on him, I showed him up for the buffoon that he is. Yet I can always claim that my attack was designed to not injure him, which it didn't. As to the subsequent face injury, why that was a single blow, and who is to say how well his helmet was made?"

"So you set it up to satisfy all parties and keep your own nose clean."

"Of course, Sir Conrad. There's more to this business than meets the eye. Anyway, that dog turd was trying to throw a widow and child off their lands. He got less than he deserved. But that's not what you came to see me about. You're worried about meeting Sir Adolf next Christmas."

"Who? And when?" I said.

"They haven't told you yet? I guess that's only to be expected. The concerned party is always the last to know. It's been bandied around the circuit for weeks, so I'll tell you about it. Just act surprised when you hear about it officially, since the heralds like to think that what they do is important. The short of it is that on the third day before Christmas, you will meet on the field at Okoitz with the Crossman Champion, Sir Adolf, in a fight to the death, with no quarter allowed. He's going to kill you, so your best bet is to sell what you can and run away. That's my advice and it's well worth the twelve pence you're going to pay me."

"If I run away, a hundred forty children will be sold into slavery. I can't allow that."

"Those poor bastards are going to be sold in Constantinople whether you're a live coward or a dead hero. You don't look to be a starry-eyed fool, of the sort who memorizes the 'Song of Roland' and bores people with it at parties. You're a sensible man. Do the sensible thing and run."

"Sir Boleslaw, I tell you I can't. But look here. If this Sir Adolf is so good, why can't I hire a champion as well? I'm not a poor widow. I can afford the best!"

"No, you can't, because the best will be fighting against you. All the rest of us are inferior to Sir Adolf, and we know it. This is a rough business. A fool doesn't survive long in it, and neither do the suicidal. There's not enough money in Christendom to pay me or anyone else to go up against him in a fight to the death. What good would money do me in hell? Because that's exactly where suicides go, and fighting Sir Adolf is straightforward self-destruction! *Run away.*"

"Okay. Thank you for the advice. But I didn't come here for advice, I came here for a fighting lesson."

"As you will, Sir Conrad. But it's a waste of time."

He picked up a pair of wooden practice swords and we went outside. We were both already in armor, and that was all the athletic equipment required.

"I trust that fighting afoot will satisfy you, Sir Conrad, since my charger is being rubbed down and won't be ready for hours."

I said that this would be fine. We sparred around for a while, and I could tell that he was pulling his blows, as one would do with an amateur, and all the while pointing out various shortcomings in my style. But despite the pulled blows, I was still receiving a serious bruising while I don't think I got a good one in on him.

"Your swordwork isn't bad, if a bit slow," he said at last.

"I'm used to a lighter sword."

"More the fool, you. But your real problem is in your shieldwork. The shield is even more important than the sword, since you can make a mistake with the sword and live. That doesn't often happen with the shield. We'll work on it a bit."

I received a further bruising while he kept yelling about how slow I was. I got to anticipating his blows, but that didn't satisfy him either.

"*No*, stupid! You're covering your eyes too soon! You don't even know what I could be doing!"

"So what else could you do?" I yelled back.

"I could do *this!*"

I awoke some hours later, still stretched out on the ground. My helmet had been removed and a pillow put under my head. A horse blanket was stretched over me. I groaned.

One of Sir Boleslaw's squires got up from the stool where he'd been waiting.

"Sir Boleslaw told me that he still feels that your most sensible route is to run away, but that if you must fight, your only hope is to defeat Sir Adolf with your lance, since you have no hope with sword and shield.

"He also asked me to remind you that you owe him twelve pence."

I got up, paid the kid, and rode back to Three Walls in the afternoon.

A Herald from Duke Henryk arrived. The Trial with the Crossmen had been Arranged. I was to be In Arms on the Field of Honor at Okoitz at Noon, Three Days Before Christmas. I was to have All Property Seized in the Affray with me, including The Slaves.

The guy was actually able to talk with capital letters. He even kept it up when he was off-duty, all the way through supper. The girls were not impressed. We gave him one of the spare huts for the night, but I'm pretty sure he slept alone.

Still, the duke had gotten me a longer stay of execution than I had expected.

I'd been trying to spend at least an hour a day talking to Anna, though often I couldn't spare that much time. It was fascinating to talk to a member of an alien species.

She was very fuzzy about her ancestry. She was definitely of the seventh generation since the creation of her species, yet she always talked about her ancestors in the first person, as though she had been the first one created. She was perfectly capable of using second and third person with regard to everyone except her direct ancestors. Furthermore, she always used the feminine forms on them, never the masculine. I couldn't figure it out.

In most ways she was simple, down to Earth. She had no interest in philosophy, nor could she see why anyone would. Mathematics beyond simple arithmetic, theology beyond the simplest moral rules, scientific theory or anything else the least bit cerebral were completely uninteresting and totally beyond her.

Yet she was by no means stupid. Given a practical problem, she never failed to come up with a practical solution. A case in point:

U KENT PUT LENS EN HOL, she spelled out. Her spelling was as atrocious as she had warned it would be. Furthermore, it never improved.

"I can't put the lance in the hole," I agreed. "Yes, that about sums up the main problem."

I KEN.

"You can skewer the quintain? Anna, you don't have hands. How could you hold a lance?"

PUT HUK EN SADL. PUT HUK EN BRYDL. PUT BRYDL EN ME. PUT LENS EN 2 HUK. I PUT LENS EN HOL.

"You think you can? We'll try it girl! I'll have the saddler work up those hooks right now. I bet he can have it done by morning. Good night, Anna, and thanks for the idea."

We were on the practice field half an hour before Sir Vladimir. We tried out Anna's idea, and it worked, every time. She was as deft with a lance as Sir Vladimir.

Furthermore, her guiding the lance left my right hand free to do other things, like having my sword drawn and hidden by my shield. If Anna's lancework didn't get the bastard, I'd be there a half second later with my sword!

We were practicing this double-hitter plan, striking the top of the post with the flat of my sword after Anna threaded the shield, as Sir Vladimir came out. He watched us dumbfounded.

"Sir Conrad, I can scarcely believe that you are finally scoring on the quintain. Getting in a swordstroke besides is—is fabulous! How—?"

So I explained Anna's idea to him. Sir Vladimir had taken Anna's spelling-out of words in stride, as if it was only to be expected. Any horse who could run the way she could had to be magic, and after that anything was possible, even probable. Furthermore, Annastashia had been teaching him to write. His spelling was about the same as Anna's, so it looked all right to him.

He scratched his chin. "I don't *think* it's illegal, but I wouldn't brag about the tactics you plan to use."

"Right. This is my secret weapon!"

"Well, in all events you seem to have it down pat, so let's get into some of the fine points of the lance . . ."

The weeks drifted by. It was a brisk fall day and the carpenters were assembling the combination outer wall-apartment house.

We had strung two hefty ropes from the tops of the cliffs on either side of the entrance to the valley. A framework was hung on wheels between the ropes and a system of ropes, pulleys, and winches allowed eight men aloft to use the framework like an overhead bridge crane. It gave us a "skyhook" over the entire construction area, and things were going up pretty fast. After months of preparation, when it seemed to the men that nothing was getting done, suddenly we had almost a quarter of our future home up in a single day. The happy mood was infectious.

Count Lambert and a retinue of a dozen knights arrived in the late afternoon.

"Count Lambert, welcome, my lord!" I was on the top of the building, seven stories above him. I signaled the crane operators, who quickly lowered me to the ground.

"Hello, Sir Conrad. Dog's blood, but that looked like fun! May I try it?"

"If you wish, my lord, I'll have them take us both to the top." Six men running in a huge hamster cage high above soon got us to the top. All of the foundations were visible from up there, and I pointed out where the church would go, and the inn and the icehouse, and the sauna.

"You're making good progress, Sir Conrad. In another year or two, this will be a fine town."

"Another year, my lord? These buildings will all be up in three weeks."

"Impossible! Not even *you* could accomplish that."

"Another wager, my lord? Say twenty muleloads of your cloth against forty loads of my bricks and mortar?" I'd never bet money with Lambert again, but somehow he saw goods and services in a different light.

"Done! You'll be making bricks then?"

"Yes. We found clay in the old mine, and we'll be building brick ovens as soon as we get our living arrangements set up. We've also found a seam of iron ore, and by spring I hope to be producing iron in decent quantities."

"My boy, you won't be alive in the spring. You won't be alive on Christmas. Have you forgotten your trial?"

"No, my lord. But I'm going to win."

"Your faith is touching. What's that big round stone hole?"

"That will be our icehouse, my lord. Actually, it will be three buildings, one inside another. The circular stone wall you see will be decked over and used as a dance floor. It will have a roof over it but no sides.

"A second building, four yards smaller in diameter and three yards shorter will be built inside of it, completely underground. The space between them will be filled with sawdust and wood chips, a fair insulator.

"The third building will be inside the second, and will be six yards smaller and six shorter than it. Here, the space between will be packed with snow this winter. I calculate that this much snow should take more than a year to melt. We'll have fresh vegetables well into the winter and cold beer all summer long."

"Still, that's a vast hole."

"Sixteen yards deep, my lord, and thirty-six across."

When we got down, I had Krystyana scurry off to the kitchens and see what could be done about something special for supper, and I told Natalia to spread the word among all the young ladies that if any of them wanted to spend the night with a real count or one of his knights, now was the time to get fancied up for a dance. She certainly knew his tastes.

As we went to supper Count Lambert said, "All the tables are the same height. Which is for us?"

"They're a convenient height for eating, my lord. It is

my custom here that all should eat the same food, and off the same tables. It's handy. I often tell my men at dinner what they will be doing the next day. I find that they work better if they've had time to think it out. As to where you should eat, well, eat wherever the lion sleeps."

"And where does the lion sleep?"

"Anywhere he wants to, my lord. Who would argue with a lion?"

That got a laugh, and Count Lambert settled into a side table. One of the joys of the thirteenth century was that the oldest, tiredest jokes were fresh leg-slappers.

The usual thirteenth-century dinner table was wide enough for only one person. People sat on one side and the servants walked on the other. My tables were the twentieth century norm, and there were no servants at Three Walls.

Krystyana hadn't thought to assign anyone to pretend they were servants, and Natalia's band of hopefuls was out scrubbing down and making themselves presentable.

We normally ate cafeteria-style, with attendants at the meat, beer, and anything-expensive counters, and help yourself at everything else. Now the workers were going through the line and some were eating, while my liege lord was waiting to be served.

I didn't know how to solve the problem, so I asked my boss. "My lord, may I ask you to clear up a point of courtesy? If the customs of a vassal are different from the customs of his liege lord, whose customs should be followed?"

"That depends on where they are, Sir Conrad. At the liege lord's manor, the vassal should punctiliously follow the customs of his lord. When on the vassal's estates, the liege lord should follow his vassal's customs unless these are offensive to him. In that case, the lord should so inform the vassal, and the vassal should in courtesy do as his liege lord wishes, at least while the liege lord is around."

"Thank you, my lord. You see, in my land we do not have servants except at an inn. I am not used to having personal servants, and prefer to do without them. What I am trying to say is that I don't have anybody trained to serve you properly. Would you be offended if I asked you to get your own food, as I normally do? Or shall I ask some of the ladies to serve us, even though they'll probably botch the job."

"I was *wondering* when you were going to offer us something to eat! I can't see where a walk across the room will hurt me or mine in the least." We took cuts at the head of the chow line, of course. Rank hath some privileges, even at Three Walls.

Back at the table, Count Lambert said, "So you always eat the same food as your peasants?"

"That is my custom, my lord."

"Remarkable. And you always feed them this good?"

"I'm afraid not. We usually have one meat dish at supper, and none at dinner. It is unusual for us to have ham, venison, and bison at the same meal. Krystyana is in charge of our kitchen and I suspect that, in your honor, she cooked all the meat we had.

"We're not at all self-sufficient in food here, and about the only meat we get is what the hunters bring in. I plan to bring sheep to these hills, but that's a long-term project."

"You'll find ewes to be very cheap. To increase my supply of raw wool for my mills, I have forbidden the slaughter of any ewe less than ten years old, or the selling of them outside my lands. Many are complaining that they cannot possibly feed them through the winter, but I'm not going to relent. If they have to find a way, they will."

"Perhaps I can help, my lord. For three months, I've had a small flock of sheep eating nothing but fresh pine needles. It's not their favorite food, but none of them have starved."

"Interesting, but it must be a great deal of work, cutting that many branches."

"Less than you'd think, my lord. You have to cut the tops off trees to fell the really big ones. I plan to keep my four topmen going all winter, and I calculate that they should be able to keep a thousand sheep alive."

"You must show me your ways at cutting trees."

"First thing in the morning, my lord. In about a month, I'm planning to have a big Mongol-style hunt.

Perhaps you and your knights would like to join us."

"A Mongol hunt? I thought you hated Mongols."

"I do. But that doesn't mean that I can't learn from them."

"Indeed. How do the Mongols hunt?"

"They surround the biggest area they can with all their men, and since that can be as many as a million, the area can be as big as all Poland. Then they beat the bushes, working inward, being careful to let no animal out, but not killing any either. They might spend weeks driving all of the beasts to a central enclosure. Then, under the eyes of their leader, their *Kakhan*, they slaughter every single animal in what amounts to a major battle.

"I don't plan anything so big or so thorough. We'll release all the female deer, bison, and other large herbivores, as well as the young and one-sixth of the males. We have to make sure that there will be game next year.

"Dangerous animals—wolves, bears, wild boar, and so on—will all be killed. I don't want them in my woods, hurting my people. The smaller animals—rabbits, birds, and the like, well, we'll miss so many of those in the round up that I don't think we have to worry about future generations."

"I like it. I'll come. You'll build this enclosure large enough for the kill to be sporting?"

"I'm building it right now. I plan to run them right through the main gates of Three Walls. All the area beyond will be our killing ground. My thought was to distribute one-sixth of the meat to the noblemen who participated, a twelfth to any peasants not living at Three Walls, and to keep the rest to feed my people here. Do you think that would be fair?"

"Very. I think most knights might have more than they could carry back, unless they brought pack mules, and that would be impolite. You'd be expected to provide a feast before and after the hunt, of course. You mention other peasants. Whose?"

"Well, there are Sir Miesko's people and my own yeomen, my lord, and—"

"That's something I wanted to talk to you about.

Were there really twenty-seven squatters on my land when I gave it to you?"

"It appears so, my lord."

"Dog's blood!" he swore. "There must be hundreds on my other lands! How the devil am I going to flush them all out?"

"Why not do what I did, my lord? Turn a liability into an asset. Swear them in as yeomen, take less from them than you would from a peasant, and give them less as well. You'll get something where you got nothing before, and they get the peace of mind of knowing that they are legitimate and have certain legal protections."

"An interesting thought. I'll think on it. But how the devil do I contact them to make my offer?"

"I'm not sure, my lord, but my experience has been that people of a certain type usually all know one another. If you wish, I'll have my bailiff see what can be done. He'll never admit to anything, but I'd bet that he can get your message across."

"Good, though one wager a day is sufficient. Have him come with us tomorrow."

"Tomorrow, my lord?"

"Yes. There is a certain ceremony that we have not yet done. The beating of your bounds. We must ride the boundaries of your lands so that all may know where they are and there will be no future disagreements. Sir Miesko and Baron Jaraslav will meet us at their borders at the proper times tomorrow. But for now, I am sated. Krystyana makes a good meal. Did you have any entertainment planned, Sir Conrad?"

"A dance, my lord. With any luck, you might find a lady that you find suitable for the evening."

"Excellent, but you really must get into the habit of telling the peasants what to do, rather than just asking them."

# Chapter Eighteen

THE LUMBERMEN had gotten to playing a rough game. The topmen would start to climb a tree to cut the top off, and two of the tree fellers would immediately start to cut down that same tree. The idea of the game was to see if the topmen could finish before the fellers cut the tree down under them. I told them not to do that, but they didn't pay much attention to me. I probably wasn't assertive enough. The topmen were getting pretty insufferable, strutting around, wearing their spikes *everywhere*. Maybe, deep down inside, really I wanted to see them lose.

Count Lambert was impressed with the game, as well as the speed with which my people could bring down a huge tree. Part of his philosophy, or perhaps character, was that if anybody else did anything that looked dangerous, he had to do it, too.

"You've done this, haven't you, Sir Conrad?"

"Yes, my lord, I had to show them how to do it."

"Good! Then you can show me as well. You peasants, strip off that equipment and lend it to us."

The topmen weren't happy about being called peasants, and they liked lending out "their" equipment even less. There had been a rash of jokes going around about topmen taking baths with their spikes on, as well as making love with the same gear that they climbed trees with.

But there wasn't much they could do but comply, which they did.

The count always picked up everything quickly, and we were soon at the top sawing through the tree. He worked so fast that keeping up with him, I didn't have time to get scared.

When the top came down and we were whipping back and forth fifteen stories up, Count Lambert looked down and said, "What? No one is cutting the tree off below us!"

"My lord, would you dare cut a tree when the duke was up it?"

"I see your point, but dog's blood! I think we would have won!"

We soon left to beat the bounds. Count Lambert had decreed that it should be a festive occasion, so besides all the knights present, Krystyana and her ladies came along, as well as the girls Lambert and his knights had slept with the night before, in borrowed finery, and some of them on pack mules since we had a limited supply of palfreys.

My bailiff was with us, at Lambert's request, and Piotr Kulczynski came along, since he had nothing better to do and it gave him further opportunity to gaze at Krystyana from afar. The idea was to have as many witnesses as possible, and preferably young people, who would be around longer to remember things.

Sir Miesko and Lady Richeza met us at their lands and the party went its way along our mutual border, with Count Lambert pointing out the landmarks to all and sundry. In the days before accurate surveying, this was the accepted way to record boundaries.

Baron Jaraslav and Sir Stefan did not meet us at the appointed time and place. We stopped and unpacked lunch while we waited for them, but even after a leisurely dinner, we were still waiting. Count Lambert was getting angry. "Sir Daniel! You did go to them yesterday, didn't you? You told them to meet us here and now?"

"Of course, my lord."

"Well, damn them!"

"There have been hard feelings between them and me, my lord," I said.

"They can hate you all they want, but they can't disobey their liege! Mount up! We'll go without them! Sir Miesko, stay with us as a witness."

So we finished my borders without Sir Stefan being along. In later days, I sometimes wondered if Lambert didn't assign me some of the baron's lands just to spite him. One day that border would cause me a good deal of grief.

On the trip back to Three Walls, we fanned out in hunting array and with luck took a wild boar and a bison. This was good because I had no meat in my larder with which to feed my guests, and the nearest supermarket was seven hundred years away.

It was dusk when we got back, and Yashoo had the apartment building half up. After all, it was a simple matter of assembling precut pieces, like putting together a huge tinker-toy set. I had checked every piece myself, so of course they fit right together.

Count Lambert was awestruck. "They did this much without your being here? I might as well concede our bet right now. I'll ship your twenty loads of cloth as soon as I return to Okoitz."

"I'll take it in medium-grade linen, my lord."

That gave us curtains and a spare set of sheets.

In the summer, everyone including me went barefoot, but with cold weather coming on, the workers started making shoes for their families. The usual peasant footwear was made of birch bark. You wrapped your feet in rags and laced on soles of bark with leather thongs. The soles lasted a week or two and then you needed new ones.

At first, I was saddened that this was all they had, but then I did some time studies on what was required to tan leather and what was required to cut new soles out of birch bark. A man could cut a set of bark shoes for his entire family in less than an hour. Tanning a hide with medieval methods took months, and leather soles didn't last out the season.

It was over fifty times cheaper to wear birch bark. I suspect that leather shoes became popular only when birch trees became rare. But birch trees were not that common on my lands. I had some birch groves planted, but for a few years we were buying birch bark. I found that it was useful for writing paper as well as shoes, and far cheaper than parchment.

By the time the first snows were flying, our basic living quarters had been completed. Well, we never stopped building, but the apartment house was up and the plumbing was in. I suppose I should describe it.

The building was a hundred ninety yards long, reaching from cliff face to cliff face, and was eighteen yards wide. Structurally, it was really five buildings, with firewalls between each.

The basement, with thick wooden fire doors, eventually to be sheathed in iron, stretched the full length. Because of the slope of the land, it was mostly exposed on the outer side, but it had no windows. From outside the valley, it was a solid masonry first floor. The basement was mostly in dry-food storage, except that the brewery was relocated there from its temporary building. A short tunnel sloped downward from the basement to the ice-house.

The first floor contained the passageway to the main (and only) gate, and off this passageway was a ramp down to the basement. Incoming food supplies could go directly into storage. Next to the gate was the main bathroom, which had showers, sinks, a hot tub, and a dozen flush toilets.

Then came the laundry room, mostly more sinks and draining racks. I'd had some wooden scrub boards made, a major improvement over the local practice of beating dirty clothes between two rocks. After all the trouble I'd had wheedling cloth out of Count Lambert, I had no desire to see it beaten to shreds by some ignorant women.

After that was the kitchen, where the stoves also heated the water for the other plumbing facilities. More porcelain sinks were dedicated to the business of washing dishes.

Our only source of water was the mine. We split small logs, burned them hollow, then tied them together to form a pipe. A trench was dug following the contour of the land, gently sloping from the mine to the apartment house. The wooden pipes were carefully fitted together in it and packed in clay to slow leakage.

The water seemed pure enough all summer, but I knew that would change once we hit coal. We had plenty of water head, so we built three big filters, each twelve yards high, one of gravel, one of crushed limestone and one of sand. Our water had to flow through all three before it got to us. The filtration system was probably overkill, but I had no way of testing the purity of the water, and an epidemic could wipe us out.

Below the filters was a big stone reservoir, and like everything else in the water system, it was covered with at least a yard of dirt as an insulator. A frozen waterline would have been a major nuisance.

The biggest room in the building was the dining room. It was two stories tall and could seat a thousand people. It stretched across two of the separate structures, right through the firewall and had a huge stone arch in the middle of it. I worried about this breach in our fire defenses, but it seemed important to me that we should all eat together. I salved my conscience by installing two fire hoses near the archway. A balcony ran around the second floor, connecting to the staircases going up.

The second floor went between the two-story gate passage and the dining room. It contained the nursery, the schoolrooms, and our library, once we had enough books for it to deserve that title. It also contained the store. There you could buy all of the sundries and small luxuries that most people wanted.

That was a major innovation, since except in the larger cities, you could only buy things when a peddler happened by. Sometimes housewives went for months without being able to buy pins or needles, so they tried to keep a small supply of money for buying such things whenever they were available. They called this fund their "pin money."

Since we bought in quantity and our markup was only a hundred percent, instead of the usual three hundred, our prices were generally much less than a backpacking peddler could sell for. Yet it was profitable, since one sales girl, Janina, ran the place, and volume was decent.

Prices were marked and that's what things sold for. No haggling allowed.

We treated our vendors the same way. We requested bids, specifically stating the quantities and qualities desired. We always bought from the lowest bidder, and if it turned out later that the product was substandard, we didn't ask him to bid next time. These business methods were denounced from all quarters, but since it was profitable to do business with us, our suppliers eventually came around.

Before long, where the town guilds let us get away with it, each of the Pink Dragon Inns had a similar store. Where they didn't, we often set up a store just outside the city limits, and ran it on a break-even basis. We busted more than one guild that way, but in so doing we drastically raised the standard of living.

Above the gate were my own quarters, with a small restroom, two toilets and two sinks.

Sir Vladimir stayed at my apartments, as did Krystyana, her four main ladies and a varying number of other girls.

With Krystyana managing a kitchen that fed eight hundred people, Yawalda taking care of the animals and coordinating all our transport, Janina handling the store and our stores—both buying and selling—Natalia acting as my executive secretary and records keeper, and Annastashia managing my personal household, I could hardly expect the girls to keep the place clean besides.

To do that, we brought in a half-dozen of the workers' daughters. My handmaidens had handmaidens.

But I got the use of them. Krystyana believed that fair was fair.

My apartment was larger and more sumptuous than I had originally planned, but Sir Vladimir convinced me that it was politically necessary to impress noble guests.

Anna had her own stall in the barn, which she used mostly for eating, since she preferred the usual fare of horses to that of humans. But she usually stayed with us. This meant that the stairways had to be bigger, the floors stronger, and the door handles had to be designed so she could work them, since she liked sitting in on the conversations.

Everybody was already convinced that I was insane, so what the heck. Anyway, I was lord, and rank hath its privileges. Anna was good people.

Over the rest of the buildings were apartments, four stories of them. The typical apartment was nine yards long and three yards wide, although they varied somewhat in size, according to the size of a man's family.

Bachelors usually bunked four to a room, as did bachelorettes. As time went on, and the ladies discovered that it was possible to be single and survive without social stigma, more and more of them stayed single longer. Some of them even held out until they were eighteen, but I get ahead of myself.

On each floor, apartments were arranged in clusters of five, around a stairway that zigzagged between floors. On the second of the four floors, the hallway was much smaller and there was a restroom. Two toilets and sinks for twenty families.

By the standards of the twentieth century, it was a crowded, substandard slum dwelling. By the standards of the thirteenth century, it was fabulous luxury, and everybody, including the people who lived there, thought I was crazy to build so lavishly.

The Pink Dragon Inn Number Three was running under the command of Tadeusz's second son, Zygmunt Wrolawski. This was a smaller version of the inn at Cieszyn, and at about the same level of plushness. It had stables for animals and thirty rooms for rent, mostly for merchants.

But the inn was essentially a workingman's bar, for a man needs to get away from his family occasionally, and to fraternize with other men. The costumes of the waitresses encouraged that and eventually the place went topless. One waitress tried it on her own and without any encouragement from me. She made more in tips than all the others put together. In a week, they were all doing it.

Somehow, despite the lack of a nudity taboo, and despite the fact that we only had the one shower room and men and women used it together, and despite the fact that beer was far cheaper in the dining room not two hundred yards away, the men still preferred to have their beer brought to them by a pretty bare-breasted girl.

The topless fad spread to all the other Pink Dragon Inns, and when it did, profits increased remarkably.

The men paid for their pleasures. The inn recaptured over forty percent of what I paid out in salaries, and the store took in another thirty-five. Most of the rest was saved. That is to say, they could leave their salaries uncollected and draw interest on it, although we had to resort to certain subterfuges to get around the Church's silly usury laws. The workers claimed damages against me to the tune of eight percent a year for not paying them on time, which was, of course at their option. It's not like I ever missed a payroll.

As things turned out, salaries were only a small part of my net outgo. I soon yielded to pressure for better pay for foremen and general foremen. It really didn't cost much at all. I got most of it back through the inn, the store, and the savings bank.

Then there was a barn for our eight horses, thirty-six pack mules, and fourteen milk cows. Yawalda was in charge of the animals and transportation.

I had insisted that all of our animals be well fed, not for any economic reason, but because of basic decency. I refused to allow any animal of mine to be mistreated. That was contrary to the usual medieval custom of using animals as scavengers, and keeping them underfed so they'd keep at it. So people said that I was crazy; when they noticed that the milk cows continued to give milk all winter long, instead of drying up for lack of food, they claimed it was magic on my part, but they still thought I was crazy.

We also kept two hundred chickens, which lived mostly on table scraps and kitchen waste. Krystyana was a tight-fisted little manager. I am partial to fresh eggs in the morning, and had breakfast served at dawn. More and more people started joining me at it, especially when I moved the dinner hour from ten to noon.

Besides being what I was brought up to be used to, the three-meals-a-day system has certain advantages. Most of the ladies worked half a day. The ten o'clock dinner hour came in the middle of the morning shift. During the winter, many of the men were working at logging operations too far away to come back for a hot lunch. At least we could give them a hot breakfast.

What's more, I liked it that way and I was lord.

I suppose I went a little overboard on the design of the church, but we had all these huge logs and it seemed a shame not to do something that pushed them to their structural limits.

And though our population was still well under a thousand, it would continue growing. Building more apartment houses was to be expected, but a community ought to have one church. If you have two churches, you have two communities.

So we built a church that sat four thousand.

I thought a long while before I decided on a name for the place. I called it the Church of Christ the Carpenter.

Imagine two big A-frame buildings, each as long and as high as it is wide, crossing in the middle, and you have the shape of it. Four massive masonry pillars went down to bedrock, and supported the structure, one at each corner.

The four huge triangular walls, each eighteen stories high, would eventually be in stained glass, but for now they had to be boarded over. Even without the glass, it was impressive, as a church should be. No fancy statues or bright paint, just huge rough logs high in the hills.

Without a traveling crane, getting those logs in place was a problem. We deliberately left several big trees standing right within the construction site. Those trees became the masts to which we attached ropes and pulleys to haul up the biggest structural components.

Once the central pyramid of our four biggest logs and a massive wooden central hub was up, and could be used as a support to haul up the rest of the parts, we carefully cut down the original trees. There were some tight moments when they were felled, for if they came down wrong, they could wreck the structure, and we would not be able to set it up again. But I guess that God didn't want his church to fall over. It worked.

We built the church pretty much from the top down. The roof went up first, then the walls, finally the floor. I don't think that the carpenters ever stopped shaking their heads over that one, even after it went up on schedule.

I had the pews, altar, and communion rail permanently installed, as opposed to the usual medieval practice of making them movable. Nobody was going to use *my* church for a beer bust, as happened elsewhere.

A month after Lambert's visit, the Mongol hunt went off very well, I thought. Over forty knights accepted my invitation, including the Banki brothers, which Janina, Yawalda, and Natalia appreciated. And Friar Roman had come from Okoitz to observe.

With all of my people and Sir Miesko's, with men, women, and older children going at it, we had over seven hundred people beating the bushes, backed up by the knights in case of trouble.

Starting out almost a hundred yards apart in the morning, they were shoulder to shoulder at sunset, and the valley was full of animals. Bison and wolves and bears. There were so many that during the night I had to give orders that no one was allowed out of the building. Not that anybody much cared. They were all too busy playing in the bathroom.

The showers were the biggest hit of all, with people standing under them back to back and belly to belly and using up hot water by the ton. The kitchen stoves were going full blast and nonstop, but they were still hard-pressed to keep the water warm.

I suppose it's harder to get enthused about a flush toilet, but they caused considerable wonderment. One knight complained that he washed his small clothes in one of the low sinks, pressed the little lever and they disappeared!

Natalia had counted the animals as they ran over the drawbridge and through the gate, and toward the end she had a different person counting each species.

We had over four thousand deer, eleven hundred wild boar, four hundred bison, six hundred wolves, two hundred elk (or moose, as the Americans call them), one hundred forty bears, plus lynx, wildcats, wood grouse, heathcocks, rabbits and other small game. And eight of the biggest cows Natalia had ever seen.

People couldn't believe her when she read the list, but after all, these were all the animals living on forty square miles of rich land.

They believed her in the morning when the killing began. The knights rampaged for two days, exhausting themselves physically before their bloodlust was sated. The commoners had to scurry to drag in all the bodies, and gut and skin them.

Tadaos the bowman begged permission to join in the slaughter, and I told him that he could bag a few, but I didn't want to spoil the nobles' fun. He strung his bow in an instant and fired off four arrows in as many seconds. Each came to rest in the head of an animal: three bucks and a wild boar. Every one of them was more than two hundred yards away. His shooting was still as good as it had been last fall. Then he unstrung his bow, and with a look of contentment on his face, recovered his arrows before he went back to help out with the skinning and gutting.

I had reserved all of the hides for myself, since we needed leather for a lot of things, and we exhausted all of my salt just salting down the skins. I had to buy three more tons out of Cieszyn before it was all over.

Five of our huge beer barrels were pressed into service holding salted meat. For a few weeks, we were back to having only water to drink, until more barrels were made.

The sauna/smokehouse was a nine-yard stone dome, and was packed almost solid.

The beehive coke oven had just been completed, and hadn't yet been used for coal. It was the same size as the sauna, since they had used the same centering on both. It too was used as a smokehouse, and the woodcutters were hard-pressed to find enough hickory to keep both fires smoldering.

In the Middle Ages, the most highly prized meat was not the muscle tissue but the internal organs. Everyone gorged themselves on liver and hearts and kidneys.

The kitchens turned out head cheese by the ton and I resolved that next year we'd have some sausage-making machinery. This year, there just wasn't time.

But to me, the most interesting things were the aurochs. There were eight of them, a bull, four cows, and three calves. These were huge wild cattle that are extinct in the twentieth century. The last of the species was killed in Poland in the sixteenth.

They were black with a white stripe down the back, from head to tail, and they were huge. While I was sitting on Anna, who was bigger than the average warhorse, the bull could raise his head and his eyes were higher than my own.

"He's mine!" Sir Vladimir shouted, lowered his lance and would have charged if I hadn't stopped him.

"Remember the rules," I told him. "At least one-sixth of the males must be kept for breeding, and he's the only one. Anyway, I'm going to domesticate him. Think of the meat on that animal! There must be three tons of it!"

"You'll never domesticate that beast, Sir Conrad."

"I can try."

With a lot of work and one serious injury, we managed to herd the aurochs into another valley, then cut down a few strategically placed trees at the entrance to barricade them in. Eventually, we had a good-sized herd of them, but I get ahead of myself.

Six dozen bucks were saved to provide fresh meat for us through the winter and there were no complaints when I had the female half of our catch released along with the young and a sixth of the males. We had more fresh meat than anybody had ever seen before.

Friar Roman had come from Okoitz, where he had been studying clothmaking, at the behest of his abbot.

At supper, he presented me with a beautifully illuminated manuscript of the deed to my property. It was as colorful as a church altar and radiant with gold foil.

"It's wonderful!" I said. "But where did you get all the paints and gold leaf?"

"Oh, I have quite a painting box now. It was given to me by a wealthy widow as a pious act for the Church. Actually, my vow of poverty has made me much better off than I was. Soon, my vow of obedience is going to give me command of a cloth factory at Cracow. I think perhaps I shouldn't discuss my vow of chastity, but Okoitz is a marvelous place."

It was agreed by all that we would do the hunt again next year, and people were courteous enough not to remind me that I wasn't going to be here next year.

Sir Miesko said that next time we should sweep his lands as well, and Count Lambert was seriously thinking of staging a Mongol hunt covering his entire territory.

"Think of it," he said. "We might rid all my lands of wolves and bears! Do you realize how many of my people they kill every year? It must be dozens! And the food we'd gather!"

Someone pointed out that the beaters would have to be in the field for weeks. How would they be fed and housed? How could they keep the wolves from sneaking out of the ring in the dark?

No one knew, but everyone agreed to think on it.

When it came to the division of the spoils, there was so much that we didn't bother trying to set up a fair system. I simply told everyone to take as much as they could carry. When I noticed some of my yeomen coming back for thirds, I put a stop to it.

We had skinned and gutted the wolves, cats, and other normally inedible animals and hung them up outside the gate. I said that if anybody kept dogs, they were welcome to come back and pick up the dog meat.

But when a few knights came back with pack animals, the carcasses were gone. Some peasants must have taken them for eating.

Until the time of the big hunt, the people at Three Walls had been eating a largely vegetarian diet, and that mostly grains, with only a small amount of meat and fresh greens in it. But from then on, we became meat-eaters, and over half of our caloric intake was in animal products. The children grew taller.

Later that fall we finally struck coal, and we found that we could make coke. This involved cleaning the coal of any obvious incursions of clay and stone, then baking the impurities out of it.

The beehive oven was a nine-yard dome that had a hole in the top through which the coal was loaded.

The rest of the oven was covered with dirt as an insulator, except for a doorway for extracting the coke. The coal was leveled with long rakes through the doorway to the depth of a yard and a half. Then a fire was started on top of the coal and the supply of air was restricted.

Soon the whole bed of coal was smoldering, and the dome of the oven reflected the heat downward. This eventually melted the coal, and volatile material—sulfur, ammonia, hydrocarbons—was vaporized to rise to the surface and be burned. It stank abominably.

The operator peeked through the small hole at the top of the doorway. When he saw that the volatiles had been burned off, the coal was again a solid, and the top of the bed was glowing, he inserted a brass spraying-apparatus through the top hole and fed enough water through it to quench the fire without unduly cooling the oven.

The coke, which was by then almost pure carbon, was shoveled out with very long-handed shovels. The door-way was bricked over again and new coal was loaded from the top.

If the process was done properly, the oven was hot enough to restart the new batch of coal by itself, saving a good deal of fuel. Once we got the oven working properly, we ran about one batch a day through. By spring, we had eight ovens going.

The masons could build the new ones through the coldest weather, since each was built next to a functioning oven, which kept the ground thawed, and the domes were built of dry laid sandstone. Mortar would never have stood the heat.

# Chapter Nineteen

BUT NOW it was a week before Christmas, and my stay of execution was over. I had to go and fight and kill or maybe be killed to see if a hundred forty-two children had the right to live normal lives.

My orders were to bring the children to Okoitz, and there wasn't any way around it. But I wasn't going to bring them in chained neck to neck as I'd found them. I was going to bring them as what they had become. The Christian children of Polish Christian people.

If the kids had to go to Okoitz, then their adoptive parents would go with them. That meant just about everybody at Three Walls, so we pretty much shut down the whole town, except for a skeleton crew who kept the chickens fed, the fires going, and the pipes from freezing.

But it meant that if I lost the fight, the Crossmen would have to take Christian children from Christian families, and I didn't think that even they could get away with that. Or maybe they could. But it was worth a try.

It meant a long, two-day walk for eight hundred people, but we were well fed and in good shape. It was cold, but we were well clothed and had plenty of blankets.

We had a long string of pack mules for our baggage and Sir Miesko was expecting us.

My new armor was done, and I'd made Ilya polish it like a mirror. If I had to go out and defend truth, justice,

and the purity of childhood, I was damn well going to go
as a knight in shining armor.

I had him polish my old helmet as well and was wearing it instead of the new one, which was hard to take off.
My new chest and back piece had a circular hole on top
for my head. At this hole the metal collar flanged up and
then out. The new helmet was a clamshell affair that
hinged on top, and it had a ring around the bottom that
fit into the collar flange on the suit below. Two hand-filed
bolts held the sides of the helmet together.

Once the new helmet was on, I could turn my head
from side to side, but I couldn't tilt it. More importantly,
it couldn't be tilted. With my old helmet, a heavy sword
blow could break my neck. With the new one, a blow to
the head was transmitted through the flange to my upper
body.

But the damned thing was a nuisance to put on and
take off. You needed a wrench and a helper.

Anna wore some armor as well. A face plate and a
lobstertail guard for the top of her neck were all she
would accept, and I only got her to wear that by telling
her it was pretty.

The hooks to hold the lance for her were built into
both sides of her face plate, in the hopes that their use
wouldn't be obvious on something strange to people. We
had them on both sides in case they threw a lefty at us.

Having a hook on the saddle was fine when we only
had to hit the hole on a quintain. Hitting a knight required something sturdier.

I had a notch cut into the saddlebow of my warkak. I
could set my lance in it with the handguard, or vamplate,
ahead of the notch. That put the force of the blow on the
saddle and thus on Anna, without my smaller muscles
having to get involved. We had continued practicing
every day and I figured that we were as ready as we
would ever be.

Besides the armor, which covered me from crown to
fingertip to toe, the only other thing I wore was a huge
wolfskin cloak. Anna and I must have looked pretty
awesome. We got a lot of stares, anyway.

Sir Miesko was ready for us, and had a barn set up for
the workers to sleep in. The booty taken from the Cross-

men was already at Okoitz, cooking facilities and supplies of food were arranged. Good neighbors are wonderful.

Sir Vladimir, Sir Miesko, and myself, along with all our ladies, were sitting at supper.

But Sir Miesko and his wife were still convinced that I was soon to die, fancy armor or not. When everybody who knows anything is of the same opinion, you can't help but start to believe them. For five months, everybody I met was certain that I was going to get killed. It was getting to me, and it was hard to stay cheerful. "Okay," I said. "I admit that there is some danger. I could die in a few days. So what do we do about it?"

"Have you given thought to your projects and your plans?" Sir Miesko asked.

"Well, everything goes back to Count Lambert, doesn't it?"

"It does if you make no other provisions for it."

"You're suggesting that I make out a will?"

"A will may or may not be honored. Tell me, is Count Lambert the man you would want to run your estate at Three Walls?" Sir Miesko asked.

"He might do a better job than most. Actually, I think that Sir Vladimir here would be about the best person for it. Can I make him my heir?"

Sir Vladimir looked shocked. "Me? But I'm no master of the technical arts!"

"No, you're not. But you have brains enough to listen to those who know more than you. You're a natural leader, and you care about people. Furthermore, you're an unimpeachable member of the old nobility. I couldn't leave it to Yashoo, for example. The nobles would never stand for it. No, Sir Vladimir, I think you're stuck with it."

Sir Vladimir started to say something, but Sir Miesko cut him off. "Now that that's agreed upon, the question is how best to accomplish it. I've mentioned that a will may or may not stand up. It depends on the duke's mood, which is, in truth, a fickle thing. Still, we should try it, for it costs us only a sheet of parchment.

"But I think that neither the duke nor any other of the nobility would dare to interfere with, say, your daughter's inheritance. After all, their own wealth and position depend on this point of law."

"But I don't have a daughter!" I said.

"But you could. It's obvious that Sir Vladimir and Annastashia have been in love for quite a long time. Even an old man like me can see that. They want to get married but they can't, because Baron Jan would never stand for one of his sons marrying a peasant. His wife is worse."

Vladimir rose in indignation, but Sir Miesko shut him down. "Sit down, Sir Vladimir. I've known your folks for twenty years. They wouldn't even come to my wedding, despite the fact that *I'd* been knighted only weeks before, because my lady was still a commoner."

"Sir Miesko, you are talking about my father and my liege lord!" Sir Vladimir said.

"I'm talking about an old acquaintance, and every word of it is true. You want to marry the girl, don't you?"

"Yes! Of course."

"And you, Annastashia. You want to marry this impetuous young knight, don't you?"

"Oh, yes!"

"Then keep him shut up while we work out how that can be accomplished."

"But she's not my daughter!" I said.

"She can be. Her parents are both dead. You can adopt her. Once she's your daughter and heir, even Baron Jan isn't going to stop his son from marrying the wealthiest heiress in the duchy.

"Oh, I know that your funds are low now, but I've seen what you've accomplished in a few months at Three Walls. In a year, you would have been the richest man in Poland. Even without you, what you've started there will get fabulous wealth. Any man with brains can see it.

"So Annastashia gets the man she wants, Sir Vladimir gets a wife of his choice and more wealth than he's ever dreamed of, and you, Sir Conrad, get an heir who can carry out your plans."

There was no arguing with his reasoning, so Sir Miesko got out parchment, pen and ink, and drafted both a letter of adoption for Annastashia, and a will for me, in which I specifically gave my blessing on the marriage of my daughter to Sir Vladimir.

"You really should get yourself a seal," Sir Miesko said. "A bit late now, though."

Everybody present signed everything, and Sir Miesko affixed his own seal and promised to get the duke's seal on both instruments the next day.

As the party was breaking up, I announced that I had some presents to distribute. I gave Sir Miesko and Sir Vladimir wolfskin capes like my own. "I've had a dozen of these made up," I said. "I'll be giving them to the highest-ranking people who show up at the fight. It takes six wolves to make one of these. I figure that if I can make wearing wolfskin popular, it will give people more incentive to exterminate the wolves.

"Actually, wolfskin is a very sturdy and warm material. It has two different kinds of hair in it. There are the long, stiff hairs you see on the outside and there are shorter, finer hairs, much like wool, next to the skin. A wolf really does have sheep's clothing, underneath.

"Lady Richeza, I couldn't bring your present with me. Indeed, you won't get it until spring. But I've left the design of a complete home water-and-septic system at Three Walls, along with written orders to build one for you.

"You'll have hot, running water in your kitchen as well as a new stove, a complete bathroom, and a small, windmill-operated water tower." She was speechless. Actually, I'd owed her something nice for a long while. That, and I needed somewhere to set up a showplace for our plumbing products, and *nobody* missed stopping at her house when they were in the area. I was a socialist becoming a miserable capitalist.

"As to you girls, I know what you want." I gave Krystyana, Yawalda, Janina, and Natalia each a purse of silver. They each poured it out on the table and squealed their appreciation.

I kept the purse intended for Annastashia in my hand. "As for you, daughter, you've been sleeping with a man before wedlock, and you'll get nothing more out of me until you mend your sinful ways!"

# FROM THE AUTOBIOGRAPHY OF SIR VLADIMIR CHARNETSKI

\* \* \*

For weeks my soul had been troubled. All things for me were reaching a climax, great forces were moving about me, yet there was nothing I could do to affect their resolution.

My friend Sir Conrad was going to his death, and in his dying I would be failing in my oath to the duke to protect him with my life.

My brother Jan had visited me at Three Walls, informing me that my father's anger was even greater than I had feared. Months after the battle with the Crossmen, he was still shouting for my damnation. Never would he bless my marriage to Annastashia or to anyone else.

And lastly, my love was with child. Our child, perhaps my son, was growing in her, and unless I soon took bold action and defied my father, my son would be born a bastard, to be scorned all of his life, and my love would be labeled a strumpet.

I could not stay and marry her in defiance of my liege lord, nor could I go to some foreign country, either. The sum of my wealth was the nine silver pence that I had carried from my home last Easter. Not a penny had I spent since leaving that blacksmith. And nine pence might buy us a single night's lodging on the road. If we left, we would starve within the week.

If I asked it, I knew Sir Conrad would lend me money—rather give it to me—for once he was dead, there would be no way to repay him.

But part of my oath to the Duke Henryk was to report to him anything needful of Sir Conrad's doings. While I had seen the need to report nothing, I was in fact spying on my friend. How then could I with honor accept his money?

Then in but an hour at Sir Miesko's table, all was resolved. Sir Miesko's wisdom and clerkish knowledge and Sir Conrad's goodness days before his own death had resolved my impossible difficulties. I was in something of a shock, and perhaps did not behave quite properly. Even after it was all over, they had to raise me up to put Sir Conrad's death-gift fur cloak on my shoulders.

I had thought Sir Conrad's withholding of the purse from Annastashia to be a mere jest, and in fact he told me later that it was. He wanted to assure Krystyana and the rest that they were not being dropped from favor.

But when I put my arm around my love to lead her to our room, she became quite stiff. She removed my arm and told me that I was acting in unseemly fashion. Then she went off and slept with Yawalda.

We arrived at Okoitz the next day as the sun was setting.

The town was vastly overcrowded, and had not arrangements been made in advance for the housing of the peasants, they would have had to stay outside and freeze.

The entire membership of the Franciscan monastery from Cracow was there, along with many other citizens from that city.

Perhaps a third of the nobility of the entire duchy had arrived or had said that they would come. The Bishop of Cracow had come, and it was said that the Bishop of Wroclaw would soon be arriving.

And of course, merchants of every stripe and product had come sniffing after the profit to be made. Every one of Count Lambert's noblemen was there or would arrive on the morrow, and most brought their wives. This host included my father and mother, but thanks be to God in heaven my Uncle Felix was with them.

"Greetings, my father and my liege," I said to my father formally.

"Vladimir. So you've come to watch the mess you've made," he said coldly.

"Father, the duke—"

"I've talked to the duke, as well as to the count! Somehow you've gotten them both on your side. But to think that my own son would make an oathbreaker of me, it's—"

He suddenly turned and walked away. My mother looked quickly back and forth between us, then fled after my father without saying a word.

Uncle Felix looked at me and said, "I'll talk to you later, boy. Keep your nose up." He went after them.

Sadly, I stared in the direction they had gone. Perhaps I had underestimated my father's anger and intransigence.

I had left Sir Conrad's party to speak with my parents, and in that incredible crowd I did not soon find them.

I know that most of the people had come to see God's will done, that is to say, for a serious purpose. But when old friends meet after months or years, the meeting must needs grow jovial, and the place had the feeling of a carnival wherein I was the only stranger.

As I passed a niche between the church and the castle, where Count Lambert had set some benches, I heard familiar voices speaking. I kept to the shadows and listened.

"I tell you, the man saved my life three different times. Remember when my boat was on the rocks on the Dunajec River, kid? If Sir Conrad hadn't come along our bones would still be there!

"And a few days later at Cracow, the night I paid you off, he was there with a candle and woke me just as three thieves were about to cut my throat and steal my goods!"

"I hadn't heard about that, Tadaos," Friar Roman said.

"Just like him not to say anything about it. I tell you, Sir Conrad is a saint."

"Well, that's for the Church to say. But there's no doubt that this whole mess would never have occurred if he hadn't heeded my pleadings and gone to Sacz to get you out of Przemysl's donjon," Friar Roman said. "He led me to God! I was a sinner before I met him! I was a Goliard poet who sneered at the Church and all that is holy. But his goodness was the example that turned me from my old ways. And his generosity! Do you realize that every day for a week he took every penny he earned working at a job that did not suit him, and gave it to me so that I could eat and have shelter at night? And in return, I brought him the message that will result in his death."

"He never saved my life," Ilya the blacksmith said. "Fact is that one time he almost ended it, when he took off the end of the anvil I was working on with one swipe of that skinny sword of his."

"Did that really happen? I thought it was only a story," Tadaos said.

"It happened. But I'll tell you, Sir Conrad has taught me more about the craft than my father ever did, and my father was a master. I tell you he's too good a man to let die!"

"He's not going to die, not while I can draw a long-bow. You've all seen me shoot. There's no man better at it in the world than me. It's a gift, I tell you. A gift from God. And now I know why God gave it to me.

"I mean to be at the top of that windmill of his on the day of the fight. From there I can hit any man on the tourney field, though none of the Crossmen would be-lieve that an arrow would fly that far, let alone kill a man."

"I've got arrow heads that can punch through any armor," Ilya said. "Even that fancy new stuff I made for Sir Conrad. You're welcome to them."

"I'll take them."

"It won't work, Tadaos. Too many people have heard of your shooting, besides those who have seen it. You haven't exactly kept it a secret!" Friar Roman said. "They'd find you and hang you, and it wouldn't do Sir Conrad a bit of good. Worse, they'd probably call foul on Sir Conrad, and kill him because of your doings."

"There's got to be a way."

The three conspirators were silent for a bit. Then the friar spoke. "If the Crossman was killed by a man, they'd catch him sure. But if it was an Act of God . . ."

"What do you mean?"

"What if golden arrows were to come down from the sky, killing the evil-doers? Isn't that what this trial is all about? To determine the will of God?"

"But I don't have any golden arrows," Tadaos said.

"You will have." Friar Roman opened his painting kit. "I think I have enough gold leaf left to cover about eight of them."

I stepped out of the shadows. "I have heard enough. You varlets are planning a mockery of all that the trial by combat stands for."

"It stands for grown men fighting because they don't have brains enough to settle their differences peacefully!" Ilya said and stood. The muscles rippled huge in the blacksmith's bare arms.

"And it stands for killing the finest man in Christendom because he had balls enough to free those poor children from the Crossmen," Tadaos added. He joined Ilya.

"You filthy peasants! You would speak like this to a true belted knight?"

The little friar stood up between us three big men. "Brothers! Christians, remember you are all brothers under God!" The little man's courage impressed us all, and the two big peasants backed off.

"You, too, Sir Vladimir," he said. "Come, join us. We need your help."

"I should join with peasants to besmear the knightly order?"

"You, too, are in Sir Conrad's debt. Word has it that he has arranged for you to marry his adopted daughter, and thus become his heir. Are you the kind of man who would wish a good friend's death so that you could collect his gold?"

"Of course not, dammit! But—"

"Then sit down and join us. We need your aid, and so does he."

"Just what do you expect me to do?"

Friar Roman said, "Now, here's my plan..."

So thus it was that I found myself riding across the tourney field in the cold of a winter's dawn, waiting to be shot.

The frivolities at Okoitz had lasted well into the night, and the field was completely deserted.

Tadaos had been sure that the weight of the thin gold would throw off his aim, and wanted some practice shots.

Since all was for naught if he missed, Friar Roman had spent the night carefully covering four arrows, and I was up with my shield hung on my lancetip, prancing around on Witchfire to give him a moving target. It is remarkable, the things a true knight finds in the path of duty.

The first arrow fell two yards too low, and I began to wonder if I would die out there. An arrow two yards to the right would pierce my heart.

I tapped my shield four times to the ground in the signal to tell the bowman how low he had shot. He was so far away that he could not see his arrows.

The second just missed the bottom of the shield. Good. It seems Tadaos's problems were in range rather than direction. I might survive. I tapped the ground once.

The third struck my shield fair on, and I raised my arm to the bowman. The fourth struck a finger's width from the third, despite the fact that I had Witchfire at the gallop.

I dismounted to recover the arrows, for we had agreed on at least three practice rounds.

But as I recovered the last, I saw Sir Lestko riding out to me. I could tell it was he by the armorial device on his shield, though I could not have done this with most knights. In the West, it is the custom for a knight to wear his personal device on his shield and elsewhere. In Poland, one wore the device of one's family, and these must be awarded by the duke, or the king, when there was one. In all of Poland, there were less than a hundred of them. But Sir Lestko's people were from the Gniezno area, far to the north, and he is the only one of his family in the duchy.

I hid the arrows behind my shield.

"Sir Vladimir! You're up early! What, has your lovely intended thrown you out into the cold?"

"You might as well know, Sir Lestko. Word of the foolishness will be out soon enough. When she was a peasant girl she was easy, warm, and willing. Now that she is Sir Conrad's daughter, she is altogether too proper, and won't even hold my hand until the wedding! And my father has not yet approved our marriage! I tell you there is very little justice in the world."

Sir Lestko laughed, as I intended him to do. "You poor bastard! Still, what she's doing is right, you know. As Sir Conrad's daughter, she must act with decorum for his honor and yours. And you, my friend, should do what every proper son of the nobility has always done."

"And what is that?"

"Salve your pains with another wench! Come along! There are skads of them available in Okoitz! Indeed, I have a spare to lend you. When it's raining soup, the wise man puts out his bowl!"

I promised to join him shortly, and we rode together toward the town. Dozens of people were out by then, and further archery practice was impossible.

It was agreed that Tadaos would shoot only when Sir Conrad was in trouble, likely though that event was. Perhaps there was still some shred of hope.

# Chapter Twenty

░░░░░░░░░░░░░░░░░░░░░░░░░░░░

FROM THE DIARY OF CONRAD SCHWARTZ

I'd withheld the purse from Annastashia mostly as a joke, since I was trying to lighten up the party. The others were treating it like a wake, and my own at that.

Also, whenever I gave one of the girls something, the others always wanted the same thing, and I was not about to have Krystyana, Janina, Natalia, and Yawalda falling into the role of daughters. They were too good as bed partners.

Thank God I'd never had Annastashia. She was already involved with Sir Vladimir before I met her. Otherwise I'd have incest on my conscience along with everything else.

Nonetheless, Annastashia took her role as my daughter seriously, which was probably for the best. Much of what I was doing in this century was flying in the face of convention, but it would not be wise to affront the institutions of the Church and the family. It made things a little rough on Sir Vladimir's lovelife, but he could stand it. Too much else was at stake.

Okoitz was more crowded than the streets of New Orleans during Mardi Gras, and much of the same attitude seemed to infect the crowd. I had the feeling that I was the sacrificial lamb that everybody had come to see slaughtered.

Oh, everybody was polite, vastly polite, entirely too polite. Every person in that crowd was convinced that I was going to be dead in a day and a half, and they all tried to make my last few hours as sticky sweet as possible.

It took an hour to get my people settled in with the peasants at Okoitz, even with the advance arrangements I'd made. The best we could get was a roof over everybody's head and minimal space on a dirt floor. People had to lay spoon fashion, back to belly, to all lie down at the same time. At least nobody was going to freeze. That much body heat could melt a snowdrift.

Then I looked up Count Lambert to report in. He was with the duke.

"Well, boy. Quite a crowd you've attracted," Duke Henryk said.

"Yes, your grace. I suppose I should feel flattered."

"I wouldn't be. Most of them are here to see the blood fly, and they don't much care whose. What on Earth is that you're wearing?"

"Your grace, I once told you that I would show your people how to make better armor. Well, this is an example of it."

"It's pretty enough. I'm sure the ladies will be impressed. The question is whether it can stop the Crossman from making an impression on you."

"I suppose we'll know that in a few days, your grace."

"I suppose we will. You brought the kids with you?"

"Yes, your grace."

"Where do you have them chained?"

"I don't, your grace. I mean they're not chained. They are with their families."

"Their families are dead. Crossmen don't leave survivors."

"Their new families, your grace. Every one of them was adopted by a family of my workers at Three Walls. I said that I'd make Christians out of them, and I have. Every one of them has voluntarily accepted Baptism. They are now Christians, and members of Christian Polish families."

"You said that you would make the horse sing, and by

God you have!" The duke laughed. "So when you're dead, the Crossmen will have to face the bishop to get them back! That's rich! You intend to keep fighting even after you're dead! Yours must be a deadly people, Sir Conrad."

"That depends on how you mean that, your grace. The people here seem to consider war a sport, to be played with sporting rules. They enjoy it. Mine hate war. We hate fighting. We haven't started a war in five hundred years. But when we must fight, we fight in a serious, deadly way. I don't mean that we fight well. We don't. Our children don't grow up dreaming of performing valorous deeds on the battlefield. Our maidens don't compete hard for the favors of fighting men. Our young men don't spend all their spare time discussing strategy and tactics.

"So when war comes to us, we fight poorly, inefficiently. But we go into it willing to take casualties, willing to die. We fight long wars, and we win."

"And how long are these wars?"

"Once we fought for a hundred thirty years, when the very name of our country was erased from the map. And we won."

That silenced the conversation for a bit. Then Count Lambert said, "You say your maidens don't get excited about military men. Who then do they chase?"

"The answer will surprise you, my lord. Many of them scream and run after musicians."

"You're right, Sir Conrad. I'm dumbfounded. Musicians?"

The duke said, "Ah. There's his excellency, the bishop. I must inform him about your Christianizing of the Pruthenians. It'll be fun to watch him squirm!"

With the duke gone, I thought I'd be able to slip out, but Count Lambert wouldn't hear of it. He dragged me around half the night, introducing me to people. I went into stimulus saturation in about five minutes, and so have no idea who the last hundred people were that I was introduced to.

I was surprised that despite the crowd, I was given a room to myself. Part of it was my status as a sacrificial lamb, but I think that at least some of the reason was that this was the room where Mikhail Malinski had died, and people had attached something stupid and superstitious to it.

Janina, Yawalda, and Natalia were off somewhere with the Banki brothers, so Krystyana and I had some peace and quiet to ourselves.

I met Father Ignacy the next morning and invited him back to my room as the only quiet place in Okoitz. After hearing my confession, he said, "That was quite a feat you accomplished, converting those Pruthenians."

"There wasn't much to it, Father. They were homeless children. We gave them warmth and love. The religious instruction and conversion came naturally."

"Nonetheless, it is the first success the Church has had with the Pruthenians in three hundred years! As a stratagem to keeping the children free, it just might be successful. The Bishops of Cracow and Wroclaw are both convinced that the Church must retain this victory. They have asked my abbot that my brothers arm ourselves with staves, that we might defend the children with force if necessary!"

"Then if that's so, do you think that they might talk to the Crossmen, and maybe stop this fight? I'll gladly give back their furs, amber, and other goods. I don't want to kill anybody, and I certainly don't want to be killed. I can't let them have the children, but if the Church is going to protect them even if I lose, what is there to fight about?"

"A worthy thought, Sir Conrad. I'll present it to their excellencies." He got up to leave.

"One last thing, Father. Is there any news of the Church's inquisition of me?"

"I'm surprised that you concern yourself with that at this time, but yes, there is news. I told you that at the request of the bishop, the report was sent to the home monastery in Italy. Well, the home monastery has returned it, saying that no, the proper channel for such a report would be through the secular Church hierarchy. So with great promptness, my abbot sent it to the Bishop of Cracow, who sent it to the Bishop of Wroclaw, as your lands are in Silesia and thus in the diocese of Wroclaw."

"You mean that it was in Italy, but rather than send it

to Rome, it came back to Poland? Incredible!"

"Isn't it though! Who would have thought that a letter could have traveled all the way to Italy and back to Poland in only a single summer and fall? You can almost see the hand of God speeding it along! But I must go now and request audience with their excellencies, to inform them of your offer."

So the Church bureaucracy was as screwed up as anything the stupid Russians had ever dreamed up.

The Crossmen arrived about noon. There must have been a thousand of them, all in battle armor and on warhorses. Their baggage train stretched for miles, and you would have thought that they were on a campaign in enemy territory rather than come to witness a trial.

They set up a city of tents outside Okoitz, on the other side of the tourney field. It wasn't the usual medieval hodgepodge, but as neatly laid out as any modern camp, or Ancient Roman one, for that matter.

Unfortunately, their camp was upwind of our town, and occasionally a vast stench wafted in from them. On asking about it, I was told that as a mark of their austerity, it was a rule of the order that the Crossmen neither shaved nor bathed. Ever. No wonder they were so mean.

I saw the two bishops with their entourages go out to the camp. Apparently my offer was being delivered. I also saw my old enemy, Sir Stefan, and his father ride out there. At least all my enemies were in the same camp.

The afternoon went slowly, annoyingly, with too many cloying well-wishers wanting to speak sadly to me.

Some bastard of a merchant had set up a *parimutuel* gambling stall, betting on the outcome of the fight. The odds were running thirty-eight to one against me. He had two parchment lists, recording who had made each bet and the amount, and two open-top barrels where the money was thrown for all to see. When the fight was over, the merchant would take a twelfth of the whole and the pot would be divided among the winners in accordance to the size of their bets. Two armed guards watched the barrels. The barrel containing bets on me was very low. I still had twenty-six thousand pence in Count Lambert's strongroom, so I went and bet it all on myself.

I'm really not a gambler, but there are some bets that you really can't lose. My wager changed the odds to eight to one, but what the heck. If I lost, I'd never miss it, since I'd be dead.

Finally, I went back to my room and stationed Natalia at the door to keep me from being bothered. The girl was a genius at it.

Why was everybody so damn convinced that I was going to die? I was going to win, dammit!

I kept telling myself that.

At supper, the Bishop of Wroclaw informed me that the Crossmen had flatly turned down my offer. They felt that they had to avenge the blood I'd spilt, Sir Stefan had convinced them that I was a warlock, and anyway, their champion was undefeated.

"Of course their champion is undefeated, your excellency. Every champion is undefeated. These are fights to the death. The only champion not undefeated is dead!"

Everybody thought I was making a joke and laughed.

"Be that as it may, my son, your conversion of the Pruthenians was a wonderful deed for the glory of God. But it places the Church in an awkward position. I shall have to defend those children, possibly against the Knights of the Cross, who are after all another branch of the Church! It would help matters considerably if you could see fit to win tomorrow."

"I shall make every effort to satisfy your wishes, your excellency." I bowed and thought, *What a pompous ass*!

"Thank you, my son."

During the meal, I gave out the remaining wolfskin capes to the duke, his son, and to seven counts, including Lambert. I explained why wolfskin was such a suitable material, and why, if they became popular, it would reduce the wolf population. They seemed to accept the gifts in memory of me, but I tried.

After supper, I went out to the stables and gave Anna a very thorough currying. I spent a few hours with her. She was the only person that wasn't convinced that I was soon to die. She knew that we were going to win!

It was a bad night, with Krystyana bawling most of the time. I had to threaten to throw her out in order to get some sleep. I even suggested that she go find Piotr Kulczynski. That shut her up.

In the morning, I said confession again and went to church. The place was half filled with Crossmen, with them on one side of the center aisle and the duke's nobles on the other. Just like a wedding, except for the stench.

When it was time for communion, the ushers brought only me and one Crossman to the communion rail. He apparently was the man I was to fight at noon.

We looked at each other and we each recognized the other at the same time. He had ice blue eyes and his nose had been broken. There were scars on his forehead and cheek and his very long, very blond hair was still greasy.

On my very first day in the thirteenth century, I had been bashed on the head by a Crossman. This was the very same bastard!

The protocol of communion did not permit us to speak, which was probably just as well. After the mass, the Crossmen immediately left in a body, so I had no chance to talk to my opponent. I wouldn't have known what to say anyway.

At noon, we were ready. The weather was cold and overcast, with very low-flying clouds. Good weather for a fight. The sun wouldn't be in my eyes and there was no danger of overheating.

The tourney field was a square about three hundred yards to the side, and marked out with little flags on sticks. A few centimeters of snow had fallen the night before, and the field was a flat, pristine white. It was hard to realize that three months before, the field had been gold with grain. Now we would fertilize it with blood.

The Crossmen lined the two sides of the field closest to their camp, and the Poles lined the other two. Nobles sat on benches in front, and at the duke's request, none of them was armed except for the ubiquitous swords. He was afraid of a fight starting. One that he would lose.

The commoners stood behind the nobles. The clergy was in a group around the two bishops.

A crossbowman was stationed at each corner of the square, two from the duke's guard and two from the

Crossmen. Their job was to kill the man who committed a foul.

Heralds had been scurrying around for days getting things organized, and I suppose that they had done a fair job. Not that I would have known a good job from a poor one.

The sext bell was rung, a trumpeter played something stirring, and the two head heralds came out with parchment scrolls. I had spent quite a bit of time writing my proclamation, since it had to state what I thought the fight was about. Protocol had it that the Crossman declaration was to be read first, and the duke's herald, the one who talked in capital letters, read them both, since the Crossmen's herald didn't speak Polish.

"Know all You Present, that on the Second day of August, in the Year of Our Lord 1232, the Notorious Brigand, Sir Conrad Stargard did Feloniously and with Malice Aforethought Attack a Caravan of Goods, the Property of the Teutonic Knights of Saint Mary's Hospital at Jerusalem.

In this Evil Attack, he Murdered Five of the Members of our Holy Order, and Maimed a Sixth Member for Life, while these Honorable Men were Peacefully Attending to the Business of Our Order.

"We Pray to God that He may Strengthen Our Champion's Arm, that he might Smite the Brigand Sir Conrad, and Recover for Our Order All our Property, Including the Heathen Slaves.

"May God Uphold the Right."

I knew about their proclamation, of course, having read a copy of it the day before. Part of the deal the duke made was that Sir Vladimir was not to be mentioned. I think the reason that the Crossmen went along with this was the size of his extended family. Having a feud with that many people would have been awkward even for the Crossmen.

That last business about the heathen slaves was new, however. They weren't backing down a bit.

Then the same herald read my proclamation.

"Know all of you present that on the Second day of August, in the Year of Our Lord 1232, I, Sir Conrad Stargard, Came upon Seven Crossmen engaged in the

Criminal Act of Abusing Children, having One Hundred Forty-Two of them Chained by the Neck, with Bleeding Feet and Whip-Scarred Backs. I Attempted to Free the Children, as was My Christian Duty as well as My Duty to my Liege Lord.

"I was Attacked by the Crossmen, Seven against One. But God was On My Side, and I was Victorious.

"I saw to it that The Children were Adopted into Good Christian Families and Received Proper Religious Instruction. They are now All Christians and may not be Returned to their Previous State of Illegal Slavery.

"I Hold that the Crossmen are an Evil Order Masquerading under the Trappings of Piety.

"I Hold that they Trade with the Infidel Mohammedans, the Very People who now Hold the Holy Lands against All True Christians, and that Their Order was Supposed to Fight.

"I Hold that they are Invading the Pruthenians for No Other Reason than Greed. They make No Attempt at the Religious Conversion of these People, but Instead Murder Them, Man, Woman, and Child.

"I Hold that This Evil Order of Crossmen must be Disbanded, and its Former Members Banished from Poland. Further, I Hold that Slavery is an Offense Against God, for Man was Made in God's Image, and God's Image Must Not Be Degraded!

"May God Uphold the Right."

The duke had said that I was stupid for not mentioning the booty, and that there wasn't a chance in hell of the Crossmen being disbanded or banished. Not in the Duchy of Mazovia, anyway. He liked the precedent it might set for him in his own territory, but it only had effect in the unlikely event that I won.

The bishop had said that my theology was questionable, but let it go at that.

I wrote it and I liked it. Mentioning the furs and amber would have lent a note of crassness to my proclamation, and anyway, my possession of them was understood.

The heralds went to the other side of the field to read the proclamations to the Crossmen in German, with the duke's herald reading mine in German. He might be a blowhard, but he spoke nine languages. You could see ripples go through the crowd of Crossmen as my proclamation was read. Good. Consternation to the enemy!

The bishops each gave a short sermon, a prayer was said, and at long last we could get on with it.

I wasn't eager to either fight or die, but this waiting was getting me in the gut. Still, a blast of raw fear hit me as I realized that in minutes I would likely be *dead*.

Another trumpet blast, the heralds left the field and the marshals shouted, "Lay on!"

I flipped down my visor, lowered my lance and we were off. *Do it by the numbers! It's just like practice!* I shouted silently to myself, trying to convince myself that I wasn't scared shitless.

As Anna and I thundered toward our opponent, I laid the lance in Anna's hook and the notch of the saddle, as we'd done a thousand times in practice. Then I drew my sword as stealthily as possible and prepared to give the bastard the double-hitter we'd practiced so often.

Anna's aim was perfect as always. She hit his shield dead center and then all hell broke loose.

My only reaction was one of total surprise. I couldn't figure out what happened, but somehow I was flying through the air! The impact with the frozen ground was brutal, armor or no armor. I lay there, stunned for a moment, until I got my wits back.

I got up, shaken. The snow wasn't thick enough to break my fall, but it was enough to hide my sword! I ran back to where the train wreck had occurred, but I couldn't find my sword. My lance was shattered. I had no weapon except for the dagger I had taken from a thug in Cieszyn last spring.

Looking up, I saw my opponent had turned his horse and was coming back at me with his lance lowered. I drew my dagger and waited for him. There was nothing else I could do.

Anna circled around and saw my predicament. She raced back and attacked, not the Crossman, but his horse.

In seconds, she ripped a major hunk of flesh from his rump with her teeth and broke both of the stallion's rear legs with her forehoofs.

My opponent went down in a sad heap. The crowd of Crossmen started yelling "Foul!" and "Witchcraft."

Apparently, Sir Stefan had done a lot of talking with them. I half expected a crossbow bolt in the back, but the marshals decided that I wasn't responsible for my horse when I was dismounted, dumb animals being what they thought they were.

Anna ran back toward me and in passing she kicked my sword up out of the snow. It popped up like a golf ball hit by a nine iron and flew toward me handle first. I had to drop my dagger to catch it, but I didn't need the dagger any more. At least I thought I wouldn't.

Then she stood back and watched, supremely confident that I would win.

The Crossman was out of the wreckage in a hurry. His horse was screaming in pain, but he didn't bother giving it an easy death. He came running at me.

"Take care of your horse!" I shouted at him. "I'll wait here while you do!"

"I do that later! First I make sure I kill you dead this time!"

There was nothing I could do but meet him.

The bastard was good. He would have made an Olympic-grade fencer easily. Even swinging a heavy hand-and-a-half bastard sword, he was faster than I was with my light watered-steel blade. What's more, he knew how to use a shield much better than I did.

He got one past my guard and slammed a blow into the left side of my head. It might have killed me had I been wearing my old helmet. As it was, it spun my helmet to the right about ninety degrees and bent the collar ring such that the helmet was jammed in that position. I couldn't turn my head! Looking forward, *I was blind*! I could only see by looking over my right shoulder!

I discarded my shield and fought him fencing-style. It was all I could do. You have to be able to look straight ahead to fight with sword and shield. A roar went up from the Polish side of the crowd, but I had no time to think about that.

He got blow after blow past my defenses, but Ilya made me a fine suit of armor. Most of the time I barely felt them.

"Die, you hell-spawn bastard! What do it take to kill you? Wood stick in heart?"

I didn't have the breath to spare to answer him.

It was his shieldwork that was stopping me from hitting him back. Every time I got a chance to strike at him, that damn shield was there. My sword had amazing cutting power, but it couldn't do much when the whole edge was hitting the flat of that leather-covered plywood shield of his.

*Okay*, I told myself. *Go for the shield! Chop that sucker to kindling!* Focusing on the shield, and catching it on the edge, I took a few major chunks out of it.

Then I got the chance to swing a big one right down the middle. I took it. My sword went down through the center of his shield, then stopped halfway. And stuck.

I tried to pull my sword free, but it was stuck fast and he wasn't about to let go of his shield.

To make matters worse for me, *my* sword was the only thing I had to block *his* sword. He wrenched his shield and my sword from my hand and swung his sword at me.

There was nothing I could do but step inside his swing and try to handle the problem karate-fashion.

There is a karate blow that is demonstrated slowly, but never practiced. You twist your opponent's right arm with your left hand so that his arm is straight and his elbow is downward, then you strike upward with the palm of your right hand. Done properly, this breaks his right elbow. This wouldn't have worked on me because the hinges on my elbow caps wouldn't bend that way. But he was in chain mail.

For all his mastery of the sword and the lance, the Crossman had never considered the possibility of unarmed combat. It worked. His elbow gave way with a satisfying pop.

He dropped his sword and I quickly picked it up. He made no attempt to run away, as many men would. He just stood there.

I didn't want to kill him, but this fight was to the death. No quarter was to be asked or given. If I didn't snuff him, the freedom of a hundred forty-two children would still be in question.

I took his sword and swung it with all my might sideways at his neck. He didn't try to stop me.

His dying word was, "*Bastard!*"

He crumpled to the snow, and the emotional reaction of all that had happened hit me. My hands and legs shook, I could barely stand, and all my sphincters let loose.

Somehow, *I was still alive!*

The crowds on both sides were cheering and shouting, but they didn't seem important, and I ignored them.

With both hands on my helmet, I managed to twist it around so I could look forward. Standing on his shield, with both hands I was able to pull out my sword. It was tightly wedged, and I think that it wasn't the cutting that stopped my blade from going all the way through, but the friction on the sides. When I had it out, I could see that I had not only cut through half the shield, I had cut through half his left arm as well. He couldn't have dropped that shield. Shield, sword, and arm were locked into a single unit.

I was pretty sure his neck was broken, but with so many children at stake I didn't want to take any chances. I raised my sword and took his head off with a single blow. It didn't bleed much. I guess he was already dead.

My lance was lying shattered on the ground, and I reconstructed what happened. I had bought my lance a year ago, figuring it was a useless piece of paraphernalia. I bought the lightest one possible. Sir Vladimir favored a light spear, so he didn't mention anything. But Sir Vladimir goes for targets like the eyeslit, and Anna had trouble reaching that high.

There was a gouge on his shield that must have been made by my lance. Anna had hit her target dead on, but on impact my spear shattered and his didn't. I never had a chance to swing my sword; it was knocked out of my hand when I went flying. I wouldn't have thought it possible to be knocked over the top of the waist-high cantle of a warkak, but that's the way I went.

I went and decapitated his horse, which was still screaming.

The Polish crowd was cheering wildly, including, I suppose, even those who had bet against me. The Crossmen were shouting hoarsely in German, but I couldn't understand them, except for more shouts of "foul" and "witchcraft."

All I knew was that it was over and that I had won.

Then the German crowd opened up and four armed and armored horsemen wearing black crosses on their white surcoats charged me with their lances lowered.

## FROM THE AUTOBIOGRAPHY OF SIR VLADIMIR CHARNETSKI

On the day of the trial, my fellow conspirators and I were all at our assigned positions. Tadaos was lying hidden on the roof of the windmill. Friar Roman was among the clergy, ready to cry out "An Act of God" and "A miracle" and such like. I was among the nobles ready to do the same.

Ilya was set to run out on the field and try to recover the gold-covered arrows, for we were sure that they could not stand close inspection. Surely God would use something better than gold leaf!

When the fight was on, Sir Conrad's lance shattered at the first impact. I cursed myself for never making him get a new and stronger one!

He was unhorsed, and the Crossman started to come around to finish him off, but still Tadaos did not fire!

Talking to the bowman later, he said that he did, but he never saw where the arrow fell, as he had hid himself immediately after loosing his shaft. When he looked up, he was surprised that the Crossman was still alive, but Sir Conrad and his opponent were locked in such tight combat that he was afraid to shoot again for fear of hitting Sir Conrad.

My friend looked sure to lose, but then to the wonderment of all, he discarded his shield! A roar went up from the crowd, for we all knew then that Sir Conrad was merely toying with the Crossman, that he was so sure of victory that he could afford a jest!

In the end, he even left his sword stuck contemptuously in the Crossman's shield and destroyed the man with his bare hands! And then gave the man the mercy blow with his opponent's own sword!

The crowd was wild! No one had expected such prowess of Sir Conrad, although he had said all along that he was going to win. Shortly after Sir Conrad's victory, he gave mercy to the Crossman's horse, for that animal had been injured by Sir Conrad's amazing mount.

We thought that all was over when four more Crossmen, fully armed and armored, charged onto the field and at Sir Conrad.

Cries of "Foul!" went up, for this was a foul beyond all imagining! But the marshals had already ordered the crossbowmen to uncock their weapons, for fear of accidental discharge. They ordered the crossbowmen to shoot the transgressors, but it takes some time to wind up those ungainly weapons. Time that Sir Conrad did not have!

Far away on the roof of the windmill, Tadaos was more prepared. He loosed four shafts at the evil-doers, watched the arrows go through the low clouds and then come down exactly on target!

Every one of his golden shafts hit its man square in the heart! They crumbled as a group and their riderless horses ran on both sides of Sir Conrad, while he stood there unmoving.

"It is an Act of God!!" Friar Roman shouted, falling to his knees. "We have seen a miracle to the glory of God!"

I too was shouting, "A miracle! A miracle!" Soon everybody was doing it as Tadaos quickly descended from the windmill and hid his bow and remaining arrows.

As planned, Ilya was first on the field. But when he grasped an arrow to pull it from the dead man's chest, it bent in his hand! The arrows were truly made of soft, *pure gold*!

Ilya fell to his knees and prayed.

# Interlude Four

I HIT the STOP button again.

"I don't believe that shooting, and I'm too much of an agnostic to believe that you have a truly documented miracle here. Your fingerprints are all over this, Tom! What gives?"

"Well, of course I did it. I couldn't trust Conrad's life to one medieval bowman, no matter how good he was. You don't think I could let those German bastards murder my own cousin, do you?

"For a long time, I've had a section of engineers working on advanced weaponry, just in case we ever needed such a thing. We've never had to use it, which is good, but rather frustrating for the engineers. They were delighted when I gave them this assignment.

"The golden arrows were the easy part. Just some thrusters on the arrowheads and some microelectronics to guide them, then a temporal circuit to get rid of the high-tech stuff afterward.

"Getting rid of Tadaos's arrows was the hard part. They had to do some weather-control work to get the low cloud ceiling to hide our ship, then detect and take out some small, uncooperative targets. After that, well, would you believe thirty-caliber cruise missiles?"

"I thought that you were so sure that Conrad would be alive eight years later," I said.

"There are so many unknowns floating around this

243

mess that I just couldn't take the chance. Maybe he could be both killed and stay alive. Is that any stranger than both saving and abandoning that child?"

"So you faked a miracle. It's hard to believe that even from you!"

"Look, kid. One man's miracle is another man's technology."

He hit the START button.

# Chapter Twenty-One

FROM THE DIARY OF CONRAD SCHWARTZ

I had gone into the fight knowing that my cause was just, and with the feeling that God was on my side. I had been scared, but somehow, I had won.

Then suddenly I was looking sure death in the face.

And then, just as suddenly it was over, and my mind couldn't handle it all at once. Like that farmer in the High Tatras, I was just stunned by all that had happened. Miracles are something that happen to someone else, far away, and a long time ago. They don't happen here and now to one's self.

Long afterward, there were nagging doubts in my mind about what really happened. I knew what an advanced technology should be capable of. If someone could make a thing like Anna, faking a miracle would be easy for him. But I never really knew.

Father Ignacy said that perhaps it was both faked and real. That God works in His own ways, and sometimes He chooses to work through men. And if so, why not through men of a different time and place?

Most of the people of the thirteenth century had no such doubts. They *knew* that God was talking to them. From the sidelines, there was much praying and wailing, but I just stood there on the snow, my mind strangely blank.

The bishops came out and claimed the gold arrows for the Church. After some little debate as to whether the four dead Crossmen should be treated as holy, for they had been the object of an Act of God, it was decided that they had been cursed by God, and were hauled off to be buried on unhallowed ground without Extreme Unction, though their arms and armor were claimed by the Church.

The duke went before the crowd of Crossmen and told them that their order had been cursed by God. He ordered them to disband and to disperse, for they were banished forever from Poland. Fully a third ripped off their uniform surcoats on the spot and rode off west, back to Germany. I heard one say that he'd wanted a bath, anyway. The balance, crasser and more worldly, packed up their gear and returned to their headquarters in Turon, Mazovia.

All told, the Crossmen lost about a quarter of their total force of men to desertion when this affair became well known. It was the more honorable and religious of them that left, of course; the worst bastards knew when they had a good thing going, and weren't about to change.

Then the duke addressed the Polish crowd, and said that from that day forth, slavery was forever banned in Poland, that Poland was now the land of the free, and that any slave need only set foot on our soil to be free. The duke was a rough old SOB, but you had to love him.

Before they pulled out, a Crossman, the commander in his fancier surcoat, came and talked to me.

"Your witchcraft and trickery won't stop us! Duke Henryk has nothing to say about what goes on in Mazovia and the Pruthenian forests. If we can't send our slaves through Silesia, we'll find another route!"

I stared at him for a moment, then said, "Then I'll have to plug that route, too."

"Do that and we'll just stop taking prisoners!" Then he went away.

Across the field, I saw Sir Vladimir and his father. They were in each other's arms, crying on each other's shoulders. Uncle Felix was standing nearby. A few hours later Baron Jan came to me and formally asked for the hand of my daughter for his son. Of course, I gave my blessings. No mention was made of a dowry, though I asked what he thought of Sir Vladimir swearing fealty to me.

Baron Jan said that if Vladimir wished it, and Count Lambert did not object, he would be willing to transfer the allegiance. Just before the wedding, it was done.

I checked on the wager I had made on myself, and discovered that the odds against me had gone back up to fourteen to one. I was two hundred thirty-eight thousand pence richer. It is not comfortable to be the only person in the world who believes something to be true, but it can be very profitable.

As they were weighing out my money, the herald of the Bishop of Wroclaw announced that the posting of bans for the marriage of Sir Vladimir and Annastashia had been shortened from six weeks to three days.

The duke awarded all of the booty won from the Crossmen to me, without even reserving the share normally due to Count Lambert. I gave Sir Vladimir half of it as a dowry.

We stayed on at Okoitz, and the day after Christmas there was a wedding. The bride I gave away was *radiant*.

# About the Author

Leo Frankowski was born on February 13, 1943, in Detroit. He wandered through seven schools getting to the seventh grade and he's been wandering ever since. By the time he was forty-five, he had held more than a hundred different positions, ranging from "scientist" in an electro-optical research lab to gardener to airman to chief engineer to company president. Much of his work was in chemical and optical instrumentation, and earned him a number of U.S. patents.

His writing has earned him nominations for a Hugo, the John W. Campbell award, and a Nebula, but he hasn't won anything.

He still owns Sterling Manufacturing and Design, but got tired of design work several years ago and now spends much of his time writing and pursuing his various hobbies: i.e., reading, making mead, drinking mead, dancing girls, and cooking.

A lifelong bachelor, he has recently inherited a teenager and lives in the wilds of Sterling Heights, Michigan.